Silver

HAV
OF 5~ ~~~~ ~~~~~~

OF

EROTIC DOMINATION

If you like one you will probably like the rest

A NEW TITLE EVERY MONTH
NOW INCLUDING EXTRA BONUS PAGES

Silver Moon Books Ltd
PO Box 1100 London N21 2QW

Distributed to the trade throughout North America by
LPC Group, 1436 West Randolph Street, Chicago, IL 60607
(800) 826-4330

If you like one of our books you will probably
like them all!

**Write for our free 20 page booklet of extracts from
early books - surely the most erotic freebie yet -
and, if you wish to be on our confidential mailing
list, for forthcoming monthly titles as they are
published:-**

Silver Moon Reader Services
PO BOX 1100 London N21 2QW
or
PO Box 1614 NEW YORK NY 1016

or leave details on our 24hr UK answerphone
0181 245 0985
International acces code then +44 181 245 0985

<u>New authors welcome</u>

www.silvermoonbooks.com
www.thebookshops.com/erotic

THE CONFESSIONS OF AMY MANSFIELD first published 1998

Copyright Rachel Hurst

The right of Rachel Hurst to be identified as the author of this book has been asserted in accordance with Section 77 and 78 of the Copyrights and Patents Act 1988

CONTENTS

THE CONFESSIONS OF AMY MANSFIELD

by
Rachel Hurst

Bonus Pages

Free first chapter downloads of all our books
http://www.silvermoonbooks.com
http://www.thebookshops.com/erotic

THE CONFESSIONS OF AMY MANSFIELD
by Rachel Hurst

ONE

My father married me off to Mr Mansfield as soon as I was eighteen years old. As a dutiful daughter I went willingly, even though Mr Mansfield was more than twice my age and I had only met him twice. I was of course nervous because, like any girl in 1849, I knew very little about what to expect except that I would go to his bed, and that something would happen concerning my body.

The ignorance in which I was raised did not tell me much of what that something was, except that it was something to do with my private parts and my bosoms. I knew my bosoms were important in some way. They had grown quite prominent over the last couple of years, and pretty well every gentleman I encountered spent more time looking at my chest than at my face. A number of young men had even sneaked opportunities to feel them, which was quite disturbing because, although utterly shocking of course, it set off the oddest feelings in me. One especially bold young man had actually ensnared me in a corner once, and kissed me and squeezed my bosoms quite a lot, which left me feeling quite weak and dizzy when at last he desisted!

For my wedding night, which was spent in Papa's house, I brushed my hair until it sang, and put on a brand new linen nightgown, with puffed sleeves and pretty blue ribbons at the neck. I was, I confess, excited and nervous at the same time, and my breasts felt strangely tight at the thought that my new husband would soon be touching them.

I wondered for a moment which side of the bed I should get into. I had never shared a bed except with my dolls. I decided to go to the far side; Mr Mansfield would then be nearest the door. I also debated with myself whether to extinguish the candle. I decided against; Mr Mansfield would need to see what he was doing when he followed me up.

He took ever such a long time to come upstairs and I grew anxious, for I knew a bride was required to make herself pretty for her husband so that he would enjoy the mysterious 'it' I had been told would consummate the union. I had tried hard to make myself pretty, and Mr Mansfield was not there to see me.

As I waited for him all the hints and nudges and winks span slowly in my imagination. There built up in me a combination of nerves and allure. Nerves because I knew no more than that my new husband would use my body in the act of consummation, though quite how he would use it nobody had ever told me. Allure because echoes of those oddly tantalizing sensations when those naughty young men had fondled my growing bosoms wormed their way into my imagination.

When at last Mr Mansfield lurched through the door I knew at once that he was rather tipsy. I was lying flat on my back with the covers to my neck, and by instinct I screwed my eyes shut as he loomed above and looked down at me.

I heard him lumbering about, peeped through my eyelashes and instantly screwed my eyes tight shut again, for he was pulling off his breeches. By the time the mattress bounced to tell me he was getting into the bed, I was trembling like a leaf in the wind. He blew out the candle.

I lay very still, ready and willing for him to do whatever it was a husband does to his new wife to 'make her a woman'. Even so when he rolled over, breathing wine-fumes on me, I was aghast when he straight away thrust his hand up between my legs! I squealed, but he cut me off with hot, wet

6

kisses.

He grabbed at my breasts. He hauled the hem of my crisp nightgown up to my waist. He mauled at my private parts. He got above me. He got between my knees. He pushed something against me. Forced me open. He grabbed my bottom and pulled me on.

It hurt, and I lay rigid and terrified as he stuck something deep into me, and pumped it in and out, in and out, and jerked, and made me hot inside, and suddenly got off me, and rolled over, and went to sleep.

At that time, I did not know a name for what it was Mr Mansfield had done, nor why he had done it. I only learned much, much later that words like 'fuck' and 'shag' and 'cock' existed.

Trying to rationalize it, I assumed that what Mr Mansfield had required do to my body was what I had heard called, mysteriously, my 'wifely duty'. He did it again during that first night, and once more before we rose on the morning. It did not hurt so much as it had the first time, but I was still rather sore. It was more uncomfortable than painful, although the way he grasped and squeezed my breasts and the cheeks of my bottom did bruise me rather.

He shagged me several times in our tent on both nights of our journey to his trading post. I got used it as the weeks passed; got used to having him clamber into bed some time after I had myself retired, feeling me about a bit, even pressing his finger into my private place, then throwing my knees apart, and pumping his cock in me. He did it pretty well every night, and often again before rising in the mornings.

I confess I became somewhat puzzled as the weeks passed. Shagging was obviously very important to my husband, but somehow he seemed rather ashamed of it. It was not the sort of thing one could talk about over breakfast, or even in the quiet time after dinner. As for myself it became

7

confusing. To be honest, I came to look forward to that moment when my husband would rub my titties and then shag me, but also irritated that it never went on long enough.

You may think me a woman of loose morals, but honesty obliges me to confess that being shagged felt nice except that it always seemed to stop too soon. Feelings would start up in me as Mr Mansfield pumped away, but then he would jerk into what is called a 'come', and roll off me and go to sleep, leaving my sensations up in the air, to coin a phrase.

It became even more confusing when Mr Mansfield lost his temper with me. He had a very quick temper. I learned how quick hardly a fortnight after reaching the trading post. He came in for supper late. I had heard raised voices from the trading room, but had thought little of it. Then I spilt the goblet of cognac he always required as an aperitif.

Instantly, he was up and at me. Before I knew what was happening I was down across his lap, my skirts were thrown up, and he was belabouring my bottom with a very heavy hand! I had of course been spanked by Papa when I had misbehaved, but this was much worse. My husband was in a fury. He actually ripped the tie-ribbon of my drawers in hauling them down, and spanked my bare bottom for what felt like a hundred years, oblivious to my wails and pleas.

It then became very strange indeed. He pushed me, sobbing, off his lap, and as I dragged myself to my feet, using the table for leverage, I saw with astonishment that he was tearing at his breeches. Still without a single word, he shoved me back across the table, threw up my skirts, and shoved his cock up me. And we were not even in bed! But what was strangest was that, even though he was rougher than usual and pumped very quickly, those stirrings he had sometimes awaked in me before, and always left unsatisfied and mysterious, came over me thick and fast!

When he fucked me again later on in bed, it caused in

8

me the most astonishing sensations of hotness and liquidity and pulsations, as though my body - and especially that part he was pumping in and out of - had taken on a life of its own. It was like nothing I could ever have imagined! Everything in me seemed to be throbbing and churning, and I could only gasp. Even when he reached his sudden jerking finish and rolled off me, the wild sensations continued in me, and when I pressed my hand to the place he had just left little ripples of deliciousness took my breath away.

Next day he was, if anything, more indifferent towards me than usual. It was very puzzling.

Lest you think too badly of him I must hasten to add that my husband did not spank me very often. Seldom more than once a week; and of course every husband has the in-alienable right to chastise his wife should he wish to do so. What was so puzzling about it, though, was that every time he spanked me he would immediately tumble me onto the floor or back over a table and shag me, and then shag me again with great vigour when we retired to our bed. And the strangest thing of all was that the shagging felt more intense after a spanking, and my titties would become all tight and tense, and my head would grow dizzy, and I would want him to keep going.

Still, I did not actually enjoy being spanked, and certainly did not like my husband's daytime indifference towards me, nor the isolation of our abode. One of my few pleasures, and I suspected it was an illicit one so I never mentioned it to my husband, was observing the native Africans who called upon my husband to buy and sell things. They were invariably very tall men, and slender, with glossy skins and proud bearing. What made my observation illicit was that they seldom wore more than a loincloth and jewellery of bronze and bone, and perhaps a blanket around their bare shoulders.

On one occasion after I had been married for several months, one of the natives brought with him his woman. He was a tall, muscular fellow, while his wife (for that is what I assumed she was) was quite diminutive. She wore no more than a brief apron to cover her womanly parts, and I stared fascinated at her unashamed nudity. Then I had a flashing, unbidden vision of this big warrior shagging his little wife as Mr Mansfield did me, and suddenly I was all hot and tight in my breasts, and rushed away in shame and embarrassment.

Naturally, I castigated myself roundly for thinking such a thing as I had. Proper ladies do not have such thoughts! Nevertheless, I have to confess that echoes of it did sometimes return to my unruly brain when warriors visited the station to trade, and I even found myself wondering whether they did 'it' in the same way as Mr Mansfield did it to me, and what it might be like for their wives.

Or for me.

I was actually imagining other men, and natives to boot! It shocked me, and I begged for forgiveness for such forbidden thoughts in my bedtime prayers. But I could not prevent them haunting me in those moments when my husband rolled off me and my hand would descend to ease the feeling of sudden coolness, or emptiness or whatever it was down there.

I even found myself having to resist doing what my then Governess had spanked me for, for like all girls I knew how certain kinds of touchings can feel exciting, which is probably why they are forbidden.

Then, six months or so into my marriage there came trouble. The King of Benin rebelled against British demands. A punitive force had been sent out. My husband straight away determined I should be sent back to the safety of Lagos. Which is where my story really begins.

10

TWO

We were to travel on horse-back, such was our hurry to escape marauding savages. I was accompanied by two troopers and a corporal. The weather was good, though as always rather hot. The corporal was a very pleasant chap of about twenty-five I guessed. He hailed from the East End of London, somewhere I had never seen, and regaled me with amusing stories about hawkers and street-criers and such as we rode our horses through winding defiles, climbing higher into the mountains all the while.

We stopped around the middle of the day. The troopers gathered wood and lit a fire, on which water from one of their canteens was boiled for tea-making. We ate cold meats and bread and cheese from our rations, and relaxed in the air, which was cooler now we were higher up. Really, it was just like a pleasant picnic.

Thus, the attack when it came was as horrible as it was sudden. Out of nowhere, a spear suddenly pierced one of the poor troopers in his neck. Then there were shouts and clashings. The corporal rushed for his weapons and the other trooper was wrestling with one of the dozen warriors who had fallen upon us. I felt an awful blow to my head, and knew no more.

When I came to myself my head throbbed horribly and my arms felt numb. It took me a minute to realise why, and to begin to awaken to the true awfulness of my situation.

My arms were numb because I was hanging by my wrists from the bough of a tree. I straightened my legs to take the weight off my rope-bound wrists and looked dizzily about me. There was no sign of my escort. Instead of three cheerful British soldiers, I saw a dozen fierce African warriors, naked save for loincloths, squabbling loudly amongst themselves over what looked to be our little party's weapons and equipment.

Then one of the warriors noticed that I had regained consciousness, and I became very scared. He shouted above the hubbub. They all turned and looked towards me. As one, they rose and moved slowly to form a half-circle around me. Some were grinning. One of them, a very tall man with a barrel chest and intricate patters of scars on his face, stood close in front of me. He pulled a long knife from a scabbard strapped to his thick, bare thigh.

The warrior raised the knife. I closed my eyes and, with a sob, commended myself to my maker, unable to defend myself in any way because of the way I was tied up.

Instead of the death blow I heard a deep-throated chuckle and felt a big hand grasp my bosom! My eyes flashed open. He had put the knife away, and now proceeded to toy with my person. He fondled my breasts for what seemed a very long while, and much more gently than my husband ever had. It had the strangest, most shameful affect on me, for though I was very scared, and knew instantly what was surely going to happen to me, I began get those hot tingly feelings. When he slid his hard hand down and began to rub it against the front of my skirt, right over what I now know is called my quim and the tops of my legs it got worse, and I felt a lurching tension deep inside.

It was awful, for although I was tied up and being molested in the most outrageous manner before the eyes of a dozen native rebels, there were growing in me the same sensations Mr Mansfield had sometimes aroused, and as I had felt when I imagined that tall warrior with his diminutive wife. Blushing to my hair-roots at my unruly reactions I hung my head and stared at the dusty ground, for I could do nothing to defend myself.

Then his hands were off me. He pulled out his knife again and I clamped my eyes tight shut, knowing my time had indeed now come. Instead, my wrists were suddenly cut loose; so suddenly that I tumbled forward into the arms of the man who had first fondled then released me. I looked up in wild surmise as he lifted me off him and set me on my feet. The others had formed a wide circle around me and he, too, now stepped back.

He made peculiar gestures with his hands, as though undoing buttons and shrugging off garments. I was confused, for he was naked save for his loincloth. Then I understood and was frozen at the enormity of it. He wanted me to remove my garments! Here, in a clearing in mountain woodland, encircled by rebel warriors, I was being required to take my clothes off!

I knew instinctively what was going to happen to me. I screeched at them and flailed my arms, warding them of. They only laughed. The big man who had molested me grabbed me by my hair. He pulled my face close to his and stared into my eyes, moving his big knife meaningfully through the air. I understood.

As I removed my clothes they removed theirs, though their undressing was very much quicker than mine. By the time I dropped my frock to the ground by my feet they had done the same with their loincloths, and were standing stark naked before my eyes.

My state became very peculiar. It would have been easier for me if they had simply grabbed me and ripped my clothes off, for having to removed them myself, desperately aware of their eyes on my every movement, wild, forbidden feelings had time to take hold in me.

I had never seen a man naked before. Everything between Mr Mansfield and me had happened beneath the bedcovers, as though it was shameful. These men stood proud. I knew what they were going to do to me and (should I be ashamed to confess it? I suppose 'proper' society would say so!) a lurching hotness sprang to life in my breasts and belly.

13

As though they were telescopes, my eyes flicked from one man to another and then to the next and the next and the next. And always they looked to only one place, and my hotness grew more tense and confusing.

When at last my fumbling fingers managed the last ties of my drawers and I was able to get them off and drop them onto the rest of my clothes in their pile on the ground, I bowed my head and stood still, trying to hide what I could with my hands and to stop my blood racing. Even at that awful moment I knew it was not racing because of fear, or at least not only because of fear.

The man who had cut me down, whom I guessed to be the leader, approached me. I shrank back instinctively, mesmerized by the thing bobbing at the join of his long, muscular thighs. I knew it to be a version of what my husband used to shag me with, but it seemed to be so very big! That it was in fact bigger than my husband's cock was proved beyond any doubt moments later.

My impressions (I was still beyond the capability of thought!) told me that he was about to pull me to the ground and have his way with me. Instead, he rummaged in the pile of my clothes, pulled out my frock, and spread it out on the ground. His unexpected thoughtfulness distracted me, as did the fact that my body seemed to be acting of its own accord.

He gestured for me to lie down. I panicked and turned to run, but I was surrounded by grinning warriors. The leader grabbed me by my hair and threw me to the ground face down. Suddenly a stripe of fire burned across my bottom. He was beating me! Beating me with one of the ropes they had used to hold their loincloths! There came another stripe, and another. I screamed and struggled but he was far too strong for me. It went on for ages, until I was sure my poor bottom had no skin left on it and I was biting the grass into which my face was being pressed.

Then, as suddenly as I had been thrown down, I was

hauled to my feet. Tears were streaming and, all thought of dignity gone, I was frantically rubbing my flaming backside with both hands. An age of torment later I became aware that the man who had beaten me, and so much harder than my husband ever had, was holding something out to me. It was my chemise. I wiped my eyes and blew my nose, and tossed the garment back onto the pile of my other clothes.

He gestured again towards where my frock was spread. I had no choice. I lay down, wincing from the soreness in my behind. It became as though time itself had slowed as he moved to kneel between my splayed legs. His cock was gleaming and much too big, and seemed to be hypnotizing me with its central eye. I expected him to fall on me and shove in, as my husband had used to. Instead, he reached for me with his hands.

He touched me, there, between my legs, but softly. A jolt of galvanic sensation shot through me as he began to move his fingers on and then in me. Nobody had ever touched me like this. In only moments I was panting and squirming my hips. It was like nothing I had ever felt before. Being spanked had knocked all resistance out of me. He could do with me as he liked. The trouble was that my body was responding in the most shocking manner.

Behind closed eyes I felt the touches change. I was very warm and moist down there, and he came into me without resistance. He stretched me, but it was the opposite of hurt as he moved slow and deep. Some tiny part of my brain knew that what was happening to me was 'a fate worse than death', but even that part died to silence as the dizzying sensations he was stirring in me took me over.

I know I became wanton. My body was moving to meet his. He was filling me, moving in me like a swell of the sea. I think I cried out as great churning spasms shook me and my sheath churned on the instrument ploughing it. When my ravisher jerked into those spurtings I was used to from

Mr Mansfield at the end of a coupling, it was like an earthquake compared to a sneeze. I think for a moment I fainted a little.

They took turns. All of them. I went into a trance. The wild sensations brought out in my body by the first of them did not quite die, and strong echoes of them crested in me again and again. My body was welcoming the way they were invading me, responding to their hard hands on my breasts. They were crowding around to have the next go at me, and I did not care.

My mind knew it could not be so, of course. These were savages and I was an Englishwoman. Yet my mind seemed to have no control at all over my body, which bucked and writhed and seemed even to push itself up to welcome the next questing cock. I felt very ashamed of myself when at last they finished with me, or, rather, later on when I rose out of my swoon and found myself still naked and splayed out on the grass even though no-one was holding me down.

I was in a state when they took up their march around sunset. My hips were stiff and sore, my quim was puffy and over-sensitive and my breasts ached from the way they had handled me. They bound my wrists with ropes, leaving a long end to lead me by. They did not give me any of my clothes back, and I felt shockingly self conscious as I was lead along by my bound wrists, my arms pulled forward so that I could not even hide my parts with my hands. That bit became especially disconcerting when what they had spurted into me in their pleasure began to leak out and trickle down my legs.

The pace they set was not especially quick, but as you can imagine it was hard for me to keep up. One of the men following along behind solved that problem very simply by cutting a thin switch from a shrub. Whenever I lagged or drooped a few sharp whacks on my sore bottom spurred me on very effectively!

What with the awfulness of my situation and the after-effects of what they had done to me earlier, I quickly became exhausted. The first few times I stumbled and fell, a volley of stripes from the switch would get me quickly scrambling to my feet again. After several hours, however, I was too weak to rise, or even to cry out at the way the man whacked my bottom.

Through a haze, I felt myself being lifted up. I was thrown across a broad shoulder as though I was no more than a sack of flour, and the men set off on their march again.

What with the after-effects of my ravishment and the bouncing of the shoulder against my ribs, I had little consciousness of where or how I was taken. I had a vague impression that the party stopped a couple of times so that one or two of the warriors could indulge in a quick shag, but I was like a limp rag and they cannot have got much pleasure from me.

I came fully to myself, and then only dimly at first, when I was taken into some kind of hut, and was dumped unceremoniously onto a sort of palliasse by the warrior who had carried me. I shrank back from him, suddenly awake and scared that he was going to rape me again. He simply turned and walked away, leaving me alone and exhausted.

I cowered against the mud wall of the hut, sure that soon they would be back. I could still feel the echoes of them inside my body. I was certain they would not leave me alone for long. Shamefully, the thought was not as horrifying as it should have been in a well brought up Englishwoman. I expected at any moment for the hut to be filled with naked warriors, all eager to fuck me.

To my growing surprise, it did not. Several hours passed and nobody came for me. I must have fallen asleep, for when I came to myself again I could see bright sunlight through the hut's low doorway. Still nobody came for me, and I be-

17

gan to wonder what on earth was going on.

At last the doorway darkened. I cowered back against the wall, certain the men had come back to use me yet again. Instead, it was a pretty young girl wearing a tiny flap of cloth at her loins and a wide smile. She handed me a wooden platter and a large pottery ewer, patted my shoulder as though in sympathy, then turned and left the hut.

The platter bore some kind of porridge with bits of cooked meat in it, and the ewer was filled with water. I suddenly realised that I was famished, and fell on the plain fare as though it was a banquet. The water was cool and delicious, and I must have swallowed at least a pint of it before putting down the ewer and turning to the food.

My wrists were still tied and the girl had left me no spoon or other implement I could eat with. My hollow tummy did not let me stand on ceremony. Kneeling on the earthen floor of the hut like an animal, I scooped up the food with my fingers, hardly even chewing as I gulped it down. It was plain and rather salty, but to me it tasted of heaven. I resisted licking the platter clean, but I did wipe as much of the porridge up as I could, and licked it from my fingers. Then I drank the rest of the water and sat back on the palliasse feeling replete.

Strange as it may seem, I did not review my situation as I sat there. My mind was more or less a blank. Perhaps it was protecting itself from the awfulness of my predicament. Perhaps it was hiding away from the thought of how I had reacted to being used by a dozen excited warriors, and the prospect of it happening again, which it surely would.

The sun was low when at last they came for me. Again, I cowered against the wall, sure that I was about to be raped. Again, I was not. A warrior grabbed the rope attached to my wrists, hauled me to my feet and pulled me out of the hut.

At once I was surrounded by a mob of laughing, chattering children and women. It was so embarrassing! They must never have seen an Englishwoman before, and to judge by they way they crowded and called, their eyes wide, their grins enormous, certainly not a stark naked one such as I was. Lots of hands touched me, and being tied the way I was made it impossible to protect myself.

The man leading me moved through the crowd rapidly, but the villagers still had plenty of chances to prod me and bounce my bosoms and slap my bottom. By the time I was hauled out of the crowd and stood once again amongst the group of warriors who had captured me, I was in tears of humiliation.

THREE

The group set off without preamble, with myself being led along by my wrists again. I was much better able to keep up this time, being rested and less stiff, so the switch was little used on my behind. It still felt awful being led along naked in the midst of a group of fierce Africans, but then it got worse.

When we came to a brief halt I realised that I needed to go. Perhaps it was a function of shock or something, but I had not felt the need to answer the calls of nature since my capture. Now, suddenly, I did. Urgently.

But how could I convey my need? These men did not understand English and I knew not their language. Becoming somewhat desperate I nudged the man nearest to me and pointed towards some nearby bushes, trying with my eyes to make him understand my need. He did not comprehend until, blushing with embarrassment, I gestured and mimed.

He grinned and nodded. He took up the rope binding my wrists and led me behind a bush. But he stayed, holding the rope and smiling. I was going to have to do it in front of him! How awful! I could not! It was too shaming! But nature was not to be denied. Blushing to my toes, I parted my knees and squatted, my wastes rushing from me for what seemed an eternity as the silent warrior looked on. If I wanted to die of embarrassment then, I did so even more when, having finished and straightened up, he tore a handful of grass from the ground and, bending me forward, wiped my bottom for me. Oh, how small and helpless I felt at that moment!

Then what I should have known was inevitable happened. Unable because of my embarrassment to look him in the eye, my own were downcast. Being so innocent I did not at first register the fact that his loincloth was bulging until he took my arm and drew me across behind another bush.

Even as he turned me and began to press me back towards the ground; even as my spinning head told me that this was awful, shameful, my loins felt as though they were swelling, opening. I tried to push him off of course, but my wrists were bound and he was much bigger and stronger than I. He was big elsewhere also. I knew it was useless to resist but honestly made an effort to do so. He easily pushed my knees apart. He pulled up his loincloth. He reared most awfully, his manhood thick and swollen. I gave up and felt my legs loll apart as he moved down onto me. He was ever so big. He was undeniable. I span away from myself as he invaded me. He was very vigorous, much more so than my husband had ever been.

He took his time, moving deep, pressing and sort of circling. It was awful because, though what he was doing should have been appalling and forbidden my body was behaving shamefully. It was responding to him. Moving to meet him. And those overwhelming pulsations I had felt before, and did not understand, were irresistibly swelling up in me.

I stared up at him as he thrust at me, astounded at the way my body seemed to be clinging to the thing he was impaling me with, moving to his overwhelming rhythm. When he thrust harder, jerked, ground my spine onto the soil beneath my back, and pulsed his heat into me, the most astounding sensations overtook me. The muscles of my thighs went into spasms. My loins cramped and melted. My legs wrapped themselves around him. My belly convulsed. I cried out, and for a moment or two left this world in a stunning wave of glorious fainting.

I know now that these, this one and those during my ravishment the day before, were my first ever real climaxes, or comes as they are called. Then, I did not know that sexual climax was even possible for a woman! At the time, I was shattered and stunned. I remember groaning as, his pulsings over, he withdrew from me. I remember wanting him to stay. I remember bursting into tears as he hauled me to my feet, weak kneed and still shuddering from what I was feeling. I remember being completely confused at what my body had done. I remember the way my skin welcomed the touch of his hard hand when it cupped my bottom as he gestured me towards where the rest of the warriors waited.

I was mortified at the way they looked at me and nudged one another and grinned. It was very clear that they were aware of exactly what had just gone on. My head was spinning with all sorts of confusions. I had just been taken in the most peremptory manner, and my unruly body had responded quite unbelievably. A dozen near-naked African warriors, their muscular bodies glistening in the moonlight, were now casting their lascivious eyes over my bare form and (I am forced to admit it, for I have vowed to be honest) my loins gave a lurch at the thought of what might now happen. A lurch of something that was other than just fright.

I tried very hard to keep marching briskly as that night wore on. That it was chilly helped, but mostly it was because I was nervous about what would happen to me if the party stopped to rest and eat. The party did stop, thrice before morning and, to be blunt, they fucked me. Marching became

21

more testing after each rest because, well, they were all vigorous men and my body had behaved shamefully with each one who shagged me.

The first time, which to judge from the moon must have been around midnight, we stopped in a little glen surrounded by thorny shrubs. The warriors lounged around on the grass and rummaged in their animal-skin bags, bringing out bread and cold meats to eat, of which I was given an ample share. I was handed a goat-skin water-bag, from which I drank gratefully.

Then a hand fell on my shoulder.

Without any need for thought, I knew what it meant. I had been anticipating it and was already hot and trembling. I got to my feet and followed the men a little way off. There was no point in resisting. They did not even bother to take me behind the bushes, but spread me right there where the others could see. There were three of them. They took me not as the first one had, slowly, but with eyes screwed shut, teeth clenched, and shoving hard and fast. At least this time, though, I was lying on grass and my spine was not being rubbed raw.

Once again, to my shame and confusion, my body went off into that spinning wildness I had experienced earlier, and before long I know my hips were bucking up at the man shagging me, and I cried out. Several times. No, I must be honest. I have to confess I cried out quite a lot, especially when each of them writhed into his climax, and made me jerk like some animal, eager to engulf him, to drain him even.

I did not know what was happening to me, or even who I was. I had never felt such sensations as I was now overwhelmed by. Mentally my situation was appalling. I was the naked captive of African savages. They were raping me, one after the other.

Bodily, something else was happening. I remember very

22

clearly a moment of lostness and emptiness when one of them, having finished his climax, pulled out of me too fast, followed by a feeling of wild joy when he was replaced by another, filling me again, and pumping at me. It was unbelievable to me that a civilized Englishwoman should feel such animalistic things, especially in such circumstances. But I did, and it stunned me.

My self-control had reasserted itself by the time of the next rest-break, and the following one. I was taken aside by several of the warriors each time, and they had their way with my body, but at least I now had control of myself and was able to observe, almost dispassionately, what was happening.

I learned then that a woman can do that. It was, in a way, as though I was outside somewhere, watching what was being done to me, and even watching my own body's reactions to it. I saw them lead me a little way aside and gesture me to lie down on the ground. I saw myself raise my bound hands above my head as if some-one was holding them. I saw myself spread my legs, my quim puffy and gaping. I saw the eager grins on their faces as they pulled off their loincloths one after another. I saw my body writhing beneath them. Saw their thick members ploughing me.

At the same time, every physical sensation seemed to have been multiplied enormously, and was not at any distance at all. Though my eyes and my mind seemed to be watching from a mile away, my body registered every single sensation. The way their cocks stretched my sheath and moved in me. The way I became moist and clinging. The way my loins began to move to match their urgent thrustings. The way ripples of sensation coursed through me. The sharpness of the grass beneath my back. Even the clouds moving across the moon above their heaving, pumping shoulders as they fucked me. Everything was clearer than crystal.

One of them took my left breast into his mouth as he

23

bucked in me, and bit my nipple in the last moment of his throes. It hurt, and I was bruised next day, but at the time it signified nothing save an additional point of voluptuous sensation, for my body was boiling and I was conscious of little save the heat he was pumping into me, and how my body was welcoming him.

I sound wanton and you may condemn me, but I plead in mitigation that I was, like so many girls of my generation, very ignorant about physical things between men and women. I was the captive of men I had been told were savages and headhunters. They were doing to me what my husband had done, only more so if you see what I mean. I was shocked and horrified of course, as a lady should be, but the trouble was that my body would not obey my mind and actually seemed eager for their thrustings inside me. Several times I was overtaken by such intense sensations, such clenchings and writhings when they pumped their hotness into me that I came near to fainting. I have to confess I even began to feel a tinge of loss when they withdrew from me!

It was an enormous intensification of those vague feelings my husband had aroused in me when he required my 'wifely duties'. He had never taken those feelings to their conclusion, however. These men, these unknown savages who were having their way with me there on the ground under the open sky, did bring those feelings to their conclusion. Stunningly so. So stunningly that my mind reeled away and I could not even think about how my body had responded.

By the time daylight came and we reached another village, I was once again in something of a trance. I was limping a little, for they had all taken turns on me during the night's march, and I felt stiff about my hips and very puffy and sore between my legs, but it did not seem to matter a farthing when the village women and children rushed out, laughing and ululating, to greet our party. I knew I was the centre of attention. Of course I was! How many African villages in the year of our Lord 1849 had witnessed a naked white woman being led captive into their midst! But somehow, it did not seem to matter to me.

The human mind is a strange and powerful thing. Somehow, without consciously working at it, my mind, or perhaps my urge for survival, had reached a conclusion. I was alive. A captive, true, and an abused one to boot. But I was alive. I intended to remain so, given the chance. If to do so I had to allow these people the freedom of my body, so be it.

My mind still shied away from the knowledge of how my body had become ecstatic nearly every time they had their fun with it.

I was put into a hut, given some food and water and once again left alone for the day, although this time my wrists were untied. My feet had become scratched and grazed during all the marching but a young girl gave me a bowl of cool water to bathe them in, though there was, of course, no soap. Between my legs was sore and puffy, and stickiness extended down my thighs where the men's jism had seeped out of me during the march. The water was a blessing, and I washed myself as thoroughly as I could, even going inside a little.

Again I slept an exhausted sleep, and was awakened with food and water when the sun was low in the sky. The man beckoned me up and took me out of the hut. There was a milling crowd and many hands reached out to touch me all over as I was led to the group of warriors who had charge of me.

My hands were tied, this time behind my back, and to my even greater consternation a rope was tied loosely around my neck. For a while, as the warriors discussed something, the long end of the rope was left hanging down my front, between my bare breasts. Then one of the men took up the end of the rope and I was led off, for all the world like a dog on a leash.

I was mentally prepared for another night like the last - hours of marching interspersed with breaks for rest and water, and the men taking turns to shag me. I was wildly wrong. It turned out to be much, much worse!

After only about an hour's marching I espied the glimmer of a fire ahead of us. As we got closer I made out that there was a tent and a large wagon. There were figures moving around the camp fire. From their silhouettes they looked to be robed like Arabs.

Suddenly I felt terrified. After more than two days and nights, and all they had done with me, I had become almost accustomed to being naked among these African men. But to be seen like this by others was horrid and shaming!

I hung back, but a sharp tug on my leash and a whack on my behind from the inevitable switch urged me forward. A hundred yards from the camp I was made to halt. Another rope was put on me, this one linking my elbows. It was pulled tight. I blushed at the way it pulled my shoulders back and made me push out my chest. It felt as though my breasts were on offer, as it were. Ever since my chest began to swell a couple of years earlier, and especially since gentlemen had begun to look at my bodice so much, and younger men to even make sneaky attempts to feel me, I had been somewhat embarrassed about the size of my breasts. With my arms trussed behind me thus, they seemed to stick out an awfully long way, and to tremble a lot as I was pulled by the halter around my neck into the circle of firelight.

The figures I had seen were indeed Arabs. Unlike the natives in the villages we had stopped at, these men did not crowd around at the sight I presented. In fact none of them moved away from the fire. I was pulled over to a tree and backed up against its thick trunk. The long end of my leash was taken around the trunk and re-tied at my neck so that I was held fast, unable to move at all except to shuffle my feet and clamp one knee across the other in instinctive reaction to my shameful exposure.

My captors had joined the Arabs by the fire and the man who had tied me in this helpless position went over and sat down with them. There ensued an animated discussion, with much extravagant waving of arms. It was obvious that I was included in whatever they were talking about, for the one I had come to think of as the leader of the Africans, the big one, kept pointing in my direction.

It became even more obvious when he and one of the Arabs rose and came over to the tree to which I was bound so uncomfortably. I could not understand a single word they were saying as they loomed over me, but somehow I knew what was in their minds.

The Arab man grabbed my breasts in both his hands. He squeezed and slapped and bounced them as though he was testing fruits. It hurt, and when I cried out he grabbed my cheeks, forcing my mouth to stay open, and inspected my teeth as though I were some animal he was considering for purchase.

He said something and the African man grabbed my left ankle, pulling it up to the side before I had a chance to react. The Arab turned his attention to the place that was now made helplessly vulnerable by the way the African was holding my leg high and wide. I shut my eyes in shame and horror as the robed man knelt and parted me with his thumbs. I could feel his breath on my thigh as he inspected me closely. He ran course fingers along my slit, between my body lips, then thrust a finger into me, making me yelp with shock and discomfort. He parted my nether lips with hard fingers and peered up me. He even sniffed me! I wanted to die of embarrassment!

Then the hands were off me and my leg was let go. By the time I had the strength to open my tearful eyes, the two men were back near the campfire. The discussion continued, though not so noisily. Several of the Arabs went into

27

one of the tents and emerged hauling long, heavy-looking crates. The lids were wrenched off with some kind of crowbar. Guns were taken out, guns like the carbines I had seen British soldiers carrying back in Lagos and Benin.

A number of them were passed from hand to hand among the Africans, and put to shoulders as though aiming, and waved about with obvious excitement. The guns were placed back in the crates and the lids re-nailed. Then, the Africans who had captured and possessed me over the last two days and nights picked up the crates, each one between two men, and walked away from the camp.

It was only when they were nearly out of sight that I realised with horror what had happened. For a silly moment I thought they had simply forgotten about me, tied there to the tree on the edge of the camp. Then I understood, and nearly fainted. I had been abandoned to these Arabs! Bartered, naked and helpless, in exchange for guns - guns which would probably be used to fight my fellow British!

FOUR

Even before the party of warriors had disappeared, one of the Arabs was approaching me. I think it was the same one who had examined me so crudely earlier. With a large, curved knife he cut through the rope which bound my neck to the trunk of the tree. Without ceremony, he grabbed my halter and dragged me over to his companions by the campfire. I was grateful for the heat from the fire for African nights can be rather chilly, but not for the attentions I at once received.

Talking to each other all the while, they checked me over as though I was no more than some piece of goods, which I suppose I was if the truth be told. Again, my mouth

28

was pulled open and my teeth and tongue inspected. My breasts were squeezed and tweaked and bounced, and my nipples tugged painfully. I was grabbed by my hair and bent forward. My feet were kicked apart. Hands mauled at the cheeks of my bottom, slapped them, pulled them apart. Fingers probed me, causing me to squeal. A stinging smack soon shut me up.

A lot of fingers examined me as I was held there helpless and humiliated to tears. The way I was positioned, bent low and with my feet wide apart, my private parts were shamefully available to them. Some of them even probed my nether entrance! It was horrible! And some of them had ragged fingernails, which scratched me sorely.

I expected that when they finished this debasing examination they would throw me to the ground and take turns in shagging me. Was certain of it, in fact. There came a by now familiar lurch of unruly wantonness deep inside me at the thought.

Instead, I was dragged upright by the man holding my hair. He said something to me, sounding harsh and frightening, though I did not understand a word, then turned me and cut off my halter and the ropes binding my wrists and elbows. As I flexed my arms to ease the cramps he grabbed me again by my hair and pulled me towards the wagon standing behind one of the tents.

He hauled me around to the back, tears stinging my eyes from his fierce grip on my hair. He shoved me forward and made me climb up into the wagon, shoving his hand between my legs to propel me up and in. I sprawled on the floor of the wagon in the most undignified manner imaginable.

The man leapt up into the wagon too, and my hair was grabbed again as I was pulled up and pushed backwards to sit on some kind of bench. The wrists which had so recently been cut free were taken and locked into some kind of manacles; I could hear chains clinking and the metal was hard and cold on my wrists. Then my arms were raised up, and I felt the manacles being fixed to something above my head.

The wagon was pitch dark and I could see nothing, which made the whole thing more terrifying. I heard the man dealing with me grunting, a low, animal sound. His hand slapped at my breasts and then shoved down between my legs, as though to demonstrate ownership. I heard him chuckle when I cried out as his harsh fingers invaded me.

When the awful Arab man left after fingering my quim most lewdly for several minutes, I struggled to recover myself and tried to sense my surroundings by scent and hearing, for I could still see nothing in the blackness of the wagon. I was soon certain that I was not alone. Muted snuffling noises could be heard. I could discern the scent of other bodies than mine; could feel their proximity. It was not until hours later, by which time the camp had been struck and the wagon had rolled and creaked for ages, and the dawn was coming up, that I was able to see the predicament I was in - a predicament in which I was not alone.

Within the wagon, their wrists chained like my own to hooks high up near the roof of the wagon, were several other girls. Like me, they were manacled and naked. Their heads were drooping in misery at their fate and, as the hours dragged on and the wagon creaked and bumped and grew stuffy in the heat of the African day, my head drooped as well.

At around the middle of the day the wagon lurched to a halt. One of the Arabs jerked open the canvas flaps that enclosed the back of the wagon and sunlight poured in, temporarily blinding me. I felt rather than saw him clamber up into the wagon. There came the rattling of chains and my arms were freed from the hook, though not from the manacles, the other girls likewise.

The man shouted something and banged the cane he

carried against the wooden floor. Wearily the other girls began to struggle to their feet. Since I was nearest the back of the wagon I hurried to follow suit, assuming we had been ordered out. Several other Arabs were standing around outside, and when I hesitated the cane landed very hard on my bottom. I veritably dived out, and sprawled all ungainly to the ground for the wagon was high. I blushed at the men's laughter as I scrambled to my feet. The manacles prevented me from rubbing at the stripe of agony across my bottom, else I would have done so with no thought for dignity!

They gave us water, which was blessedly welcome even though it came in a communal bowl and was brackish. The other girls, all young Africans, had surely experienced this before and knew what I did not, for they instantly plunged their faces into the bowl and began slurping, even banging their heads together to make room. In only moments, my thirst and my will to survive driving me, my own head was down among theirs and I too was slurping up the water without a thought for how humiliating this was.

When the cool water almost gone there came a shout. I was so busy drinking I did not register for a moment, until the cane once again cut down onto my unsuspecting bottom, making me scream at the sudden fire of it. I leapt to my feet to join the other three girls, who were standing in a line, their manacled hands clasped at their navels, their feet wide and their heads bowed. Another cut of the cane fell on my buttocks, and I hastened to adopt the same pose.

My eyes were flicking about wildly as I tried to take in the scene. There were at least four men, all swathed in the flowing white robes of desert Arabs. Each carried a long, thin cane. There were three girls other than myself, all young and African and naked and manacled. My heart came very close to despair as I realised that this was nothing else than a slave train. I had been sold to Arab slavers in exchange for a few boxes of guns! What my fate was to be now did not bear thinking about.

That journey in the stuffy, rattling wagon, took an age; two weeks at least. The cargo of miserable women was added to several times, until the wagon was uncomfortably crowded, all of us naked and with our wrists chained to the roof-hooks except when we were let out to be watered and fed at the middle of the day, and again at night. The nights were the most trying.

The routine was always the same. A couple of us would be set to gathering wood or dried dung or anything else combustible for the two fires that were to be built - a large one for cooking, a smaller one for outside our captors' tent. Another pair would be sent to fetch water, for we always seemed to stop near a stream or water-hole. The rest would hurry to erect the Arabs' tent and arrange the carpets and cushions within, then set about preparing the ingredients for our meal - invariably a great pot of porridge-like stew with a few vegetables chopped into it, some lumps of fatty meat which always made the stew greasy, plus a lot of salt. Our captors prepared their own, much more succulent meal of breads and kebabs and beans and fruits.

Then, while the food was cooking, we were made to run around the wagon. One of the Arabs would stand beyond each of its corners, cane in hand, and we girls were made to run round and round and round, spurred on by plentiful swipes if we slowed or stumbled. At first I thought all this running was just gratuitous torment, but later it occurred to me that, as shrewd businessmen, our captors were simply keeping their herd of naked women fit and trim.

Lest you wonder why we did not attempt escape, the reasons are simple. We were in the middle of relentless African bush. We were naked. We were manacled. And besides, we had been set a chilling example.

One girl, a tall and spirited creature, did try to run off a couple of days after she was put with us. They caught her within the hour, and dragged her back by her hair. With many shouts and cuts with their canes, they made the rest of us form a line to watch the proceedings.

The girl was huddled sobbing near the foot of a nearby tree Two of the Arabs grabbed her manacles and hauled her to her feet. They attached a long rope to the chain between her wrists, threw the end over a high branch, and hauled the struggling girl up until only her toes were touching the ground.

Then they began to beat her, two of them, ignoring her screams and her frantic writhing and kicking. Their blows fell indiscriminately as she twisted and span, catching her back and thighs as well as her poor backside, and even striping her breasts and belly. They stopped at last when she fainted, only the heaving of her chest showing that she had not passed away. The rest of us huddled together, trembling with shock and whimpering from the savagery of it. It was a salutary lesson, and none of the rest of us ever even thought about escape after that.

After our enforced run around the wagon for the purposes of fitness, we were allowed to feed. We ate like animals. There were ten of us at the end, all fighting to get our hands and faces into the communal bowl of stew while our captors relaxed over their own meal. One had to fight or go hungry, for there was never enough to go round. One very big girl always got most. She showed no compunction in shoving the rest of us aside so that she could eat her fill, and she was so much bigger and stronger than us that she had no difficulty in keeping us out of her way. What puzzled me for the first few nights, until I understood a long while later what the relation between two women can be, was that she always made room for a particularly delicate little creature, with huge eyes and a nervous manner, to eat beside her. The pair always looked almost grotesque, the one huge and muscular, her great breasts swinging as she gobbled the stew, the other tiny by comparison, her backside tight and her breasts hardly more than buds.

When our communal bowl had been scraped and licked clean, another bowl was provided; a bowl of water from which we were allowed to drink and wash our hands and faces.

The sleeping arrangements for we females were very simple. A rope was tied to our manacles and then to one of the spokes of the wagon's wheels. That was when the awful bit happened. As we lay there, ten of us by the end, naked, our arms stretched above our heads, our bodies exposed, our captors would move around us as though inspecting items on a butcher's slab. They would pick one, or sometimes two. The girl would be untied, hauled up by her manacles and taken off to the tent.

I was chosen any number of times. I suppose it was because I was the only European. It must have been that, because several of the others were much prettier than me. The contrast between their appearance and mine was dramatic. Each of them was tall, one or two reaching almost six feet I judged, whereas I reached hardly more than five. Their skins were dark and glossy, reflecting the firelight as though they were made of metal, while mine is very pale and I am plagued with freckles. Their hair was tight and black and curly, much more sensible than mine, which was long and unruly and of a hue which got me teased as 'ginger' and 'carrots' when I was a child. The contrast between myself and the other girls automatically drew our captors eyes in my direction, and they were not easy on me.

The first time I was taken to the tent was a lesson to me, or perhaps a demonstration of an unconscious resolution I had reached. Or perhaps it was just a woman's instinct to survive. Together with another girl, one of the very tall ones, I was pulled up from the wagon and dragged off towards the tent. Since the man had taken a very thorough feel of my intimacies before grabbing me, I knew exactly what to expect. I was more wrong than I had ever been in my entire life!

The tent was large and lit by several brass oil-lamps. The three men already inside the tent were lounging on sheep-skins and sharing a water-pipe as the fourth shoved us inside. I could feel the tall girl beside me trembling in antici-pation of what was about to happen to us. I was trembling myself. I told myself that these four could not be harder on me than the dozen warriors who had sold me to them. It did not really make me any less nervous.

One of the men clambered to his feet and approached. As I knew was inevitable, he came straight for me. I man-aged not to cower when he reached forward and began to play with my breasts, though I know I blushed to my toe-tips as he squeezed and bounced me, turning his head to grin and call to his companions. I could not prevent a little squeal of pain when he pinched my nipples and pulled them; pulled them so hard I almost staggered and fell against him.

He laughed aloud at my discomfiture, and did it again. He spent a long time pinching and tugging at my nipples, grinning down at me as I blushed and winced. From the cor-ner of my eye I saw that the other girl had been taken to the side of the tent, and was already on her back with one of the men very vigorous between her long legs. I knew I would very soon be in a similar situation, but stood as still as I could, knowing I had no choice if I was to survive, while the man pinched and tugged at my nipples until I had tears in my eyes.

I knew he was going to shag me, and found myself wish-ing he would stop tormenting my nipples and get on with it.

FIVE

I was confused when instead of shoving me down onto my back, the man who had been playing with me suddenly grabbed me by my hair - what a curse thick hair can be! - and forced me to my knees. With his free hand he pulled aside his robe and there, right in front of my face, was his thick cock pointing out at me like the neck of a tortoise.

He jerked my head forward and his thing actually bumped against my face. I was shocked beyond measure. I jerked back and, despite the pain from the way my hair was being pulled, glanced up at the man. He was making strange motions with his mouth and his loins. After a blank moment I understood, and was amazed. No-one could ask such a thing! What he was indicating was beyond imagining!

I squirmed and struggled, almost pulling my hair from my head in my panic. The man released my hair and stepped back his robe falling to cover him rampant cock. My relief was very short lived.

Amidst shouts and scuffling my manacles were grabbed and I was hefted to my feet, then off them. My wrists were dragged painfully high. My manacles were hooked over a thick peg protruding from the central tent-post, and I was left dangling. More shouts and the other girl, released now by the man who had shagged her, scuttled across on all fours and grabbed my ankles with strong fingers.

She held my legs still. From the corner of my eye I saw the man who had handled me so brutally rummage in a thick bundle. What he came up with made me catch my breath. It was a rod rather like an English horse-whip, but thin and perhaps four feet in length. From the end hung a loop of leather perhaps another six or nine inches long. He swished it through the air several times, as though for practice. The noise it made was awful!

So was its effect. Stretched out between the manacles hooked over the peg and the other girl's strong hands holding me fast, I watched with growing terror as the man took up position to one side of me. There was no preamble. He simply raised his whip and brought it down across my backside.

It was as though a fiery brand had landed on me and stayed! How the other girl managed to hold on to my legs I cannot imagine, for I bucked and kicked like a wild thing. He beat me very fast in his anger, the only pause being when someone shoved a rag into my mouth to gag my screams.

I came back to consciousness lying on the ground, water having been splashed on to my face. The man who had whipped me was standing over me again. He reached down and took a handful of my hair. He did not need to pull hard to get me up onto my knees. I had been beaten in both senses. He pulled his robe aside.

I did not know what to do. Or rather, I did not know how to do what he obviously required. The very idea of such a thing could never possibly have occurred to any well brought up young woman. Mind you, the idea of having a man thrusting his cock into one's private place would have been equally unthinkable before my arranged marriage to Mr Mansfield only six months ago!

A man's parts are strange close to, especially as close as these now were to my face. He had two handfuls of my hair and was pulling me on. His thing was thick and sort of lolling in front of me, a drop of clear fluid dewing its single eye. I had to lift it between forefinger and thumb to do what he wanted. He began to stiffen almost as soon as I touched him.

I was very nervous. I licked my lips and reached out my tongue to him. He tasted strange, tangy. I licked the purplish, plum-like end, still not quite knowing what to do - or perhaps simply not wishing to admit it to myself. He jerked my head forward a bit, pressing my lips against what I had just been licking. Nervously I opened to him.

I gagged as he pushed himself into my mouth. I had no recourse but to go with him, for I dreaded another beating. He jerked my head backwards and forwards. I understood. It was just the same motion a man uses when he is taking his pleasure between a woman's legs. His size and the depth of his movements forced me to suck and swallow. It was strange and alien, but I had no choice in it. The notion that a man might want to pleasure himself in a woman's mouth in the same way as he did her private place confused me, but at the same time a part of my mind saw the logic of it.

Even as I performed this act for the first time I began to understand the sense of it, for both are soft and warm places. Then again, I also came to understand, pretty quickly, than men are not very fussy about where they get relief when their manhoods are excited!

That first time I was incapable of understanding much except that my behind was on fire, that a man was shagging me in my mouth and that I was trying desperately not to gag and choke. I lost my fight when he jerked into his come, for he shoved ever so deep, right to the back of my throat, and it was impossible for me to swallow fast enough as he pumped his jism into my gaping throat.

He was grinning as he stepped back and put himself away. Some of his stuff had seeped from the corners of my mouth and dribbled down to my chin. I wiped it off with a finger. I could not think what to do with it. I did not dare wipe it on the rug I was kneeling on. I did the only thing that seemed possible, and licked my finger clean. Already a second man was advancing on me, grinning salaciously and pulling open his robe.

With this second man, I learned that if I moved my

38

head of my own volition he did not pull so hard on my hair, nor push so strongly with his cock. By the time the third of them put his hands on my head and pulled me forward my mind was back in control, and I knew what I needed to do. I bobbed my face up and down on him, and sucked on him, and used my tongue. It was much easier then, for he let go my head, and did not pump at me to make me gag, and I had some measure of control over what was happening.

With the fourth of them, even though I was feeling sick from all I had been obliged to swallow, I dared to use my hands as well as my lips and tongue. He came off very quickly, and I felt a wave of relief as, my fingers rubbing his thickness and my mouth sucking like mad on the plum-like end of his thing, he did his spurting and I swallowed it all.

'At least,' I thought, 'it is over.'

It was not of course. As soon as I had gulped down the last man's spurtings I was hauled off to one side and tossed down onto my back. At once one of the men was on me, shoving my legs wide and pushing into me without ceremony. He was not near so urgent as I was used to; indeed, he moved slow. I supposed that it was because he had already reached at least one climax in my mouth, and possibly another in the other girl, and thus was not so much in need of quick relief.

He took his time, moving in me slow and deep, his hands gripping my bottom to pull me on. I was able to look at his face, all screwed up and tense with the pleasure he was getting from me. He had a big nose pitted with blackheads. His moustaches and beard were matted. I began to think him ugly until what was happening between my legs, in my belly, started to take over.

My body began to swell to an urgency. The sensations set off by the cock moving in my sheath began to dominate everything. My breasts felt hard as his hands fondled them. The muscles of my belly and thighs began to ripple and spasm with that strange, honeyed, overwhelming force that, nowadays, always seemed to rise in me when a man was shagging me. My head span. My loins bucked. I felt him jerk into his come, and my whole being became a rain of golden electricity as I writhed with excitation until I felt I must surely die.

A woman's climax is so deep, so profound, that it is indeed a kind of sweet dying, and at the same time the most glorious, shattering, skylark sensation anyone can possibly experience. And it goes on longer than a man's. I knew this more or less at once, for when the man who had sent me to this Elysium had finished he pulled out of me straight away, causing me to mewl a bit with disappointment. But then his place was taken by another, and at once I was bucking and gasping again, and my belly was matching the rhythm of the organ ploughing me.

It was a long night. Each of the men took turns to fuck me, and one even made use of my mouth again - which tasted strange and took a long time, for he had already had any number of comes. It was only next day, manacled and half asleep in the back of the creaking wagon, that my weary brain began to become reflective. It was a rather incoherent reflectiveness to be sure, and it kept swimming in and out of my consciousness as I dozed and came awake again, but before the end of the day I knew myself much better than I had before.

My cloudy thoughts circled around the strange, overwhelming and - honesty compels me to confess it - glorious sensations which had overtaken me when I was being shagged. Some of the time it had been almost as though while pleasuring themselves by doing what they were doing between my legs, the men were also pleasuring me. Things had happened in my body which I could still hardly believe. The sheath into which they repeatedly shoved themselves became welcoming, and seemed to writhe and convulse with a strange kind of rapture at their invasions. The sight, out of the corner of my eye while one of the men bucked between my legs, of the beautiful African girl sucking and fondling a hard cock set off a deep-seated lurching in my belly which caused the man shagging me to grin and bellow out loud as he reached his climax. And that in turn had set off another convulsion in my own body.

What kind of woman had I become? Was I a wanton? A hussy? Why had those reactions which my husband had occasionally awoken in me now become so overpowering? And so frequent! I could not come to an answer. All I can say is that soon, when we were taken out of the wagon in the middle of the day to be fed and watered, I found myself looking at the men differently - and watching to see how they looked at me.

Why the way they looked at me should have been significant I could not have put into words. What I can say is that the expression on the face of one of them, any of them, as his eyes moved from my bosoms to my legs, as he smirked and licked his lips, would cause me to blush and make my nipples harden.

As I have said, the journey in the wagon lasted at least two weeks. I was taken into the men's tent for the night many more times, always with one or more of the African girls. It became clear very quickly that our four Arab captors took particular pleasure from the enjoyment of my mouth. Each of them required that particular service on each of the nights I was taken into their tent, sometimes to stir them up to take the other girl, sometimes as a preamble to shagging me. Towards the end of our journey I was even required to suck thick manhoods during our mid-day stop.

It may seem shameful to you, but I tried hard to please in this respect, not only from dread of that awful beating being repeated, but because I learned that if I performed well and eagerly the men would not grab my hair and drag me on and choke me and, more importantly, I had some

41

measure of control over that moment when they began to jerk and spurt. At least I no longer gagged at it. Also, honesty obliges me to confess that the taste of them and of their salty jism spurting on to the back of my tongue became not unpleasant.

One of the many difficulties about that journey was that I did not speak the language and none of the others spoke English. I could respond to the shouts and gestures of the men - they were usually pretty explicit, and often accompanied by a sharp swipe from a cane. What was worse was that the other captive girls could talk to each other, but I could not.

Questions burned in me, but I could not ask them. Were these men really slave traders? Where were they taking us? Where had the other girls come from? Had they been captured and sold like me? What was to be our fate?

The other girls could talk to one another and did most of the time, in whispers because the men sometimes became angry if they heard conversation. I was isolated from this consolation, and felt very lonely and dispirited because of it.

In fact I cried a quite a lot during that awful journey. But then, as I think will always happen when numbers of people are in the same distress, one of the other captive girls tried to comfort me. We could not speak each other's language, but there is an unspoken meaning in the eyes, and hers were tender and comforting. She hugged me, and helped me to eat the greasy stew we were fed at night before lying down around the wagon or - often in both our cases - were taken into the men's tent for a night of sucking and shagging. We managed to sit beside each other in the wagon as we creaked and bumped towards wherever we were heading. With our wrists manacled to the hooks near the roof we could not touch or hug, but we managed to sit close, shoulder to shoulder and hip to hip, and I drew strength from her.

She was a sweet girl and very pretty, a little younger than me I guessed, with pert little breasts, a charming shy smile, and the deepest, loveliest eyes. The lumbering wagon in which we spent each day was hot and cramped and stinking. Our wrist manacles, which were not even removed when we were taken into the men's tent at night, chaffed and grazed our wrists. The food never varied from that greasy stew. We were beaten at the least excuse. Yet through it all, though she was as harshly treated as any of us, my new little friend showed as much concern for me as for herself.

Her care made the difference in me between unhappiness and despair, and I wondered from whence she drew such loving strength. I was only able to repay her inadequately by nursing her as best I could after she had been dragged off to entertain the men in their tent for yet another a night, this time without me.

They had been very hard with her, and she had been in a sorry state when they hauled her back. Even through the coffee-darkness of her skin I could detect bruises on her hips, and the insides of her thighs and on her sweet little breasts. To judge by the weals on her poor bottom, they had used their cane on her an awful lot, and she hissed and flinched when I smoothed some of the congealed fat from the stew over them, that being the only palliative I could think of.

SIX

The journey ended at last in some kind of town of mud-brick houses. The first we knew of it was when we were hauled out from the cart at evening and herded, canes flying freely, into a great walled yard like a prison and, with men shouting and encouraging us with long canes, were herded

43

into a large room with brick walls and an iron door, where at last our manacles were removed. It felt wonderful! The men were very eager in the use of their canes though, and several of us were hissing and clutching at our stinging bottoms by the time we scurried into the room.

There were other women already there, cowering naked and round eyed. The iron door crashed shut, and what little light came in through the narrow slits high up in the walls began to wane. My new friend and I huddled in a corner together, and our hearts sank.

We were kept there for several days, and each day more women and girls were herded in until there must have been half a hundred of us of all shapes and sizes, though I was still the only European - a fact which assured that I got a lot of attention, from the other women as well as from the guards.

Each morning the iron door would crash open and some guards would bring in a great cauldron of stew, which seemed to be made mostly of beans and lentils with the occasional piece of meat, and a basket of flat, unleavened breads, which they set down in the middle of the room. We soon learned that, apart from the bath-sized container of water near the door, this was all we would get until night, when a similar mess would be brought in to us.

The scene when that food was brought in and the guards left was from a nightmare. There were no bowls or spoons or anything else, and there was no standing on ceremony. The women fought like cats to get their share of the food! The bigger, stronger ones literally kicked their slighter sisters aside or dragged them back by their hair.

The big woman who had been in our wagon was by far the best at this fierce contest of naked, shoving and wrestling women. She showed no compunction about punching and elbowing other women aside, and once she was at the cauldron she was not to be moved, her heavy breasts swaying as she bent over the food, her great haunches banging from side to side to keep others away and allow her little friend to eat beside her. I have to confess, a little guiltily, that I soon learned to cheer her on, for she also favoured and assisted those of us who had been in the same wagon with her.

It was another example of how people in the same straits help each other, and I admired her for it. Had she not held others off and made space for me I would probably have got no food at all, being among the smallest women in that awful dungeon. Mind you, I did learn to scratch and bite with the best of them whenever one of the other women tried to snatch away my hard won meal!

Incidentally, it was during several of the nights in this foul dungeon that I witnessed a scene which greatly puzzled me and which I did not fully understand until a while later. The big woman who had looked after her little friend during our wagon-journey and now fought for our food for us, was lying off to one side, her little friend curled up within her muscular arm.

A movement caught my eye in the pale light from the high openings in the wall. It was the big woman moving and patting her little friend on her tight little bottom. To my astonished curiosity, the little one, lithe and quick in her movements, span around and wriggled on top of her protectress' big body.

The big woman's knees rose and parted as the young girl's body wriggled on to hers, her own slighter legs moving to either side of her friend's lolling bosoms. The girl seemed to have her head pressed down between her partner's heavy thighs, and it seemed to be bobbing and moving - though, then, I could not think for the life of me why or to what purpose.

It was too dark to see very much, and it was clearly a

rather private thing so I did not stare. I could not help keep peeping though. As well as the pretty young girl's head bobbing in the strangest of manners, the big woman's hands seemed to be doing something between the girl's legs.

There was only one answer to what they were doing, but at the time my mind could not encompass the possibility of it. I was to learn better before long.

For myself, I had come very low. As I have said, being the only European meant that I got a lot of attention from the guards. It seemed that in this place they had absolute rights over we women captives. Those rights extended to entering our dungeon whenever they fancied, and indicating the woman they required with a sharp swipe of their canes. All too often it was me. Their chosen one would then have to follow them docilely to their selected spot to be raped, often by several of them - and to show willing into the bargain. As I learned the very first time I was selected, it did not pay to seem reluctant: they were very free with their canes, very free indeed!

Captive, naked, in a place I knew not whereof, I would surely have despaired and tried to end it all had it not been for the sweetness of my little friend and the hearty support of the big woman. I never knew their names, but I knew their natures and loved them for it.

After the morning battle for food we were taken out and obliged to wash ourselves down like cattle, with swabs and buckets of water, each bucket shared by half a dozen of us. We were then made to trot in a circle around the main part of the barn for exercise, all of us in a mob as though we were racing against one another. The men guarding us wielded goads and canes which they did not hesitate to use on us if we failed to keep moving at a satisfactorily quick pace.

The sight of fifty or more women and girls prancing naked around that barn, their breasts and bottoms jiggling, must have been hugely entertaining for the dozen or more men who guarded us. All of them grinned as they watched us, and all of them were free with their canes, usually picking out a particularly pretty and nubile girl to swipe as she trotted past, making her squeal and grab her sore bottom. I myself came in for a lot of this, presumably because my white skin attracted the eye. I was certainly not the prettiest among us, nor did I have the best figure.

Some of the captive girls, especially the younger ones, were enviably lovely as to their bodies. Dark, glossy skin stretched tight over long, slender backs and high, firm buttocks. Slim, curvaceous thighs and calves like gazelles. Breasts small and firm, or full and swaying. Arms slim and strong, hands with long, delicate fingers. Oh, how I envied them their grace and strength as I chased them around that awful barn, my own too-large titties bouncing uncomfortably, my hair flapping around my shoulders, my lungs heaving as I struggled to keep up with their seemingly easy pace.

The only respite a girl had from this hour of exercise was if one of the guards grabbed her arm and pulled her aside. It was a mixed blessing, for although she could then get a rest from the running, the guard would make very free with her panting body, mauling and feeling and fingering to his heart's content. I was even obliged on several occasions to put my hand inside a guard's cloak and rub his stiff cock while he pulled and tweaked my breasts. At least, though, I was not made to kneel down and suck any of them as some of the other girls were - right there in public too!

Somehow I found the strength not to buckle under this regime, but ran determinedly, and suffered the stripes of their canes across my backside, and kept still for their gropings, and rubbed their cocks. I tried not to think about the way my body got all hot and unruly when they played with me. It is shameful for a respectable Englishwoman to get bodily excitement from the fact that a total stranger is thrusting his fingers into her quim just because he has the power to do so, whether she wills or not. But I did. Often, if one of the guards had fingered me rather thoroughly, my legs would become almost too weak for the running, and my lungs would be panting.

Finally, after an age running round and round, when they were satisfied that their beasts, we gasping females, were exercised enough to keep us fit and presentable, we were locked away again until we were fed in the evening.

My dreadful certainty as to what was going to happen to us was confirmed on the fourth or fifth morning. We were fed and watered as before, and washed down, but this time there was no forced exercise.

Instead of being made to run around, we were made to stand in a wide circle. A tall man with a black beard, wearing a fez and the usual flowing robes, though his were black rather than the usual white or striped, entered the barn-like hall and began to inspect us.

He pointed to me at once, for I stood out as the only white woman among the crowd. Instantly, a huge guard grabbed my hair and I was separated out and dragged off to a large side-room. Soon, other girls were thrown in with me, all of them young, and all as terrified as I was. My sweet friend from the wagon journey was among them, and we clung to one another.

When the tall man entered, he was accompanied by a number of black-robed women. We were made to stand, and they began to prepare us for what my sinking heart knew was to be our sale. Any reluctance was greeted with a slap, and we were made to stand up straight, with our hands behind our heads, our elbows back so that our breasts were well presented. The auctioneer (for surely that was who the tall, black robed man must be) examined us each in turn.

From the corner of my eye I watched him approach the

first girl. He looked closely into her eyes and ears, pulled her mouth open to examine her teeth, searched through her hair as though for lice. Then he hefted and bounced her breasts, made her bend forward so that he could examine her bottom, then stand straight again and part her knees so he could check her by feeling up between her legs. I tried to steel myself, for it would soon be my turn for this humiliating inspection.

After his examination of each girl, the auctioneer gave some orders to the black-robed women, and the girl was taken aside to be individually prepared.

One girl, very tall and with full hips and great proud breasts, had her nipples painted white to emphasize them, and a white stripe was painted along the crease of her sex. Another girl, whose skin was so dark and glossy it was almost blue-black, was oiled all over so that she glowed.

I myself was the centre of much attention. I was the only European, and they fussed around me. My mind tried to shrug off the rueful thought that their attention was because I would probably fetch a good price.

The auctioneer took his time examining me. He pulled my eyelids wide, and stuck his fingertip into my ears. He scrabbled around in my hair for a long time. He pulled my mouth wide to check my teeth and tongue, which he actually gripped between his fingers and pulled out quite painfully. He kneaded my breasts and the cheeks of my bottom. He knelt down and pulled my knees apart so that he could examine my quim. It was very detailed and very humiliating. He pulled my body lips almost painfully wide and peered up me. He thrust hard fingers into me, even moving them in and out several times as if to make absolutely sure of my physical state.

He grinned smugly at my little gasps and the way my sheath instantly got moist, then signalled to the women. I was taken aside, blushing from the shame of his imperious examination. My hair was washed, then brushed and brushed and brushed until it almost floated about my head and shoulders. My nipples were teased and tweaked and pulled to make them stand out, and then painted red. My nether lips too were teased and then painted. They even painted around my eyes, though what for I could not think.

Then we were all lined up, each looking nervously at the others. The auctioneer looked us over, walking slowly down the line of naked girls and eycing each of us from top to toe. He felt a breast here, a bottom there.

He paused in front of me, and examined me again, with shameful minuteness. He cupped and jiggled both my breasts. He went behind me and pulled the cheeks of my bottom apart, and pushed a finger into me. He slapped a hand on my private place, and sank several fingers into me as though once again checking my tightness and flexibility. He smeared my paint in doing so, and I had to be painted again. I had to fight back tears of humiliation, not only at having to suffer such a callous examination, but also because he had grinned knowingly when his fingers discovered that I had again become moist. At last, having thoroughly fingered and felt me, he stepped back and clapped his hands.

The black-clad women who had combed and painted us re-appeared like a flock of bats. They put squares of cloth on our faces beneath our eyes, and tied them around the napes of our necks, the strings going over our ears so that the masks did not slip down. Then they wrapped voluminous cloaks about our shoulders and tied them at our throats. The cloaks were black, and reached to the ground, and did not smell very fresh. Even so, it felt wonderful to be covered up for the first time in weeks. If I had known that the purpose in covering us was to make our subsequent uncovering all the more noteworthy, I might have felt differently.

We stood like strange statues, all of us now cowed and entirely concealed except for our eyes and hair, all of us

50

looking nervously towards the tall figure of the auctioneer..
A figure clad exactly like we were floated in to stand beside
him. He pointed at us then at her, not using words because
probably few of us would have understood him. He gestured
from this new woman to us several more times, then nodded
his head emphatically and clapped his hands once, loudly.

The woman's hands appeared from between the folds
of her cloak. She swung her arms out, spreading the black
material wide and exposing her naked body to us, then bent
and parted her knees in the lewdest of poses, thrusting her
belly towards us. The auctioneer clapped twice, and she
closed her cloak and returned to the humble stance all we
others were in.

The auctioneer again pointed to her then to us, and
clapped his hands. The woman repeated her performance.
The message was already clear. Several of the girls copied
the woman's demonstration.

The man clapped twice, and all of the women covered
up again. His eyes raked over us from left to right. His face
was stern. Several of the African guards who were standing
by the wall moved forward, swishing their canes. He clapped
his hands again, harder. All of us whipped our cloaks open
and parted our knees, and pushed our bellies forward to display ourselves. He made us do it a dozen times, as if we
were in a rehearsal.

We were. A rehearsal for this man's slave auction.

SEVEN

I am a coward, I know I am, at least in so far as such things
as this were involved. I learned it when I held back from
following the frightening auctioneer outside. I knew by then
that there was a crowd out there, and we would be displayed

51

to them and sold off, and I could not face such a fate.

I screamed out my panic and ran, and tried to hide, which was very stupid of me because it was obvious to the greatest fool that there was nowhere to run. I was caught. A huge man grabbed me up as easily as though I was no more than a kitten almost before I had got half a dozen steps. He held me off the ground, and carried me to the auctioneer. Words were exchanged. I was tossed to the floor and a foot landed on my neck. The back of my cloak was whipped up. A searing fire burst across my backside as they began to beat me with a wide leather strap.

I screamed and struggled, but to no avail. I was whipped and whipped from my waist to the backs of my knees until I had no strength even to beg for mercy. At last it stopped, and I was hauled sobbing to my feet. The auctioneer lifted my chin with his forefinger and his eyes pierced mine. What I saw there terrified me.

He knew I was defeated. His dark eyes bored down into mine, gleaming with triumph at my submission. He grinned, and slowly clapped his hands. As if in a dream, my hands moved forward and parted my robe, and I displayed myself for him, knees bent and spread. He looked me up and down. He reached a hand down very slowly, making sure I knew exactly what he was going to do. I gasped as he slipped his fingers into me. I did not dare move. After a triumphant minute of fingering me he nodded as though I were a pet who had successfully learned a new trick, and turned away, ordering one of the crow-like old women to refurbish the paint around my eyes and between my legs where his hand had smudged it.

When I was signalled to go outside I went silently and without protest.

The other girls were waiting in a huddled group near the foot of some wide wooden steps that led up to a high platform. There were a number of fierce-looking guards watching over them, whips and goads clutched in their hands. The girls and women stood still and silent, their heads bowed, unable to do anything to avoid whatever fate awaited them.

To my surprise, there were several African men there also. They were all tall and well muscled, and might have been well capable of overpowering the guards had their wrists not been manacled behind their necks, and had they not looked as cowed and miserable as we females. Unlike us, they were naked, and their bodies had been oiled to show up their lithe musculature. Had they not been so downcast, they would have looked magnificent. To be honest, I have to add that I could not resist peeping again and again at their tight bottoms and, when they turned, the blatant malenesses that nestled at the joins of their thighs. It made me feel distinctly warm, and a little ashamed of myself.

I could not see over the platform, for it was too high, but I could hear the murmur as of a large crowd, and my tummy turned to warm water. The auctioneer mounted the steps and disappeared onto the platform. I heard his voice speaking loudly, and the crowd quieted. He spoke for a long time, and then a gong sounded.

At once, one of the men was pushed by a guard towards the steps. He began to mount slowly, his head bowed. The guard gave him a single stroke across his backside with the cane to speed him up. He disappeared onto the platform, and after another short speech from the auctioneer I heard the bidding begin.

It was very quick, for after only a few minutes the gong sounded again, and the second man was sent up, and then the third. Now it was the turn of we females.

Our treatment was different. When the gong sounded this time, guards stepped forward. Each took hold of a girl and hauled her up the steps. We were taken up in threes. The selling of the girls took much longer than that of the men. I was kept waiting 'til the very last group, and by the time it came for we final three to be taken up, I was trembling like a leaf.

The sight that met my frightened eyes when we reached the platform fulfilled all my imaginings. Dozens and dozens of robed men thronged the floor of the auction space, all looking up at us greedily. I saw several women, too, which shocked me. Kneeling among them were the girls who had already been sold, their robes gone, their heads bowed. The male slaves were there too, kneeling at the feet of their various new owners, all of whom were women. For an instant I was dizzied by the notion that these poor men, kneeling naked and cowed beside their new owners, had been purchased for carnal purposes. I had a vision of one of these women sitting so smugly with her new purchase kneeling beside her. She was rolling with fat and in at least her sixties, and I imagined her summoning the magnificent creature she had just purchased to service her on pain of a flogging. It made me draw in my breath - and stirred me too, if I am honest.

As I struggled to clear my fuzzled mind, the guards pushed us towards the front of the platform. The auctioneer paced back and forth in front of us talking loudly. I suppose he was extolling our value, for at one point he touched my shoulder, and a little later he fanned out my hair to show it off. He seemed to spend more time on me than the other two, I supposed because I was white and my hair was long and ginger, in contrast to the neat black curls of the others.

When he had finished his speech the auctioneer moved to one side of the stage. With the long staff he carried, he tapped the first girl on her shoulder and she stepped forward to the very edge of the stage. The faces of the crowd of buyers craned upwards. The auctioneer clapped his hands. At once, the girl swung her arms wide to part her cloak, and bent her knees and pushed her belly forward in that lewd pose we had been taught. The upturned faces became greedy.

There began a cacophony of shouts and calls as the crowd began bidding. The girl stood absolutely still in her blatant pose as her price was set. It must have been a high price, for the bidding went on for a long time. At last the auctioneer banged the end of his staff on the stage. He called something, pointed to a grinning man to the left of the stage, and clapped his hands twice.

The poor girl, who had been holding her awkward pose for a long time, slowly straightened up and closed her cloak. One of the guards immediately took it off her. Naked save for the square of cloth hiding the lower part of her face, she was led down some steps at the side of the stage, and was taken possession of by her new owner. I shuddered, both for her unknown fate and my own.

The sale of the second girl was surprisingly quick, and then it was my turn. I had become numb from sheer nerves. I obeyed the tap of the auctioneer's staff on my bottom as though I was a marionette. A sea of faces leered up at me. From a thousand miles away, I heard the auctioneer's hands clap. Like an automaton, I opened my cloak, and parted my knees, and pushed my belly forward, displaying - nay virtually offering - my most private of parts to hundreds of greedy eyes.

It was as though I was not inside my own head. I could see the faces leering up at me. I could see myself displayed to them, my arms wide and my belly thrust forward to give them the best possible view of my exposed womanly parts. I could pick out individual features and voices in the crowd - a high-pitched yelp here, a pock-marked leer there, a tongue wetting the lips of a gap-toothed mouth. Only the slaves who had already been sold were not staring at me ravenously.

Then I was surprised to hear, as if from a distance, the double clap which told me to close my cloak and stand straight again. I did so, puzzled because I was sure the bidding for me had not even started yet. Then I began to learn that my sale was to be different from those of the other girls.

The auctioneer came up behind me, talking loudly to the crowd all the while. He reached around, and untied the cloak at my throat. He held it closed for long moments, then suddenly flung it aside. The crowd shouted and applauded as I stood before them stark naked except for the little square of cloth covering my face below my eyes. Somehow, the veil made me feel even more blatantly naked.

He took my arms and raised them up, linking my hands on the top of my head and pulling my elbows back, so that my breasts were thrust forward. Still talking loudly, he reached round and cupped my titties in his hard hands. He bounced and fondled me and pulled at my nipples in the lewdest manner. I shut my eyes to escape from my humiliation - and from the hotness that was building inside me.

His hands released my breasts, and ran lingeringly over my ribs and flanks and belly. Through a mist of embarrassment, I heard him clap his hands. I could only obey, but I was disconcerted for a moment, for I had no cloak to throw open. Then I guessed what was wanted, and I bent my knees and pushed my belly forward with my hands still behind my head. I felt his hand cup me between my straining thighs. I felt him part my folds for the crowd to see.

He clapped twice, and gratefully I straightened up. He turned me round and bent me over. He nudged my feet apart. His hard hands spread my buttocks. A sharp finger traced the length of my cleft, tapping the tense pucker of my rosehole, and pushing against the lips of my exposed quim. My mind span away from me. There was no part of my body he did not feel free to display for the pleasure of his customers. He even drew the crowd's attention to the weals left on my flesh by my beating earlier, tracing his fingers across them, calling aloud and laughing. I wanted to die.

At last, he made me straighten up, and turned me to

face the crowd. There was a moment of stillness. The auctioneer banged his staff. There came a cacophony of shouts and a forest of waving arms.

My sale had begun.

Never, not even when I was first captured, had I felt so helpless and despondent. Standing stark naked on the auction stage, before a ravening crowd of potential buyers, my heart froze in my chest. My fate would be sealed by whoever paid highest for me, and once again I had no control over what would happen to me.

Instinctively, and with no conscious intent, my shoulders rounded themselves, and my legs pressed themselves together, one knee overlapping the other in an effort to hide at least something of my nakedness. I felt a sharp rap on my bottom from the auctioneer's staff. Angrily, he gestured me to straighten up, and put my hands behind my head, and get my feet apart.

I obeyed. I had no option. He pulled my elbows back so that my breasts were thrust forward. I could feel the eyes of the crowd crawling over my blatantly displayed nakedness. Nothing of me was hidden.

The bidding was loud and rapid. Some part of my brain that was not numb with humiliation wondered how on earth the auctioneer managed to keep up with it, such a babble was there.

The noise began to change. Most of the crowd seemed to have dropped out of the bidding, and it had got slower. I could make out individual voices now, and see hands raised. Ugly, grinning faces turned from me to the auctioneer as he registered their bids. Other faces showed annoyance or anger as their bids were topped.

At last, the bidding became a contest between three would-be purchasers. I looked from one to the other as their bids were called. One was a hugely fat man, quite young, his cleanly shaven face sweating beneath a white turban. The second was an old man so cruel-looking the very sight of his eyes made me shiver. The third was a woman who had already bought several girls, who knelt on the ground beside her, their heads bent low.

I found myself observing with a strange detachment, a sort of resigned calm. One of these three would buy me, and decide my fate. I had no choice in it. I felt I did not even care. Whichever it was, I was lost. I only hoped it would not be the old man with the cruel eyes.

Except for these three, the whole crowd was silent, as though watching some tense contest. The voices bidding could be clearly heard. The gaps between bids grew longer, and I knew I had reached a high price. For some reason it gave me a perverse satisfaction. If one of them was going to possess me, at least it would be at a steep cost!

The fat man dropped out first, and the bidding became a contest between the woman and the cruel-looking old man. I found myself taking sides. The woman scared me, but the man terrified me much more. They bid slowly, and my heart stopped whenever the woman hesitated. First one then the other would listen to the opponent's bid, look down to think, then bid in return. It got slower and slower, and I got more and more nervous.

The man called something to the auctioneer. The woman shouted in response. There was a flurry as both of them mounted the steps to the platform. They both came close, addressing one another as though they were arguing. They spoke to the auctioneer, who nodded and bowed as though giving some concession. He reached forward and removed my face-veil, and the realization of absolute nakedness in front of this mob swept over me.

It may sound silly I know, but the presence of that little square of cloth below my eyes had seemed to give me some protection, a sort of anonymity as it were. With it gone I felt exposed and vulnerable and absolutely helpless.

The woman and the cruel looking old man took turns to examine me as though I were a prize specimen in a cattle market - which I suppose in a way I was.

The woman felt my hair, and hefted and bounced my breasts, and looked close into my eyes. Her own eyes were dispassionate, for was I not just a piece of goods? She checked in my ears and pulled my mouth open to inspect my teeth and smell my breath. She made me get my knees really wide, and pulled the lips of my quim apart with callous fingers. She actually peered up into my exposed sheath, and tweaked me with a fingernail. It hurt, and I hissed at the discomfort, but she only nodded. She bent me forward and pulled the cheeks of my bottom apart, and kneaded them like dough, even pressing a fingertip against my little rose-hole.

The old man with the cruel eyes was worse. He too checked my eyes and my teeth, but when he examined my breasts he let his fingernails dig into me, and he pulled and rolled my nipples harshly. He went behind me to inspect my bottom, pinching and squeezing me, pulling my buttocks apart and thrusting a finger into me so harshly I cried out, for which I got a whack across the shoulders with the auctioneer's staff. He returned to my front and ran his dry hands over my belly and thighs. He too parted my nether lips, but not to merely look at me, for without warning he thrust several fingers into me. I was unable to stop a whimper of discomfort and humiliation at his invasion, and for a second his cold eyes lit with amused satisfaction.

The crowd was enjoying the spectacle of this helpless white woman being humiliated, and was baying for more. There was a lot of shouting and laughter. The man fingered me for a long time, time enough for my blushes to reach my ankles and my sheath to become moist, he was toying with me so salaciously. At last, he took his hands off me and turned to the woman.

They spoke to each other, ignoring me, then went down

from the platform again, to resume their former places. Then, his voice higher and louder than before, the cruel-looking old man made a loud bid. The crowd gave a rippling gasp that told me the bid was very high, and my heart sank. It stopped entirely as the woman dropped her head.

No! Please no! I screamed inside my head. Do not let him have me! I stared at the woman, willing her with every fibre of my being to raise her head and bid again, for I knew from the way his eyes had lit when I gasped at his fingering of me that my fate at the hands of the old man would be hard indeed. A lifetime of breathless agony passed. I knew I was doomed. Then, heavens! she slowly lifted her head. She looked across at her opponent and spoke, very quietly.

The crowd gasped. The cruel old man bowed his head and waved his hand dismissively. The crowd cheered and burst into applause. My head lit up with joy. The woman had won!

How unimaginably strange we humans are. Only a short while ago I had been in despair at the thought of being sold off like an animal. Now, I was so happy at being bought by the woman rather than the old man that all I felt was a gratitude so deep I could have kissed her feet!

Grateful to be bought as a slave! How far had you sunk, Amy!

EIGHT

I was still weak with relief as I was led down from the platform and handed over to my new owner. I sank down onto my knees beside the girls she had bought earlier. The one next to me put a comforting hand on my shoulder, and I almost burst into tears at my release.

It was not long before I discovered what kind of release

it was.

As I was led down to her, my new owner must have seen the relief in my eyes, for she smiled and shifted her shoulders smugly. When I knelt on the ground beside the girls she had bought earlier, she looked down at me almost kindly.

Very seldom after that did I see any signs of kindness.

With my sale, the auction was over, and the square slowly cleared of its throng. The woman - I never did learn her name, though her other slaves referred to her as something like 'Memmisaab', and I learned to do the same - spoke an order, and the other girls stood up. I hastened to follow suit.

Two fierce-looking African men bearing bunches of clanking chains in their hands came up to us. My ankles were manacled. An iron collar was locked about my neck and a heavy chain linked from it to the collar of the girl in front of me. My arms were pulled up, and my hands locked behind my neck with iron bracelets, as were those of my fellow slaves.

A whip cracked. Memmisaab walked off. With the guards in close attendance, and whips cracking, and chains jangling, we slaves shuffled along behind her.

She took us a long way, through crowded streets where people ogled and called out at the sight of naked slave-girls shuffling along behind their owner. I felt horribly exposed, for all the other women in the streets except we slave girls were clad in voluminous robes from head to toe, with only their faces showing - and some even had those covered below the eyes.

Later, when I discovered the nature of the establishment to which we were being taken, I realized that by leading us naked through the town our new owner was doing nothing else than advertising that she had some new girls - some 'new stock', as it were.

The woman led us around many corners, along alleys, across squares. The manacles cut my ankles. I could only shuffle, and it was torture to keep up without falling. I did stumble several times, to be hauled up roughly by one of the guards and set shuffling again. What did it matter that in hauling me up his rough hands made free with my helpless body? All was lost anyway!

At last, just when I thought the manacles would cut my feet off, and my arms were numb, and the soreness in my back from the whipping was becoming unbearable, we reached our destination.

We were led through a low door and along a corridor of rough brick. We were shoved into a cold, damp cell. Our leg-irons were taken off, and our hands released from our collars. Memmisaab stood in the bright light of the doorway. She cast a slow stare over her new possessions huddled naked and terrified against the walls. Her smile chilled me. The door swung shut, and the cell became pitch black.

It was cold. The very air I breathed was chill and damp. I heard scrabbling that sounded like rats. I began to weep. A voice whispered low in my ear. I felt the warmth of a body close by. An arm eased over my head, the chains on her wrists chinking as they moved down to hold and comfort me. Even at their lowest ebb, slaves somehow manage to comfort one another!

Whoever she was, she was warm, and the arm around me was strong. I rested my head against her shoulder, and curled myself close against her, as much for re-assurance as for warmth. I slept.

I was not aware that I slept, for I lay long awake and scared. Yet I must have, for I was startled conscious by the crashing open of the door, and the blinding sunlight that streamed in, and the shouts of the guards.

We struggled blinking to our feet. We were herded out. The other girls were taken away in a group. Alone, a chain fixed to my metal collar, my wrists manacled behind my back, naked, I was led off in another direction.

Memmisaab awaited me, and my real slavery began.

The man who shepherded me away from the other girls, one of Memmisaab's many guards, brooked no hesitation on my part. He was quick with the strap he carried in his big hand, and stinging cuts to my bottom and the backs of my thighs soon had me trotting in the direction he indicated. He herded me along winding passageways and through doorways, and finally into the large, echoing chamber in which I was to spend so much of my time for the next days and weeks.

The floor was of smooth flagstones. The high ceiling was supported by rows of thick stone pillars. Dully, my eyes registered that most of them had brackets fixed at various heights, with chains hanging from them, but my mind took no significance from it, so dispirited was I. There were other, odd-looking contraptions about the place, but I hardly had the strength of spirit to glance at them.

My gaze was irresistibly drawn towards one end of the room, where my new owner sat on a throne-like chair, which was itself standing on a rich carpet. I was led before her. She looked me over from head to foot, and spoke.

I did not understand, for it was a language I had never heard before. Suddenly my guard bellowed, grabbed me by the neck. He forced me down onto my knees and pressed my forehead onto the flagstones. He gave my helplessly raised bottom three fearsome lashes with his strap, and I bit back a scream.

I soon learned that this obeisance was a requirement when coming into the presence of Memmisaab. If one did not drop instantly to one's knees, and press one's forehead to the ground, one's backside paid for it.

After a moment or two, the pain was at my other end, for the guard grabbed a handful of my hair and dragged me upright, hauling me up almost off my feet before letting me go. I stood facing Memmisaab, fighting a desire to squirm as her eyes travelled slowly over me.

They were cold eyes. Cold, small, black eyes set in a face which might once have been handsome, but was now lined and narrow. She was a large woman, though not obese, and was richly dressed in brightly coloured cotton robes, with a silver-edged muslin scarf over her greying hair. She waved a be-ringed hand and said something to the guard. Placing big, hard hands on my shoulders, he turned me around slowly so that my mistress could inspect the rest of me.

At another sharp order, spoken in a harsh voice that was surprisingly high-pitched for such a large woman, the guard took a ring of keys from his belt and unlocked my manacles and leg irons. It felt a blessed relief to be free of them, for there were grazes around my wrists and ankles from the rough metal. My collar, too, was taken off, and to judge by Memmisaab's look of sharp irritation, my neck was also grazed.

Her inspection over, my new owner signalled again to the guard, and I was gestured to follow him. I did so, feeling very small compared to the giant man. He must have been well over six feet in height, with broad shoulders and a thick waist. He wore only a pair of voluminous pantaloons, held at the waist by a thick leather belt from which hung his ring of keys and the strap with which he had whipped my bottom. To my astonishment, his broad, heavily muscled back bore the scars of at least one lashing.

He led me to what I came to know as the bath-house, although more than mere bathing went on there. Several elderly women, black robed, awaited us. They at once gathered around me, cooing and clucking as though they had never seen a white woman before.

Whether they had or not, they soon became business-like. Buckets of steaming water were dredged out of a wood-fired boiler in a corner and poured into a tub. Its temperature was tested with an elbow, as if for bathing an infant, and I was signalled to step in. They kept me standing shin deep in the warm water, with my feet apart, and using thick cloths like flannels and a couple of shallow brass bowls wetted me all over, including my hair. Then every inch of me was soaped and scrubbed, thoroughly though not roughly. They paid particular attention to between my legs, washing me very carefully, and pulling my folds open to wash within, even at one moment pushing a cloth-covered finger up into me. They did the same to my bottom, which made me squeal with shock. Finally, I was doused with buckets of clean water, made to step out of the tub, and vigorously dried with rough towels.

The women fussed a little about the grazes on my neck and wrists and ankles, and smeared them with a soothing ointment before gesturing me to lie down on a high wooden bench. As the first woman approached, I felt a lurch of dread deep inside me. My legs were grabbed and pulled up and wide apart, and the women's attention became focused on my helplessly exposed womanly parts. They opened me and felt me about a little, slipping fingers into me and commenting to each other, and then one of them began to lather me.

I looked down between my upraised legs, astonished at such a thing, for they had already washed me very thoroughly down there. Then I screamed. One of the women had in her hand a huge razor! And she was moving it towards me!

I screamed and struggled, but they were much too strong for me. A towel was shoved into my mouth as a gag. My legs were pulled wider. Hands pressed down on my tummy to keep me still. The razor approached.

I froze as though paralysed. That blade looked horribly sharp! Held in the most vulnerable and humiliating position possible, I submitted to having my intimacies shaved bare by an unknown black-clad woman, while others held me down and a huge African guard looked on.

When she had finished shaving me the woman rinsed me and dried me carefully with a soft towel. Then she smoothed some kind of lotion on me. At first it was deliciously cool and, I have to confess it, felt nice. Then it seemed to get warm and began to sting, and in a minute I was bucking and writhing, tears streaming.

The women holding me down merely giggled and held me tighter. It felt as though the whole area they had just shaved had sparks coming off it! Soon, though, the stinging began to ease, to be replaced by a feeling of tightness and enormous sensitivity. When the women hauled me into a sitting position, and began to comb and brush my hair I wriggled from the sensations between my legs, for my quim-lips seemed to be feeling the actual grain of the wood I was sitting on.

The women appeared to be fascinated by my coppery tresses, and spent a long time fussing with them before they were satisfied. Finally, they painted my eyes with kohl, but there was no looking glass about, so I could not see the effect. It had been so long since I saw my reflection in a mirror that I had pretty well forgotten what I looked like anyway.

When the women had finished with me, the guard stepped forward. He looked me over, felt between my legs to check how smooth I was, inevitably fingering me up in the process, then led me back to where Memmisaab awaited me. A tap of his hand on my bottom reminded me, and I threw myself to my knees and touched my forehead to the floor. Another tap, this time on my head, and I stood up.

Memmisaab looked me over again and nodded, as though pleased with what she saw. She began to speak, looking closely into my eyes. Clearly, she was saying something to me, but I could not understand a single word. She tried again, in what sounded like a different language. It was still a blank to me. Beginning to look somewhat irritated, the frightening woman barked a series of single words at me, pausing after each to see whether I responded. I grew more scared with each word, and tried increasingly nervously to make them out.

Then I heard what sounded like the word 'francais' and my heart leapt. I remembered a little of the French language from one of my governesses, though only a very little. Even so, it was my chance to placate Memmisaab, and I leapt at it.

"Oui Madame, oui maitresse," I gasped, hoping against hope.

Memmisaab seemed to relax when I responded, and leaned back in her chair. She issued a sharp order, and the guard turned and hurried out of the room.

He came back after only a minute or two, accompanied by another man almost equally as large, with a long, diagonal scar running from his forehead almost to his jaw. This, I learned, was Ishbal. It transpired that he spoke a little French, and thus he was to be my principal guard and trainer.

NINE

Ishbal's first act as my trainer was to take me to what seemed to be a workshop, for a huge sweating blacksmith awaited us. Piles of metal rings of various sizes, clearly collars and wrist- and ankle-bands, lay on a bench. The blacksmith picked one up, and approached me. He looked closely at my neck, then at my wrists and ankles, and spoke to Ishbal. By his gestures, I guessed that he was concerned about my grazes. The two men seemed to be in a quandary. Motioning me to stay, Ishbal hurried off.

It was uncomfortable waiting there, being looked over

with casual salaciousness by the big blacksmith. But not uncomfortable in quite the way it should have been for one brought up to be a respectable Englishwoman!

I was stark naked and being looked over by a very large man. I could tell he was large by what was happening inside his pantaloons, which were bulging very noticeably at the front. I should have wanted to die on the spot were I a 'proper' woman. Instead I found I could only breathe quick and shallow. My breasts got tight and my nipples stood out as the giant blacksmith's eyes roved over them. His eyes moved slowly down. I could have turned away or put one knee across the other so as to hide at least something of what he was looking at. I remained exactly as I was. It was as if I could feel his eyes probing me; there, in the centre of my womanhood.

And I became hot. That by now familiar, shameful, throbbing began in my blood. I could not take my eyes off the bulge in his pantaloons. I blushed when I found myself thinking his cock must be very large, then blushed deeper at the thought of being shagged by such a man.

I had the distinct feeling that he was going to do precisely that any minute, but fortunately Ishbal was not away for long. He must have consulted with Memmisaab and got a decision, for the blacksmith did not fix a collar on me, nor manacles about my wrists and ankles. Memmisaab obviously preferred her slave-girls undamaged, for my manacles were not put on me until after my grazes had healed, and then they were light, with smoothly rounded edges that would not cut or chafe.

For now, just a chain was fixed around my waist. It was made of a bright, silver coloured metal, with small neat links, the last of which was hammered closed with a finality which told me it was not intended to be removed; ever. Four of the links were larger, thick rings fully an inch in diameter. The blacksmith adjusted the chain so that these larger rings lay one on each side, and the others front and back. They clearly had some function, but I could not imagine what it was.

When he had finished, the blacksmith said something to Ishbal, who gave a laugh and shrugged his huge shoulders. To my horror, the blacksmith picked me up as though I were a doll, and felt me all over, and tipped me upside down and held my legs apart while he sniffed and prodded and even licked at my womanly parts. He laughed, and said something, and thrust a finger into each of my entrances as though to see if I was like the women of his own race. Then he turned me right side up and casually tossed me to Ishbal, who caught me as though I was no more than a postal package.

Then my situation became frightening rather than merely humiliating. Ishbal took up a rope and bound my wrists, then lifted me up and hung me by my wrists from a metal peg high on the wall. On either side of my waist were big iron rings. Ishbal got another piece of rope and tied it between the rings, very tightly across my tummy, so that my back was held hard against the rough brick of the wall.

Then Ishbal knelt and took hold of my ankles, pulling my legs down ever so hard, so that I was stretched painfully tight. My mind was rolling as wildly as my eyes in panic about what was happening. Then I saw what the blacksmith was doing and I screamed.

He was turning away from the glowing coals of his forge. In his hand he had a long rod, the end of it sparking white hot. He was approaching me. I bucked and writhed and screamed so much that even Ishbal found it hard to hold me still.

It was a branding-iron. I cannot describe the actual experience of being branded, for I fainted at the very approach of the glowing iron. The brand lies precisely one and a quarter inches above the top of my crease, just where my mound swells to fullness. It is in the shape of a curved, wide-bladed sword, and has a little arrowhead below, pointing to my slit as though in invitation. It is not large, but it is very, very noticeable.

I regained consciousness lying on my back on a hard bench. I was tied down at wrists, neck and waist, and with my legs bound down on either side of the bench so that my knees were splayed and I could not move them. That was probably a mercy, for I was very sore down there. About every hour Ishbal or one of the black-clad women would loom over me and smooth cool unguent onto my brand. It eased my body greatly, though not my mind for I now knew with a terrible finality that I was the property of Memmisaab and had no choice about my fate.

I do not know what the ointment they used on me was made of, only that it was a deep pink in colour, smelled of pungent spices, and was very effective in both easing my pain and healing over the wound of my brand. By only the second day I could move about with only a little discomfort. By the fourth my wound had completely healed, though I was desperately conscious of the bright red, sharp-edged insignia impressed so blatantly upon my womanhood - and especially since pretty well all the guards, once I was up and about, insisted on inspecting it in great detail, and by touch as well as sight.

Once my trainer Ishbal was convinced that I was fit again I was led back to what I came to think of as the training room. Memmisaab required that all her slaves be well trained. The strap was Memmisaab's principal means of instilling order and eagerness into her girls. There are few things more effective in ensuring a girl's instant obedience than the remembrance of a strap belabouring her bottom, and few things better calculated to make her at least feign the eagerness Memmisaab required in all things than the threat of a lashing to come.

70

I soon learned to associate what I came to call the training room, and Ishbal too, with humiliation and exhaustion, and the fire caused to one's bottom by frequent spankings. Some of the time other girls were trained with me, and Ishbal would often use them to demonstrate to me things that were too complicated for him to explain, or for me to understand.

That came later, though. On this occasion we were alone in the training room, and Ishbal's first intention was to prove to me my absolute abasement, and his requirement for instant and total obedience.

He pointed to the floor and shouted "A bas, chienne! " - which my dizzied head took a moment to translate as 'get down, bitch'. He raised his strap, and I threw myself down onto the chilly flagstones. With his foot, he rolled me over onto my back. He stood above me, huge and terrifying. He pointed to my feet and made a very obvious gesture. "Haute les jambes," he bellowed. I raised my legs and parted them, getting my knees up until they pressed against my breasts.

Ishbal knelt down and began to examine me closely and with humiliating thoroughness. With rough fingers he parted my folds. He traced my shape, and thrust a finger into me, moving it in and out slowly as though exploring my reactions. He tweaked and fingered me for several minutes. He even sniffed me!

I resigned myself to the certainty that this huge man was going to assert his power by fucking me then and there on the cold flagstones. Instead, he slapped me hard on the back of my thigh, and gestured me to stand up again.

He took my wrists and placed my hands behind my head. When I rounded my shoulders, he gave me a sharp stroke with his strap across my belly. I instantly held my elbows well back, humiliated when he grinned and nodded at the way my breasts were thus pushed out. He slapped his hands up underneath them, making them bounce and tremble, then

71

pulled on my nipples.

I do not know what it is about my nipples that attracts attention so. They are neither as large or as pretty as many girls', though they do get rather embarrassingly prominent in certain circumstances. Even so, Mr Mansfield my husband had insisted on playing with them a lot, as had the Africans who kidnapped me, and then the Arab slavers, and Ishbal and pretty well everybody who could get at them ever since.

I have to confess that except when they are squeezed or pulled too hard the effect of such teasings is to get me hot and tense. Are all women thus victims to their bodily sensations? Or is it, perhaps, a sort of primeval self-defence process through which a woman's body prepares itself to be taken by a stronger one? I cannot offer a final answer.

However, to return to my narrative. Ishbal finished toying with my breasts and took me over to one of the pillars. He stood me with my back against it and used the chain around my waist to fix me in place. He made me link my hands behind my head again and nudged my ankles with his foot to make me get my legs apart.

"Pousse ta connasse," he said. I did not understand. What was I supposed to push? He repeated the order and made the most peculiar movements and patted between my legs with the flat of his hand. My puzzlement must have shown on my face, for he frowned and repeated his movements more emphatically, before patting me again and nodding his head vigorously.

It suddenly dawned on me what he wanted, and I blushed to my hair-roots. It was too awful! He whipped me once across the fronts of my thighs. "Pousse ta connasse, putain!" he bellowed. I knew that if I did not do as he wished he would beat me again, and the stripe he had already given me was stinging dreadfully. Wishing I might die of embarrassment, I began to move my hips.

72

He held the flat of his hand an inch or so away from my womanly parts. I was required to thrust myself forward and touch myself onto his hand. I shut my eyes in shame as I struggled to perform his humiliating demand. Chained by the waist and not daring to move my feet, I was obliged to roll and pump my hips in the lewdest of manners in order to obey him. Each time I managed to press myself against his hand, he tweaked his fingers into my folds, establishing very effectively in my consciousness that this part of me was to be the centre of my future world, and that it was under his control.

He kept me at it for an age, gradually moving his hand away a little at a time so that my movements were forced to become more and more wild and exaggerated.

"Pousse!" he shouted. "Pousse ta connasse, coquine!"

My back and thighs began to ache from the degrading exercise, and even as I was made to obey I realized that my performance mimicked the crudest possible of sexual actions, for I was having to gyrate my pelvis and pump it back and forth in the lewdest of manners.

The worst thing, though, was that the way I was having to move my body, and the things his fingers were doing to me began to stir up those hot sensations that had so plagued me since my African captors first stirred them up in me. I was panting and wet between my legs by the time Ishbal moved his hand away and released me from the pillar.

That was one of the exercises I was made to perform daily, as were all the girls at the group training sessions which took place every morning. That first time, though, Ishbal was as intent on debasing me as he was on training me. Each time I pushed myself onto his hand his fingers would invade me. Though my spirit hated this, my body could not but react. When I was nigh on exhausted and felt my back must break under this unaccustomed exertion, Ishbal's hand stayed on me as my loins pulled back.

My eyes flicked open in surprise at the change. His face was close to mine, his black eyes alight with some kind of triumph. He rubbed his fingers slowly and lasciviously between the puffy lips of my quim, grinning as he slid them deep into my sheath, and thrust them in and out several times - his grin broadening as I gave a helpless little moan. Then he pulled his hand out of me and raised it. His fingers were wet and slick from my juices. He moved them before my face, nodding and smiling to show his triumph. Then he thrust them at my mouth and made me lick them clean - made me lick from his thick, awful fingers the proof of his triumph and my degradation.

Satisfied that he had got me properly cowed, Ishbal released me from the pillar. With a combination of words and gestures, he got me to march around the perimeter of the room. It was a peculiar and very taxing way of marching, for he made me keep my hands behind my head and my elbows back, and raise my knees as high as my waist, with my toes pointed, at each step. It was a very difficult step to maintain, but Ishbal spurred me on very effectively with the occasional swipe of his strap on my straining back and bottom.

When I had paraded around the room half a dozen times and was close to collapse, Ishbal stopped me and gestured me over to one of the contraptions I had seen on first entering this terrible room. It was like a stool, only higher, and what would have been the seat was a yard across, the four stout wooden legs were at a wide angle, and there were straps dangling from them as well as from the seat part.

Ishbal lifted me onto it, and placed me so that I was lying on my tummy with my legs dangling. He fixed straps across me at my waist so that I was held fast. He took first one ankle, then the other, and strapped it to the leg of the stool so that my own legs were as wide splayed as those of the stool. I gave another moan as his hand stroked slowly down over the cleft of my bottom and further, to cup my helplessly exposed quim, his fingers opening me and delving as though to prove my helplessness.

Then I heard him move away. Strapped down, with my legs held apart and my hands still clasped behind my head, I could only wait in dread for what might befall me. I heard him coming back. I shut my eyes and held my breath.

He grabbed my hair and pulled my head up. In his free hand he held a whip. He moved it slowly before my eyes, tugging my hair cruelly to make sure I took a good look at the object in his hand. It had a thick, leather-covered handle a foot long and shaped like a rampant manhood. From the end hung a dozen or more narrow leather straps, shiny from use, three feet or more in length. I can describe it in detail, for it became an all too familiar feature of my existence.

Looking from my horrified eyes to the whip and back, and nodding, Ishbal made me know that this device was for me. To confirm it, he let my head drop, moved off a little, and lashed me with it. He beat me once across my back, below my shoulder blades, and I screamed. He striped me once across my backside, and it was worse. He hit me a third time across the backs of my thighs, high up, and I screamed and thrashed about on the stool as much as my bonds would allow.

He grabbed my hair and lifted my head again. His face was very close to mine, and he was grinning and nodding. He put the thicker, curved end of the whip handle to his thick lips and gave it an exaggerated kiss, then held it to my own mouth. I had to kiss it! Kiss the whip that had just set fire to my flesh!

At first I did not understand, could not believe what he seemed to want. He let go my head and thrashed me again, exactly as before, on my back, on my squirming buttocks, and on my shuddering thighs. He lifted my head again and repeated his pantomime.

I kissed the whip.

As time went on, I learned that he liked to make me kiss the whip, and the thick strap he always carried, and the canes and paddles he sometimes used on me. It was a sign of my submission which was required by my owner. She liked to enslave our minds as well as our bodies.

When I had kissed the whip that first time, Ishbal smiled almost gently, and let go my head. When he had whipped me, my arms had flailed about. He took my hands and planted them behind my head again, pressing firmly to indicate that I must keep them there. He moved round behind me, out of my line of vision. He began to touch me. I was helplessly exposed and offered up, and could not defend myself. He made free with me.

He stroked and felt and fingered me. He ran his hands over my bottom and the insides of my thighs. He parted my buttocks and ran his fingers along my cleft. He slid hard, knowing fingertips along the length of my crease again and again and again. He rolled that helpless nub of sensation I have learned to call my clitty with his hard thumb, circling and tormenting it. He slid several fingers deep into me.

There are times when the opposite of what one is brought up to think should happen actually happens. My mind was reeling with shame at what this awful man was doing to me; my body should have gone cold and my senses numb. Instead, he got me hot. I know now that there is some part of me, perhaps some part of every woman, which reacts in a manner wildly different from that which polite society would expect of me when I am helpless against the lusts of another. At the time, I was horribly ashamed of my own wanton reactions.

As Ishbal worked on me I could feel myself becoming shamefully aroused, even against my wishes. It was too horrible to contemplate, yet it was happening. Ishbal knew exactly what he was doing; he must have done it a thousand times before, to a thousand girls. He stroked me, caressed me, teased my clitty, slipped fingers into my bottom and my quim, chuckling and murmuring all the while at the wanton way my body was reacting.

When he began to penetrate me, I was already lost. He came into me slowly, thick and hard, and very rigid; pushing in, withdrawing a little, pushing in more, until I was filled and groaning, and longing to die of shame at the way my body was opening to him, the muscles of my sheath squirming on him.

After hardly more than half a dozen pushes and retreats, the retreats small, the pushes ever so firm, I began to come, hopelessly and helplessly, as it moved deep in me. So deep! In the midst of my transports I felt my head dragged up again. Ishbal thrust his hard cock into my slack mouth, and instinctively I sucked him.

Only when he had spurted his hot essence onto my tongue, and I had swallowed it all, and my body was beginning to subside, did the real awfulness of what had happened hit me and send me burning with shame. Driving home the depth of my humiliation, his softening thing still only an inch from my face, Ishbal reached over me. The object in my sheath, which I had thought was him and which had spiralled me to such an overwhelming climax, jiggled in and out a little, and was then slowly withdrawn.

He held up my head. He was grinning with triumph. Only inches from my eyes he waved the handle of his whip. It was slick and moist and shiny from my juices. How far down did he want to drive me? I had submitted so far as to kiss the whip. Now he had penetrated me with it, and driven me wild. And worse, he then made me lick and suck it clean of the evidence of my body's wanton surrender, moving it on and in my mouth just as though it were a real manhood I was pleasuring.

I could sink no lower.

As though he could read the shame and the surrender in my eyes, Ishbal grinned, murmured "Ah, ma petite chienne," and patted me on my upraised bottom for all the world as if I was his pet dog - or perhaps the 'little bitch' he had just called me, and one on heat at that. With dexterous, tender fingers he unbuckled the straps that held me. He lifted me off the stool and stood me on my feet, my legs weak. He cupped my chin in his big hand and looked hard into my eyes.

"Merci, maitre," he said, slowly and emphatically. "Vous dit 'Merci. Merci maitre'!"

I could hardly believe my ears, nor my eyes neither as he imitated a curtsey, repeating his words yet again. He had just reduced me, taken me in the most humiliating fashion, whipped me and made me suck his cock and swallow his jism, and now he was telling me I had to thank him. Telling me I had to curtsey humbly to him and say 'thank you, master'!

For an instant the Englishwoman in me was outraged. Ishbal must have detected something of it in my eyes, for his own hardened and the knuckles of the hand holding the whip tensed and his shoulders stiffened. Instantly, fright drove out any thought of rebellion and I bobbed my knees in the humblest curtsey I could manage.

"Merci, mon maitre. Merci beaucoup."

My voice felt throaty, but it had been disturbingly easy to say. Somehow, though, my mind would not address its own surprised question. Why had I called this great scarred African who had just raped me 'my' master? And why had I thanked him 'very much'?

Ishbal grinned at me with every appearance of satisfaction, and ruffled his great hard hand in my hair.

"Bon." he murmured, lifting my chin with a fingertip.

"Vous est une bonne petite chienne, et jolie aussi."

I felt myself blushing, and with shame as well. Why on earth should I be pleased that this great, ugly creature had called me a 'good little bitch, and pretty too'. Yet somehow I had. What kind of woman was I becoming!

In the most immediate sense, the kind of woman I became was an abject slave, confused, obedient and, I confess it, eager to please - even if only avoid stripes on my backside.

After that first session, Ishbal took me to a sort of communal eating room. At a long table, with benches along each side, sat a number of guards, all African, and all seeming huge. Scampering between the table and a sort of serving hatch were a number of naked women and girls, bringing food and drink to the men, and clearing away used dishes and cups.

As I followed Ishbal into the room a momentary silence fell, to be followed by a cacophony of hoots and calls as the men caught sight of me. Instantly, I felt a wave of desperate embarrassment as a dozen grinning faces turned towards me and drank in my nakedness. Ishbal gestured me to get him some food and sat down among the other guards. I hurried to obey. The aroma of the thick stew of meat and pulses made me near faint as I realized how ravenously hungry I was.

When I had served Ishbal, not knowing whether or not I was allowed to dodge the hands that groped for me, he gestured that I was to get a bowl of the stew for myself. I was so grateful, and so dying of hunger that I was even able to blot out the embarrassment of being made to eat it with my fingers, standing up on the middle of the guards' table with my legs apart, so that the guards could enjoy the sight of me, and Ishbal could bask in the pleasure of my obedience.

Afterwards, when I had been allowed down from the

table, and had cleared away Ishbal's dish, and washed and dried his hands and my own, and a number of his fellow guards had bounced my breasts and laughed with him while they felt me up, Ishbal took me to my cell. It was a tiny stone-built chamber with nothing more than a narrow wooden bunk. The bunk had a mattress, though, and blankets were luxury after my nights sleeping on the ground or stone floors. That Ishbal patted my head and smiled at me quite gently, after I had pulled the blankets over myself, somehow served to make me feel small and warm, and I slept instantly.

TEN

The place Memmisaab owned, and the source of the wealth with which she bought me and the other girls, was a house of entertainment or, to put it bluntly, a brothel.

If, as the adage has it, I slept like an infant that night, next morning saw the end of any semblance of childishness or innocence, for my training as a prostitute began in earnest.

Ishbal roused me early, by stripping off my blankets and calling loudly. A stinging stripe from his strap across my bottom instantly had me up and scampering. 'Breakfast', if you could call it that, was a steaming pottage of lentils and other pulses, eaten from a wooden bowl with the fingers, and washed down with water. Then, I was hurried along to the bath house, where the black-robed women awaited me, and I was washed and combed and polished, and had my eyes painted.

There were other girls about, lots of them, all young, and all as naked and hurried as myself, but there was no time to speak to any of them; no time, even, to do more than cast a glance in their direction. I was to learn that Memmisaab did not encourage communication between her girls. Perhaps she thought it might lead to some kind of independence of spirit. Nothing of that kind was allowed or tolerated.

After my ablutions, Ishbal casually checked as to whether or not I needed shaving yet and how my brand was healing up. I was to learn that pretty well everyone in my new world, except the other girls, reserved for themselves the right to feel us up that way. There can be few better ways of asserting control over a girl's mind as well as her body, which is what Memmisaab required, than to keep her naked and oblige her to stop whatever she was doing and open her knees whenever anybody wanted to feel her between her legs. It certainly drove home to me how available I now was.

There were half a dozen other girls there, all African except one, who had a pale coffee complexion, long straight hair so black it seemed to glow, and enormous dark eyes that flashed even wider whenever one of the guard's straps lit on her slender rump. I came to know her well as time went on.

They were of all different shapes and sizes, as though Memmisaab was catering to all tastes - which I soon learned was exactly what she was doing, for within a week, more or less as soon as my brand had healed sufficiently, I had personal experience of what kind of place this really was. A couple were like women I had seen during my time at Benin, tall, with high foreheads and straight noses, long, slender limbs and high, taut breasts.

One was much heavier of build, though not fat. She had very short hair, like a crinkly mat over her scalp. Her limbs were round and strong-looking, with thighs that looked to be near as thick as my waist. When she marched, for we were all made to march in that odd, high-kneed gait Ishbal had taught me, her huge breasts swung and bounced, and the great swells of her buttocks flexed and trembled with such

81

obvious strength you would have trusted her to hold up the building, had it threatened to tumble.

Another was tiny. When I first laid eyes on her I thought her a child, but her face and the developed ripeness of her body, though it was minuscule compared to the others, showed that she was a grown woman albeit she was half a head shorter than me, and I am only just over five feet tall. She was apparently of a people called pigmies, who are all very small, and was very popular among certain of Memmisaab's customers.

I had not time, though, to look at my fellow slaves properly, nor ever to actually get to know them, for we had all been brought here for training and for exercise to make us trim and capable for Memmisaab's business.

The exercises were particular and peculiar. Memmisaab's business was no more and no less than a brothel and I, like these other women, had been bought to perform in it. The purpose behind her demand that we be exercised and trained was simply to make us better able to please her customers with our bodies and our skills.

Stated thus baldly, the fact that I tried hard during the exercising, and strove to become well trained might make me seem low to you, my reader; might make me appear to be indeed a wanton. But it was the only life I had; the only life I could see stretched out before me. And in any case, Ishbal's strap across my bare bottom was easily enough to keep me active and at least pretending to be eager!

As to the exercises themselves, we were made to stretch and bend a great deal to keep ourselves supple and flexible. We were taught several positions which we had to adopt the instant we heard the word of command. All of them seemed designed specifically to emphasize our subservience as well as to display our bodies.

At the command 'hadja' we had to throw ourselves onto the ground on our backs, raise our legs, and hold our feet

82

with both hands so that the soles were together. In this position a woman is very open, for her knees are forced wide apart, and our trainers used it frequently so that they could examine us with humiliating thoroughness. Although Ishbal was my appointed trainer, all the guards had command over any of we females, and for a long time pretty well all of them enjoyed shouting hadja at me, and examining and fingering me while I strained to keep the soles of my feet together lest they get annoyed and spank me.

They also enjoyed calling out the commands for the other positions. 'kiffoi' meant I had to get my hands behind my head with my elbows back, stand with my feet apart, and push my loins as far forward as possible. This was a very difficult position to maintain, and they often kept me in it for a long time while they laughed and felt my breasts and fingered me up.

At the command 'pakka', I had to kneel down with my knees apart and press my hands and forehead to the floor, arching my back and keeping my bottom high. It was a lewder version of the obeisance her slave-girls made to Memmisaab, and the way we had to greet her customers, except with them we had to be facing away so that the first thing they saw of us was our upraised bottoms and offered intimacies.

Apart from the stretching and bending and that peculiar walking style, which were designed to keep us fit and supple, all the exercises were intended for nothing else than to make us more apt for the purposes of carnality.

I was obliged to strengthen my mouth and tongue by sucking on an ivory rod, and squeezing it with my tongue, for anything up to an hour at a time. Ishbal would check my progress by putting several of his fingers into my mouth and having me suck and lick them - and of course he tested and perfected my technique on his male member pretty well daily.

I learned very quickly to do my best on these occasions for Ishbal was very demanding, both as to technique and apparent eagerness. I learned how to undo the front of his pantaloons with fluttering fingers. I learned to cup and fondle his tight, heavy sack with gentle fingers, and to circle equally delicate fingers around his thick shaft, stroking it gently along its length as my tongue lapped at the bulbous end of his member.

Once again, honesty obliges me to own up that I soon began to feel a strange, deep pleasure in performing that particular act. The taste, once you are used to it and provided the man has hygienic habits, is quite alluring, as is his aroma of excitement. With this act it is the woman who is in control unless the man is so uncouth as to grab her by her hair. Ishbal never did. He would stand, or sometimes lie, perfectly still while my hands and mouth worked on him. I was soon able to take him almost to my throat without gagging. I found that if I breathed out very gently as I moved down, and sucked hard and swirled my tongue as I pulled back towards his plum, I could force a little grunt of pleasure from him. I learned the little signs of his impending climax, and how to delay it. Sometimes I kept him going for nearly an hour before he deposited his offering of joy into my increasingly skilful mouth!

Some of Ishbal's fellow trainers did hold my head. With Ishbal, pleasuring his member with my mouth became a delightful little game. With the others, it seldom was. For them, my mouth was just something to shag. No skill, no finesse, no subtlety; just a slave-girl kneeling down, a thick cock pumping away, a pair of heavy hands holding clumps of hair, and then a gulping and choking. They never took more than a few minutes, though, so it could have been worse.

What was worse, certainly at first was when Ishbal had me bend over and then thrust a thick finger into my bottom-hole. The first time he did it I shrieked and leapt up, mortified. Instantly he grabbed me in his strong arm, threw me across his knee, and spanked me soundly. After that, twice a day, I would bend over for Ishbal and he would finger my bottom while I strove to flex and relax the muscle there. It dawned on me the very first time that this particular orifice would not be ignored by Memmisaab's clients, and that it might be best for me to be flexible there even if only for my own protection. As it turned out, that entrance proved to be pretty well as popular as the proper one, and as my mouth.

I had to perform a similar exercise with that more regular entrance to my body, between my legs, except that then I would be lying on my back with my knees high and wide. Ishbal would kneel between my upraised feet and advance his hand on me. First he would part my body-lips and rub and fondle me to get me moist. Perhaps it is the automatic reaction of a woman's body to such touches, or perhaps I am deep down a wanton, but he never failed to have me damp and panting in minutes.

Then he would insert a finger into me. I was required to flex the muscles of my quim and sheath exactly as I was those of my bottom-hole, only more so. I would have to relax myself so much that he could easily insert several fingers into me, then tighten so that I could squeeze a single finger, which I was obliged to do rhythmically, in imitation of the way a woman's sheath reacts naturally when she is swooping towards a come.

Honesty forces me to confess that these humiliating performances in imitation of sex were made all the more degrading by the fact that my unruly body always responded to it. As I lay there with my legs wide, and Ishbal inserted several fingers, then made me tighten rhythmically on just one, I would become moist and hot, and blush furiously when Ishbal grinned at my unwilling arousal, and laughed aloud when peaks of excitation rippled through me and I gasped and panted into a helpless climax.

He was a skilled and experienced trainer and knew exactly what he was doing - doing to my mind as well as my body as he brought me to climax, holding my feet wide and my body working to squeeze his thick finger with the muscles of my writhing sheath. Except for the cane or strap, there can be few better ways of exerting dominance over a woman and making her aware of how licentious her body really is!

I did these exercises almost to the point of exhaustion day after day before Ishbal decided I was ready to be offered to Memmisaab's clients. He tested the level of my developing abilities any number of times. The feeling of such a large man as Ishbal enjoying one's back passage was humiliating and uncomfortable, but after a while I got used to it and was able to concentrate on flexing and relaxing for his pleasure.

It says much for my true nature that when he did me in my 'front entrance', as it were, it was always glorious, and I would buck and sob like the true slut I knew I had become!

The most demanding exercise of them all however, at the beginning at least, was the one where he fixed my chain to the pillar and made me pump my belly to touch his hand with my parts. He never seemed satisfied until my muscles were screaming for relief, and my body-lips were sopping from all his fingering, which always made him grin as I licked his fingers clean.

After about a week, when I had become quite proficient at this lewd exercise, Ishbal stopped chaining me to the pillar, so that I had to learn to perform unsupported, with my hands clamped behind my head. He also introduced a variation. It was a rod of some kind of wood, smoothed and shaped and polished, only four or five inches long, but rather thick. From one end protruded a thinner rod about an inch long, from the end of which dangled a bell.

He would shout the order kiffoi, and wherever I was I would at once get my hands behind my head and part my feet and bend my knees, in the required position. Smiling, he would part my nether lips and finger me a bit to get me moist, then insert the rod into me so that only the bell remained free. Then he would bellow the order "Pousse ta connasse! Sonnez la cloche!" He would clap his hands rhythmically, and I would have to match his pace by pumping my hips to ring the bell.

It was a fiendish device, for the bell only rang on the forward swing, and even then only if I jerked my hips quite wildly. Ishbal would clap, and I would thrust with my belly, and he would speed up and slow down, and grin as I tried desperately to match his rhythm. If the bell did not ring, if my jerking of my loins was not satisfactory, I would be spanked - one stroke for each failure.

Ishbal took particular pleasure from making me ring the bell, and often made me do it for the amusement of his fellow guards, as proof positive of my complete submission to him. It was horrible to be stopped in whatever I might be doing, and be given that awful order. To have to stand naked and helpless while Ishbal laughed with the other guards as he fingered me to get me moist, and slowly thrust the rod into me was mortifying. It was worse when he said "Sonnez la cloche," and began to clap his hands, for they always laughed lewdly when he set a fast rhythm and I had to pump my hips wildly to ring the bell in time, while their eyes crawled over my nakedness, and they felt my breasts and my thighs, and congratulated Ishbal on my obedience and the skill with which I pumped my belly.

The really embarrassing thing was that the actions I was obliged to perform, together with the sensations of the rod inside me, invariably got me worked up. And what with the way the other guards tweaked my nipples and felt my behind, by the time Ishbal pulled the bell out of me I would be panting and shuddering and close to coming.

Sometimes, after such a performance, Ishbal would take me off to an alcove, of which there were many, and fuck me - or if not him, then one of the other guards. It always sent me wild, pumping my hips and gasping, explosions bursting all over my body and mind. It was shameful, yet how I longed for it!

In Memmisaab's establishment, the guards held absolute sway after she and her clients. Ishbal and his fellows, although - as I later discovered - also slaves, held total rights over us. That included using us for their pleasure whenever and however they fancied. Their duty as Memmisaab's trainers was to ensure that we, her slave-prostitutes, were instantly compliant and, as I later learned it is called, were 'good fucks'.

To judge from the reactions of my trainer Ishbal and his fellow guards and trainers, I soon became a good fuck, especially when Ishbal had got me all worked up with the bell-ringing and playing with my nipples. The men had control of us, and responsibility for our performance. They used their straps freely to make us eager. Their reward was that, whenever they took one of us aside or, as was more usual, took us then and there, up against a wall or splayed on the flagstones, in public, the girl in question would try really hard to please for fear of the strapping that might follow.

I myself, being the only European in the place, was picked out very frequently during those first weeks. My first real lesson in this was when one of the trainers, a low-browed brute of a creature with one leg somewhat withered so that he limped, said something to Ishbal as he was taking me from the training room to my cell. I was very weary from the exercises, and hardly registered Ishbal's nod of agreement.

Thus, when my hair was grabbed, and I was pushed to my knees, and the man's member bumped against my face, I was off-put. It was only a moment or two before I understood what was required and bobbed my head forward and opened my mouth, but that was long enough. Obedience had to be instant and unconditional. Mine had not been.

The man stepped back from me. He pulled my face up towards his by tugging my hair. The expression in his eyes was one of amusement. He pulled his strap out of his waistband, and gestured. Despairingly, for I knew what I was in for, I lowered myself to lie face down on the flagstones, my arms straight out above my head, my legs straight and wide apart. He only gave me perhaps ten strokes, but it was enough. At the clap of his hands, I was instantly up on my knees and grabbing at his cock with hands and mouth. Anything rather than more fire to my poor buttocks!

He took me slowly, holding back so that my sucking would take longer, even calling out to his colleagues to come and watch as I strained anxiously at his heavy manhood. Then, just as I felt those twitches which always betray that a man is about to come, and began to work harder on him, he pulled back, and held my head up by grabbing my hair, and spurted his jism right into my face, laughing louder even than his audience of fellow guards.

Ishbal's objective, and that of Memmisaab, was to exert absolute dominance. More, to drive their girls to a stage where they were beyond mere obedience, beyond just submission. They wanted us in a condition where we were desperate to please, and where a glance that was not angry, or a half-smile, or the simple absence of a whipping, had gratitude welling up in us.

In the cold light of day it sounds inconceivable I know. Let me assure you, though, that the human spirit is much stranger and more mysterious than people think. In Memmisaab's brothel - for it was nothing else - I found my depths, and I found my weaknesses, and I found that I had somewhere a source of inner strength.

For a time, the humiliations Ishbal heaped upon me made me want to die, yet I did not. Somehow, I came to feel there was a softness in his eyes, a gentleness in his handling of me. Take, for example, when he introduced me to the douche. At the time I had no idea at all as to its purpose, and neither my French nor Ishbal's were capable of communicating it. Although I now know the douche to be a true friend to all sensible women, that first time I saw it, it was very frightening.

It was like a sort of bellows affair with a long tube to the forefront, and a bag device between two paddles to the rear. I was lying, as Ishbal had ordered me, on a low bench with my legs splayed. I thought Ishbal was going to shag me, even though he had done so only half an hour before, preceded by two of his colleagues. Instead, he brought up this strange instrument.

When he reached down and parted my quim I got tense. When he moved the device towards me I got scared. He smacked my thigh when I resisted, then slowly inserted the long, cold shaft end of the thing into me. When he squeezed the bellows of it I squealed and near fainted as warm liquid gushed up into me and then poured out again. Had the expression on his face not been kindly I would have thought he was doing something awful to me, for nobody had ever told me about douches, or that their purpose was entirely benevolent.

Ishbal did so. He began an elaborate pantomime which first had my eyes widening, then had me giggling until my ribs ached. He patted me between my legs and mimed rather frantic shagging, his face screwed up in mock lust. Then he turned side on to me and shoved out his belly, running his hands over it and waggling his eyebrows. It was that which started me giggling. When he then mimed rocking an infant in his arms and cooing like a young mother, the sight was so ridiculous it had me snorting, tears streaming down my cheeks. Even Ishbal knew it, and soon he was laughing with me.

We became more sober as he continued his lesson to me and soon, though not without some difficulty and misunderstandings, I comprehended his meaning. The thought of being got with child in this place was just too awful! Thereafter I accepted the douche willingly, even asking for it if Ishbal seemed to have forgotten.

What was much more embarrassingly uncomfortable, and what I never ever asked for, was the douching of my rear passage which began once Memmisaab made me available to her clients. It could never have occurred to a civilized Englishwoman that a man might wish to use that part of her for his pleasure. The exercises Ishbal had put me through should have given me a clue, but honestly they did not. Perhaps I am just stupid. I was to learn that Memmisaab's customers, a lot of them, did indeed enjoy riding their woman in her rear. Perhaps it stems from some perverse feeling of power over her, some wish to degrade her.

If that is truly the case, then it is certainly effective.

But again I am getting ahead of myself.

ELEVEN

There seemed to be, as my training progressed, something almost complicit developing between my trainer and me. It was as though the beatings he inflicted on me when they were necessary were held back in some way. They were horrible, and frequent, yet they seemed not actually as hard as they had been at first. I learned how right my instinct had been on the one occasion another guard had charge of me, and it made me grateful to belong to Ishbal.

This man was very tall, and thin except for a pot-belly that made him look odd and even a little ridiculous. I do not know why he had charge of me that morning, just that Ishbal was not there and this man was.

He put me through my training just as Ishbal always did. I marched around the hall with the other girls, and took

91

my beating as always (I never seemed able to please by the height of my knees or the swing of my breasts). I bent and stretched for him. I sucked his fingers. I pumped my pelvis wildly, though he did not have the bell for me to ring. I spread myself. I offered my breasts to be felt. I lay on my back and got my legs up for him. I tried so hard to please him!

Yet the harder I tried, the deeper he frowned. I became more and more nervous. I knew something was badly wrong when he kept me back when the other girls were dismissed. Ishbal often kept me back, to shag me or have me suck him, but when he did there was always a smile on his face. This man's face was dark and foreboding.

I did not know why. I had tried hard, and could think of nothing I had done wrong. It did not matter. When he had me alone and I was really scared, I made myself smile at him as winsomely as I could, and showed by gestures that he could shag me if he liked, or I would suck him off. Instead of responding as any man might to a girl obviously willing for anything, he got angrier. He dragged me by my hair to the stool on which Ishbal had first whipped me. He fixed me down. He thrashed me with a rattan cane, wildly, unbelievably. I screamed, and he stuffed a gag into my mouth. He thrashed me until I felt my head must burst. Never, never, has there been such agony in the whole universe!

Each stripe was like a white hot knife across my skin. I bucked and struggled so hard against the horror of it that my wrists and ankles were actually cut by my manacles, though I did not know it until later.

I do not know why he did it, nor what it was about me that set him off so. All I know is that I screamed and wailed, and at last mercifully fainted, and came to myself with Ishbal and some of the girls cradling me, and that I was in agony from my shoulders to the backs of my knees.

It took me a week to recover from that worst of possible

beatings, and it taught me that Ishbal was not the monster I had originally thought him. He nursed me as I lay face down, stiff and sore, upon my bed. He fed me soup, and rubbed creams onto me, and supervised the girls who were set to tend me. He even held me up to a window so that I could witness the man who had so beaten me being flogged in his turn as punishment, though it did not make me feel any better.

During the period of my recovery I had time to think. Or should I say that, as I lay on my bed, my mind filled the long periods of inactivity with rationalizing? Whatever it was, I came to see Ishbal, and the way he had treated me, in a different light.

Was he not a slave also? Had he any more choice than I in what he was obliged to do? He was Memmisaab's instrument and, if the flogging of the other man which I had witnessed through the window was anything to go by, faced far more terrible punishments than I if he failed in his duty. Yet now he was being kind to me, and I realized that his beatings of me had been light.

If he had thrashed me as the other man had, I would be dead by now!

Although we had few words with which to communicate, and although he was still my trainer, with complete power over me, there came about during the days of my convalescence a softening between us. It was almost entirely through the eyes.

I caught the softness in his as he smoothed cooling creams over the weals that striped my back and bottom. He, I think, caught the gratitude in my eyes when he was soft with me.

It made no difference to the strictness with which he trained me and put me through my paces once I had recovered, but it did, I am sure, cause him to ease off with the force, if not the frequency, of my beatings. And when he fucked me, which he did more often after I had recovered than he had before, it was more usually on his bed than with me bound to the stool or shackled to a pillar, and more gentle, and for longer.

He even stopped lending me to his colleagues, which was a blessing. Even quite early on in my time there it occurred to me as odd, and even bad business, that Memmisaab's guards and trainers, though slaves themselves, had entirely free access to the goods her customers had to pay highly for. I know that before Ishbal stopped it, I was had far more often by guards and trainers than I was by customers.

The group training sessions, at which all we girls - about a dozen and a half of us - were exercised together, took place in the mornings. After a mid-day communal meal, the other girls would be taken off by their various trainers and Ishbal would take me back to the Training Room again.

It was during these afternoon sessions with Ishbal, and after the grazes on my wrists ankles and neck had entirely disappeared, and I had been taken to the blacksmith to have new, lighter and smoother, manacles fixed around my wrists and ankles, and a collar riveted around my neck, that Memmisaab began to send for me to entertain her customers.

At first there were only one or two a day; fat, rich men who could afford to hire a white woman, for you may be sure Memmisaab set a high price on her new and unique acquisition. A girl would scurry in to where Ishbal was training me, and kneel with her brow to the floor, and give Ishbal her message, and I would be taken off to be prepared.

Busy old women would bathe me, and shave me down there, unless I had already been shaved that day, and dry me off and put that stinging lotion on me. My hair would be brushed and burnished. My eyes and lips and nipples would be painted. Musk-oil would be applied to my nether lips and the cleft of my bottom and behind my ears.

A veil known as a yashmak would be hung beneath my eyes. A sort of abbreviated waistcoat would be put on me, open at the front and not covering my breasts at all, and a skirt of fine muslin hung about my waist. This dressing up always struck me as rather comic. Used by now to always going around stark naked, to have clothes put on me when being sent off for some man's sexual gratification seemed rather ridiculous. At last, painted and dressed I would be led to the bed-chamber.

It was always the same one, and I came to think of it as my own. It was not large, perhaps twelve feet by fifteen, and it had heavy velvet drapes of deep burgundy red covering the walls. There was a dresser with a mirror and some chairs, and of course the bed.

This was of unusual construction, with a high and ornate head-end decorated with moldings of scenes of what can only be described as Saturnalia, with lots of figures of maidens having things done to them by mythical beasts, and a contrastingly low foot end. Its four thick corner-posts rising up to a canopy of fine silk-muslin, it dominated the room - as of course it should in such an establishment as this. The mattress was thickly-stuffed and hard, and covered with a silk sheet. Many pillows and cushions lay about on it. There was no top sheet or counterpane, for this was not a bed intended to be slept in.

I would be led in, and motioned to wait in the pakka position, kneeling down with my forehead on the floor, my knees splayed and my bottom towards the door, so that the customer would be greeted by the sight of my womanly parts as soon as he came into the room. There was a fine lattice in one wall, through which Ishbal watched to ensure I behaved well. He showed it to me the first time I was taken there, and by gestures and grimaces and the few words of French we shared, gave me to understand what my fate would be if I did not writhe and squirm and wriggle and look adoringly at whichever man had bought my services.

I suppose it was because I was pale of skin and had red hair and freckles that those early clients were so excited. Some of them actually jerked into their comes at the very sight of me, and I would then have to work hard to re-arouse them, knowing that all the time Ishbal was watching, and that I would be flogged if the client departed less than delighted with my performance.

Through Ishbal's very demanding training I had come to know many of the ways a woman can excite a man, and I had to be very active with them with Memmisaab's customers. I tried hard, sucking and wriggling and pumping my belly for them as though my life depended upon it. Even so, I did not always escape a spanking.

One thing I had come to understand through Ishbal was that this activity could be a mutual giving and taking of pleasure. Just as a man gets pleasure from thrusting himself into a warm and welcoming quim, so he can give it by his skill and staying power, by his sensitivity, by his touchings and fondlings, and by his recognition of his partner as an equal participant. Just as a woman gives pleasure by caressing a man with her mouth, so she gets it by the delight she generates, and the feeling of triumph when she builds him to a shuddering climax to her own rhythm and timing, and by the light in his eyes afterwards. And how well I know how much a man can pleasure a woman by fondling her breasts and her clitty!

With Memmisaab's customers it was not the same. They demanded to be pleased, and cared not about giving pleasure. I learned it with my very first client under Memmisaab's rule.

When he came into the bedroom I was, as Ishbal had

instructed me, kneeling on the rug with my head down on my folded arms, and my knees apart in the pakka position I had been taught. The man took his time about beginning on me, for I heard him moving about, and felt the draft of his burnouse as it swung about.

It was yet another signal of my complete subjection to the will of my owner and of Ishbal, and thus of this unknown customer, that I should be made to kneel thus, with my bottom in the air, and my knees wide, and all my womanly parts offered up, not hidden at all by the near-transparent muslin of my skirt, while the man looked me over and drank coffee - and while, I knew, Ishbal peered in through his lattice.

After an age, the man nudged my bottom with his foot. Not knowing whether I was doing right, I got to my feet. The man's eyes moved over me, and he gestured with his hand. I did not know what he meant, and could not understand the words he spat at me in a voice made thick by his obvious excitement at what I was offering him - or rather, what Memmisaab and Ishbal were offering, for it was I that was being offered. Ishbal's urgent whisper - "Pousse! Pousse ta connasse! Danse!" - came to my rescue in my puzzlement.

I instantly raised up my arms and began to gyrate my belly, moving about for the man's pleasure, pumping my hips as if trying to ring the bell, waving my arms about, displaying myself for him in the most lascivious manner. His glittering black eyes followed my every movement, and his tongue snaked out to moisten his thin lips.

The man suddenly clapped his hands and gestured again. He was on the bed, and he moved his feet apart, and tugged at the hem of his burnouse. Ishbal's whisper said "Sucoter! Sucoter!" I dived my head under the folds of the man's garment. I squirmed up between his parted knees.

Although he must have been wealthy, else he could not have afforded me, he had not bathed recently, or possibly ever. His odour made me long to back away. Fear of Ishbal's whip made me go on. My hands found his already stiff manhood. I guided my face towards it in the pungent darkness. I made myself suck him, though I had to fight back my distaste.

He was not big, but big enough to near choke me when he pushed my head down. This was not like Ishbal or any of the other guards and trainers I had practised sucking. They had let me get on with it, perhaps occasionally touching my head to guide me. This man wanted only to fuck my mouth; to use it as a source of self-stimulation.

Suddenly, his garment was thrown up, and he grabbed my hair and shoved me onto my back. He ripped off my skirt, and threw my legs apart, and was on me. He rammed into me like a wild beast. He gripped my breasts as if they were handles to pull me on. He rutted at me as though he were frantic, cramming himself against my splayed pelvis, his eyes screwed shut and on his face an expression almost of agony.

Thank heavens it only took a few minutes.

Even during that short time, I knew from his grunts that I must pretend excitement, and I bucked my hips for him, and groaned aloud as though he was transporting me to heaven.

His come was quick, almost like a sneeze, and he was out of me at once, and on his feet, and looking down at me with a look that showed he thought he was the finest lover on earth, and that I should be grateful for the honour he had done me by stuffing his thing up me. Poor fool! I hoped he had been made to pay well for his vainglory!

If I had begun to feel an arrogance, a sense of superiority, at this man's poor performance and my ability to satisfy him so easily, he reminded me of my true station in the simplest of ways. He grabbed my nipples in his two hands and tugged at them. I had to scramble up off the bed for fear he would pull them off, he was so rough. Then he shoved me down onto the floor so that I was kneeling as I had when he first entered.

As I knelt there wondering, through the pain of my throbbing nipples, what he would require of me next, he began to sort of fiddle about with me, back between my legs. They were not the touches of a man about to mount his woman, nor touches suggesting excitement. He just flicked his fingers at me, and got my nether lips apart, and put something cool and hard between them, and pressed me closed again.

I waited in the kneeling position until I heard him leave, then reached round for the object he had thrust into me. It was a coin! Before slapping my bottom, and laughing, and going off, the man had left a coin lodged between the lips of my quim! No finer, more devastating humiliation could be dreamed of. It said that I was worthy of a small reward for my efforts to please him, but that reward was given in just the way to show how low he regarded me!

I have managed to keep that coin by me ever since. To me, it is a symbol of how strong a person's spirit can really be. It had been thrust into me at the lowest ebb of my life, when I had been enslaved, and sold off, and beaten, and forced to perform as a naked prostitute for a fierce owner and strict trainer. Yet deep inside I knew that he, the man who had paid for my body, and who had thrust that coin into me as a gesture of contempt, was in reality less than I was.

I might well be a beaten slave; I might well be forced to serve the lusts of such as he, but he was the one who had paid. He was the one who had the need. He was the one who needed to boost his sense of worth by using and abusing a woman who had no choice in the matter.

Ishbal was not thus, for though he beat me, and made me perform my exercises, when he fucked me it was because he enjoyed it, and he liked me to enjoy it also. He beat me because he had to, and to prove my submission and obedience to the woman who was his owner as well as mine. That customer who had thrust the coin up me was so limited he thought he proved his superiority simply by having the money to shag me, and doing so. How sad!

Not all those early customers were as bad as the first one, thank heavens. Although all of them were concerned only for their own pleasure - after all, they had paid highly for the right to fuck Memmisaab's little ginger-haired English girl - their manner of taking their pleasure was much less frantic and self-centered.

I realized early on that, having paid for me, there was no real limit as to the amount of time they had me for - and no limit at all to the things they could require me to do for them.

Often I was kept for several hours together. With most customers, I was made to dance before getting down to business. I always had to suck them off, sometimes several times if I was required to re-arouse them after they had shagged me. They always shagged me, of course - sometimes in rather difficult positions, and more than once - and most used my bottom too. But it was how they had me that mattered in the end.

If they were perfunctory, treating me as a thing rather than a living person, it was always hard for me. If, though, they took their time, and were not too rough with me, and seemed pleased with my efforts to please them, it was much nicer.

The most important thing, of course, was that I should express the utmost delight in being had by them. Irrespective of what they were like - fat old merchants; handsome; ugly; warrior-types or toothless old men, it mattered not - I had to smile, and simper admiringly, and wriggle and gasp and look adoring as though their shagging of me was the most wonderful experience I had ever known.

You may think me a wanton for thus baldly describing the ways I was used as a slave of sex, and the tricks I used in my turn. The point I am trying to make, albeit clumsily, is that by taking time, and by varying things, these men whose only object was their own pleasure allowed my own senses to be aroused - and sometimes the climaxes I always pretended to experience became actually genuine.

And you must also understand the other side of the coin, so to say. I had no choice about the way I was obliged to live. I was nineteen years of age, kept naked and healthy, the whole purpose of my existence being the gratification of lust. Surrounded as I was by scenes of carnality, trained and exercised so as to be fit for sex, the only object of each day being the men who would hire my body, was it not inevitable that my own carnal instincts would be bestirred whether I willed it or not? They were bestirred. Not every time, especially when I was tired or my customer was particularly unprepossessing, but honesty compels me to admit that my body did often enjoy what happened to it.

Some of the positions my customers got me in seemed very peculiar. I learned much later that there is apparently a book on the subject, though I can hardly believe it. Mostly they shagged me on my back with my legs up of course, but I was also taken from the rear, face down, or on my side with one knee tucked up to my breasts, or with my feet tucked into the man's armpits, or on all fours from behind. Sometimes I was required to get astride, on top, to wriggle and gyrate my belly while the customer played with my breasts. It became my favourite position, for I learned that I could move myself to excite my own parts, and bring on those glorious cramps and pulsations of a woman's climax while at the same time bringing the man I was riding to his own pulsings.

There was one man who got me on my back, and when

he was deep inside me got his legs outside mine, and squeezed my thighs together and rocked in me, and that was almost as good in the way it excited my clitty, but he was the only one to shag me that way so I cannot be sure.

TWELVE

Because my price early on was high, I tended to get only older, richer customers, and seldom more than three or four in an afternoon and evening - mostly, I supposed, because they tended to keep me for rather a long time. Several of them visited me quite regularly.

One of them, a very fat old man of at least sixty, I guessed, stands as a good example of what I mean about getting pleasure through giving it. He took to visiting me in the afternoon at least once a week, and the performance was always the same.

I knelt in the pakka position of obeisance, with my forehead on the rug, so that the first thing he saw when he entered was my raised bottom, offered to him through the thin muslin of my skirt.

With the toe of his slipper, he softly touched the back of my head to show acceptance of my submission, and sat on the bed. At the clap of his hands, I rose to my feet and danced for him, rotating my hips and shaking my shoulders to make my breasts sway. He watched me avidly, and already I started to get stirred up at the way his excitement showed in his face.

At a second clap of his hands, I stopped dancing and stripped off my waistcoat and skirt. I moved close before him as he sat on the bed and took up the kiffoi position, with my hands behind my head and my knees parted and bent. I did not need the order pousse ta connasse, for I knew that, like Ishbal, this man delighted in having me pump my belly for him. Unlike my trainer, though, he kept his hand on me so that while gyrating I was actually rubbing myself against his fingers. That, too, was very arousing - as was the moment he took his hand from between my legs, and looked to see that it was slick with my juices, smiling happily.

Then he lay back on the bed, and I pulled open his pantaloons and pleasured him with my tongue and lips. He was not large in his member, and always began soft. Thus, I could take almost the whole of him into my mouth, and cup his balls in my hand, and squeeze and suck and lick, and feel the delight of him growing stiff under my ministrations.

I sucked and licked him for a long time, perhaps as much as half an hour, but he never spurted his essence into my mouth like most of them did. When he had enjoyed the sensations of my tongue and lips and fingertips long enough, and his cock was stiff enough, he tapped me lightly on the back of my head. At this hoped for signal, I climbed astride his plump thighs, and got myself over his cock, and sank myself onto him for a slow - and for me delicious - shag.

Astride and in control is for me the most wonderful way to fuck, for a girl is able to move for her own best enjoyment. That this man, too, liked me on top was a glorious bonus.

I rode him slowly, for that is what he wanted, and he took a long time to reach his delight, by which time I was already deliciously convulsing. I had to control myself, of course, and try to hide the fact that I had been coming for quite a while, for if I had gone wild on him he might have got annoyed that I was working for my own pleasure rather than his - which would have earned me a spanking from Ishbal.

After he had his climax deep in my belly, I got off and poured him coffee and served him sweetmeats while he rested and recovered. While he was thus refreshing himself, I knelt beside him on the mattress, and put my hands behind my head and arched my spine to present my breasts for him. He liked looking at me posed thus, with my head back and my titties offered out for him. He was one of the many men who enjoyed playing with my nipples and he tweaked and teased me, only a little roughly, while he drank, occasionally dropping his hand down to rub my clitty, chuckling each time I gasped and squirmed.

His refreshments finished, he lay back on the bed again, and I sucked him a second time. He took longer to get stirred up this time, and in the back of my mind I was grateful that Ishbal had made me suck his fingers so hard and for so long, for it had given me the ability to suck and lick for long periods without discomfort to the muscles of my throat, or to my tongue-root.

I knew, too, that by cupping and pressing him just below his balls, and even slipping a finger between his plump buttocks to press and tease him, I could bring him to a second erection fairly easily.

At the appropriate moment, when he felt himself capable, he patted me on my head again. and I leapt up and bent myself over the foot-end of the bed. If my sucking and fondling had been right - which you may be sure I made certain it was - he came off much more quickly in my bottom than when I had been riding him.

Last of all, at the end of at least two hours of serving him, I washed him clean, and towelled him dry, and gave his soft little member a farewell kiss. He patted me on my head, handed me a little purse with coins in it, and left.

He was a dear man, and needed to use each of my available places and have me several times in order to reassure himself he was not getting too old. And he was nice to me, given that I was his bought thing to do with whatever he wished.

Few of my customers were as nice as my sweet old man

of course, though none were as awful as the one who liked to fix me face down to the bed by my wrists and ankles, and rut in my bottom, and slap me hard when he'd had his pleasure, and walk out, leaving me there spread-eagled until Ishbal came to release me.

I never did know how much my sweet old man gave me in money, for Ishbal always took it off me. Perhaps he gave it to Memmisaab, perhaps he kept it. What right had I to question? What I can say is that, every time after my sweet old fat man, Ishbal was afire, and lost no time at all in getting me down onto the bed that was still warm from the customer, and fucking me hard and voluptuously.   Having worked two or more hours for the pleasure of my customer, being mounted by Ishbal, who was both larger and more vigorous, never failed to have me bucking and wailing in seconds as I climaxed again and again!

I got to know Ishbal deeply as the weeks and months passed. He was scarred and very big, and could have been thought ugly, but there was something about the way he treated me that brought out in me an affection for him.

True, he thrashed me daily, and sometimes very hard. True, he made me perform those exhausting exercises, and beat me when I failed to ring the bell in time to his clapping. True, he showed me off to his fellow trainers, and let them feel me up, and sometimes stood me up alongside one of their girls while our bodies and our obedience were compared and they joked about our submissiveness.

True, too, that he had his choice amongst other girls, and I sometimes saw him get one of them up against a pillar, or down on the flagstones, and shag her almost brutally. Yet it was me he nearly always chose. And when he shagged me there was something other, something more personal, in the way he took his pleasure.

With the other guards and trainers, who despite Ishbal's

prohibition sometimes managed to pull me aside unseen, and have their pleasure of me, it was always a callous thing. They would get me up against a wall, or on the floor, and rut at me, and spurt their hotness up me, and swagger away pleased with themselves.

With Ishbal it was almost a mutual exploration of the delights of the body. Yes, it is true that I would have to perform whenever and however and wherever he desired - and sometimes that was embarrassingly public - but it is also true that the way he looked at me, even when he was showing off to his fellow trainers, told me that this was a sort of compact between us. There was a softness in his eyes when he looked at me which told me that underneath it all, even though he was obliged to beat and train and debase me, even though he was by virtue of his status as my trainer obliged to demonstrate his control in public, he did not really wish it; that if he had been free to have his way, I would have been prized rather than subjugated.

With Ishbal, when he got me on my back, or made me bend over so that he could enter me from behind, there was a gentleness in his movements, and a softness, an intimacy even, in his eyes and hands that told me of a certainty that he at least liked me, and enjoyed my body almost as though he were my lover, rather than as a man who took me by right of power.

It is strange how the human spirit can find and cling to tiny comforts in even the most humiliating of situations. My own did that then, in what I came to think of as my secret friendship with Ishbal. Even when he got me strapped down, and made me kiss that twelve-tongued lash, and then beat me with it until I sobbed, even then I knew in my heart he was really my friend, and loved me, and was only beating me because he had to.

Who knows but I was right, for if Ishbal had not been

my trainer another would, and he might have been as vicious as the man who near flayed me alive that awful day.

As I have said, I believe the human spirit to be pretty near indomitable in the ways it manages to rise above even the most extreme of circumstances, and to find moments of comfort, and even contentment. I believe it because such was the case with me then.

Naked and helpless, the fact that I was English made me a target for Ishbal's fellow guards. Even though he tried to forbid them, they missed few opportunities to get me aside to shag me, or to bend me over to plough my bottom, or (a favourite with most of them) to get me on my knees with their hands gripping my hair and their cocks down my throat. Seldom was I able to walk down a corridor without hands reaching out to feel me up. Often were the times they found an excuse to beat me, for they had the right, and my white skin and submissive manner seemed to egg them on.

As well as that, news that Memmisaab had a white girl as slave spread wide, and my afternoons and evenings were soon kept busy with wealthy men who wished to see if a white girl was as good and as obedient as the black and brown and coffee-coloured girls they were used to.

Yet among it all, those moments when Ishbal's eyes met mine, those moments when he stroked my hair, or patted my bottom as if I was his pet, were lovely, and warming, and kept me going.

Among the warmest of times during my slavery with Memmisaab and also the most humiliating, strangely enough, were my dance lessons to rehearse me for the performances I was to give in the coffee-house when my owner deemed me proficient. The coffee-house was Memmisaab's 'shop window', where those of her girls who were not servicing a customer paraded themselves along a latticed cloister attempting to attract one. At one end was a raised stage where girls would dance or perform in other ways for the entertainment (and titillation) of the audience. My performance was to be a dance which included ringing my bell.

Ishbal, of course, conducted the lessons, but I was actually taught by a beautiful woman who looked as though she might have hailed from India. I had seen her in the training room many times but had never had the chance to speak to her, or any of the other girls come to that. She had the most wonderful shawl of glossy hair, so black it shone almost blue. Her eyes were huge and tilted up at the outside corners. Her cheekbones were high, and her lips full. She was quite short, only a couple of inches taller than me, but her legs were long and shapely, her waist slender, and her breasts and hips were full and luscious.

Looking at her, I wondered how on earth any of Memmisaab's many clients could possibly seek me when she was available, so much lovelier in every respect than me, I thought. And she danced like a dream of beauty.

The first lesson began with Ishbal making me show her how I rang the bell, and she watched me, and even as she did I could see in her eyes that she was already calculating how to convert this lewd performance into a dance. When I stopped, she paused, and looked at the floor, and stroked her chin thoughtfully. Then she raised her head, and began to move, and in an instant she became magic.

She was as naked as the day, and unadorned save for the collar and manacles and chain that all Memmisaab's girls wore, yet as she danced she seemed to become misted with veils of beauty. Her eyes were not here with we her audience, but off somewhere rapturous. Her body became liquid. Her arms did not so much move as ripple like warm waters. Her hips and thighs moved with such voluptuous fluidity that if she had had a bell, it would have rung of its own accord for sheer joy. Oh, I wanted to melt to the ground and kiss her feet, she was so glorious!

When it came to my turn, to the time I was supposed to mimic her, Ishbal inserted my bell, and smiled, and clapped his hands. I could not do it. Any movements I made would be so awkward, so bovine by comparison, that I was ashamed even to try.

Seeing my reluctance, Ishbal got me over his knee and gave me a spanking. When he set me on my feet again and gave the order, the other girl looked so deep into my eyes no words were needed.

"Come on," her liquid eyes were saying. "You can do it. I will help you."

And help me she did. She clapped a soft rhythm. She took my arms and showed me how to move them. She smiled at me when I got it right, and gave only a little frown when I was clumsy. With her hands, she guided my hips into the right movements. She showed me the steps over and over until I knew them without thinking.

I needed her help and encouragement all the more when Ishbal took to making me wear a peculiar plug affair in my bottom at the same time as I had the bell inserted in my front. Although it was not large, perhaps three inches long and one inch thick, I felt very crammed when I had both devices in me. It was shaped like a letter 'L' and narrowed down at the right-angle so that I could not eject it. I did not understand yet why Ishbal imposed this new burden on me, but naturally had no choice but to bear it. My understanding only came when I was finally required to perform in the coffee-house, and I confess that when it did Ishbal had to spank me to stop me laughing.

Ishbal gave my new teacher and me a lot of time together to rehearse my dance, and his smile let me know that he knew we were becoming closer than teacher and pupil.

Her name was Bennasira, if I spell it right. No other words, at least words either of us could understand, were ever exchanged, for we had nothing of each other's language. But there are languages other than those which limit themselves to words.

Bennasira spoke to me almost from the first moment in a language far deeper than mere words. Even as Ishbal hauled me up after my spanking, she looked at me with a gaze deep and knowing. She helped and encouraged me. Her hands as she guided my arms or my hips were gentle and warm. Her smile when I got it right was brilliant. Her eyes seemed to go deep into mine, willing me to try hard, and telling me that I could do it. Telling me, too, that she knew I was coming to love her.

Even Ishbal knew it, for after my third or fourth lesson in this exotic and beautiful form of dancing he began to leave me alone with this soft, lovely woman. He knew, of course. Knew that she would gentle and encourage and inspire me. Bennasira knew how I was beginning to feel about her, of course, knew it from the way my eyes could not leave hers, and how I would gaze fascinated at her breasts, and at the smooth curves between her navel and her thighs. She seemed to enjoy my fascination, and became gently teasing in her manner with me.

She let me make love to her after half a dozen or so lessons. She had coaxed and coached me. She had moved my arms and body with her soft hands. She had looked into my eyes. Looked deep, and smiled softly. After the lesson, she took my hand, and smiled, and led me to her sleeping-place.

The little cubicles we slaves were allowed as sleeping quarters were Spartan by any standards - perhaps six feet wide and eight long, containing only a bunk to sleep on and a bucket for the calls of nature, they were no more than they needed to be. Yet Bennasira's cubicle, because it was hers and no other's, had an atmosphere of warmth about it that was entrancing. Or perhaps it was just my mood, for by the time she got me there I knew I was going to be allowed to make love with my beautiful Bennasira, and my heart was singing and my breasts were hard and tense and tingling.

Her skin was of the hue of milky tea, and smooth as petals. Her lips were full and soft, and her breath was perfumed with cloves and flowers. She lay down on her bunk and allowed me to run my hands over her, and to kiss her, and breathe in the warm, heady perfume of her womanliness.

She lay perfectly still, with her eyes closed, as I kissed and caressed her from her toes to her hair. I felt like a schoolgirl at some solemn Mass or Confirmation. Her breasts were firm and full, and the aureolae around her hard nipples were dark brown and the size of crown coins. They tasted of freshness and honey, and a thrill of delight ran through me as they stiffened under the caresses of my tongue.

Her belly was smooth and softly rounded, and her navel was deep. She gave the tiniest of shivers and sighed softly as I ran my tongue in circles around and into it, and then moved slowly from her navel to the swell of her mound. Like me, she was shaved and branded, and her womanhood was a wondrous tulip of plump softness.

As I moved my hand towards her, breathless and timid at her loveliness, she eased her thighs apart for me. Her folds were plump and soft, and her crease long and pink. She sighed again, and eased herself towards me as I began to caress her. I parted her folds with tentative fingers. I dipped my mouth towards her inner lips, already red and swelling.

Ah, she tasted of heaven! Of musk and spices and womanhood. Her inner folds were warm and already glistening as I slipped my tongue along her length. She sighed when my fingertips found her soft entrance and explored it and, in

111

concert, my tongue flicked around her clitty, which thrilled me to my core by stirring and coming alive.

She began to move with me, but gently, like liquid, parting herself fully for me and rolling her womanhood gently under my mouth as I licked and sucked her, and drank her glorious ambrosia.

I knew she had risen to a climax, and was drunk on the knowledge as she rested a gentle hand on the back of my head and moved herself on my hands and mouth. Compared with a man's, a woman's come is a glorious thing, slow, and building and undulating through every atom of her being.

Not for a woman the quick tension and sudden spurtings that are a man's come. For a woman it is the inexorable winding of a glorious spring, a tightening and heightening of every nerve and sense, on and on until she must burst asunder or die. And then, Ah! a cramping and churning and a bursting of electric glory from toes to crown and back, to focus in overwhelming, throbbing, bubbling meltings deep in her womb, and which go on and on and on, rising and falling like the irresistible swell of the ocean.

It was thus with my beautiful Bennasira now as she tensed and tensed, and gave a single sighing groan, and shuddered, and I felt the muscles of her belly and thighs spasm and ripple.

It was thus with me also, for even though she had not touched me I was having the loveliest, gentlest comes of my own.

Afterwards, she was very gentle with me. She kissed me, and washed my face, and kissed me again. She held my hand as we went back to the training room. Ishbal was there, with several other girls, and he smiled as soon as he saw us. I blushed to think he had guessed what we had been doing, but blushed contentedly for I was as happy as I had been since before father married me off to Mr Mansfield.

Ishbal allowed us to spend time together whenever he could, and we made love nearly every day. Bennasira was a marvellous lover, gentler, warmer, more knowing than anybody I had lain with before, and those moments of bliss together compensated greatly for the rest of my life as Memmisaab's whore.

Lest you are shocked at me, and are wondering how I knew what to do with a woman, I have to add here that Bennasira was not the first woman I had dealings with. Memmisaab had taken me to her couch early in my time with her, and quite often thereafter. It was, I suppose, just another way of asserting her power over me. It lacked the glory of my times with my lovely Bennasira, for Memmisaab was always very free with the long cane she carried and so I always worked hard. The worse bit was that whereas Bennasira would ripple and sigh and stroke my hair when she climaxed, Memmisaab always clamped my head between her heavy thighs and bucked and held me down, almost suffocating me in her excitement. Also, Bennasira always brought me to glory afterwards and Memmisaab could not have cared less.

There came at last the time Memmisaab deemed me ready to perform my dance in her coffee house. The thought filled me with dread. It was one thing to perform before Ishbal and Bennasira, and even the other girls and guards. It was rather intimidating to dance before Memmisaab, for she was a sharp and demanding mistress, and I came to know that she would require my services between her knees after my dance was finished.

The thought of performing under the eyes of all those men, though! The thought of having to move to the sound of the flutes and tambour, and having to gyrate my body for the lewd pleasure of an actual audience, filled me with embarrassment.

I had no choice, of course, and could only stand trembling with nerves as they prepared me.

My hair was brushed out, and a heavy cap of silver chains placed upon my head. My eyes were lined with kohl, and my mouth and navel and nether lips were painted with rouge. A little bell was fixed to each of my nipples with a sort of slip-knot affair, for Bennasira had taught me how to wriggle my shoulders to make my breasts sway and bounce. My body was oiled to make my skin shine, and lastly a muslin yashmak was hung across my face below my eyes.

My lower bell, the one which had created the idea for this performance, was not to be inserted until I was actually on the stage. That was when I learned the purpose of the second wooden plug Ishbal had made me wear recently, for he re-introduced it. It was different now, though, and the very sight of it made me burst into near-hysterical laughter - laughter born as much from my nervousness as from the device itself.

It now had a bunch of huge white ostrich-feathers sticking out of its shorter end. Ishbal had to spank me very firmly to stop my giggles and to get me under enough control and to keep me still enough to insert it into my bottom without damaging me. The feathers stuck out straight behind me like a tail, and bobbed about when I moved. The sight and feel of it stopped any temptation I might have had to giggle now, for even I realised that it made me look strange and exotic.

As Ishbal at last led me off, I caught Bennasira's eye, and she smiled and blew me a kiss, and I felt a little better, though I was once again getting horribly nervous.

There must have been some kind of advertisement beforehand, for the coffee house was absolutely packed. I did not need to even see it to know, for the hubbub of voices was tremendous. My stomach lurched and my legs turned to water. I hung back. Ishbal turned, and looked at me warningly, and raised his strap. I had to go on if I did not wish to be thrashed.

Ishbal stepped through the narrow door that led to the stage, and I made myself follow, my heart in my mouth. He led me to the centre of the stage and clapped his hands very loud. Slowly, the noise died away and a rustling quiet fell over the place as scores and hundreds of eyes were turned to where I stood, naked and trembling with nerves.

When all was as still as it could be with such a crowd, Ishbal clapped his hands twice. At the signal we had rehearsed, I got my hands behind my head, and spread my knees, and pushed my hips forward in the kiffoi position, feeling my feathers waft about behind me. Ishbal kept me like that for several minutes so that the audience could get a good look at me. Then he turned me around slowly and made me wriggle so that the audience could get a good look at my tail-feathers, at which there came shouts and calls.

He turned me to face the audience again and spread my knees. There was a communal growl of lust as he ran the flat of his hand slowly down from my belly to between my legs. Keeping to the side so everybody could see just what he was doing, he parted the outer lips of my quim with his fingers. Holding up the rod, he showed it to the audience, chinking the bell to show them what was afoot, then slowly inserted it into me. I was tense and dry with nerves, and it was uncomfortable, but after sliding it back and forth along the length of my parted body-lips he got it set in me and stepped back.

He clapped his hands again, and I straightened up as much as the bell between my thighs and the plug holding my tail-feathers would ever let me. I waited, feeling all the eyes crawling over me. Then the music began, high-pitched, and quiet because Memmisaab wanted her customers to hear my bells, and I began to dance.

Something very strange happened. As the first notes of

the flutes rose up, and as the tambour began its soft beat, the image of Bennasira floated into my head. I saw her eyes, not those of the audience. I heard her voice whispering to me, and I began to move - to move just as she had taught me so patiently and with such love.

With her loving spirit inspiring me, I danced. I spread my arms, and they moved like silk scarves in a wind. I shook my shoulders, and my breasts moved and trembled, and the bells on my nipples sounded tinklingly. I wiggled my bottom, and my feathers shook. I moved my left hip forward, and touched my toes to the stage, my knee bent outwards in the way Bennasira had shown me. I thrust with my belly. My bell rang. My shoulders moved again, and my nipple-bells rang. I slid forward my right hip and thrust with my belly again, and that bell sounded.

It was perfect! In exact time to the rhythm of the tambour the high sound of my nipple-bells was echoed by the lower ring of the bell between my legs. I moved around the stage, aware of the audience but no longer terrified by them. My body was taken up by the rhythm, and by my image of Bennasira, and by a strange feeling of triumph.

Left hip, thrust; right hip, thrust; shaking shoulders and arms, to set my breasts bouncing; and all the time my bells and my trembling tail-feathers confirmed I was dancing well, as well as Ishbal or even Memmisaab could have wished. I wondered whether she was watching me from some secret place, and felt a thrill at my success.

That was not the only thrill I felt, for my nipples had become like nuts, and the bell-knots were giving me a slight and delicious pain. The lewd gyrations of my pelvis had worked on me as much as on the gawking audience, and the muscles of my aroused sheath gripped the rod inside me as though it were a lover's cock.

I felt the audience becoming tense, and there were even a few calls when I rang my lower bell especially loud. Ishbal

116

was standing in the center of the stage, his arms folded proudly, his feet planted firm, a smile of triumph on his face. Although it was not rehearsed, I danced to his side and wriggled myself close, and got my forward foot across his leg, and wriggled my torso against him, and pumped my hips to shake my feathers and ring my bell loudly.

I stepped away, and moved around, step and ring, shake and ring, the high sound of my nipple-bells contrasting with the deeper note of the bell dangling from my quim. I moved around in front of Ishbal and repeated my movements, which even I found exciting, against his other side. Whoops and yells came from the audience.

I became a wraith, and moved around Ishbal like smoke, getting close up to him and writhing my belly, moving away and swinging my breasts, and ringing and ringing my bells. I knew he might spank me afterwards, for none of this had been rehearsed, but it did not matter. Bennasira was in my body and in my heart; the rod in my sheath had become Ishbal; even my tail-feathers seemed exciting. I was lost in an exotic rapture.

I was beyond myself. I was in a dream. I had known all along in my mind that this dance was designed to excite Memmisaab's customers. Now I knew it in my body too, and was carried off by the blatant sexuality of it. If they were getting excited - which, to judge by the mounting noise, they very much were - so was I. More than them, if I am honest.

The music began to quicken. I faced my audience and swung my breasts so that my upper bells chinked like mad. I got my feet apart and bent my knees and opened myself to the audience, and pumped and pumped my pelvis, faster and faster as the tambour speeded up, until my hips were wild and the bell between my legs was sounding one continuous ringing, and the cheers were tumultuous, for as well as ringing the bell I was churning in the midst of a glorious orgasm.

Only when the tambour crashed into a final roll, and Ishbal grabbed me up, and held me out for the audience to shout and call, did I come back to myself. His powerful arm about my waist, Ishbal reached down and eased the bell-rod out of me, and held it up for the crowd to see, all slick as it was with my juices, and pandemonium burst out. They even threw money!

I was in a very peculiar state after my performance: exhausted, far more so than I had been by my many rehearsals, even though they had taken hours, and my dance on the stage only ten minutes: euphoric also, for not only did I know I had been successful, and had excited the audience, but I was still deeply aroused within myself. It was wonderful, too, to know I had pleased Ishbal, for when he grabbed me up in his arms, and hugged me to his great chest as he carried me off the stage, he grinned and nodded, and even kissed me. He had never kissed me before, and I felt so happy I hugged him until he pulled my arms off from around his neck with pretended impatience.

It shows how transported I was by the whole thing that it was not until Ishbal got me back to my cell that I realised I still had my tail-feathers firmly implanted in my bottom. Ishbal removed them with a grin before lying me down and fucking me long and hard as my reward.

THIRTEEN

The other side of the coin of my successful performance was that my services at once became much more in demand. By the time Ishbal had led me to what I thought of as 'my' bedroom, and kissed me again (those were the only kisses he had ever given me, but there were many to follow) there was a veritable queue of men eager to hire my body for their pleasure. That had been Memmisaab's intention, of course, Good business sense told her that twenty times ten (or whatever price she charged for me) was better than three times thirty from the richer men.

Luckily, my queue of customers that day were nearly all quick in their eagerness. I suppose seeing a white woman perform as lasciviously as I had just performed, and then getting her on her back with her legs up had got them high strung, for none of them took more than about five minutes - and of course, getting me cheaper meant that they were only allowed one go, as it were.

The first three or four received the benefit of my excited state, for at the first thrust of the first cock I began to pulsate yet again on the echoes of Ishbal, so pent up was I, and I kept churning into repeated comes for a long while, my head spinning and my body undulating in helpless ecstasy. After that, I drifted down and soon was conscious of little more than a succession of bodies descending on me, and of eyes leering, and of hands mauling, and of cocks thrusting up me. It was more exhausting than I could have imagined, but my body defended itself by spiralling away from what was being done to it.

By the time they finished with me, hours and ages later, they were getting little value for their money, for I was no more than a rag, a hole for them to shove themselves into, an unresisting, unresponsive receptacle for their cocks and their jism.

How a man can ever get pleasure from shagging a woman in that condition I will never understand. By the time the last one finished on me I was just a carcass, on my back, with my legs sagging limp and spread, and no life in me at all. Ishbal would have needed to whip me with spiked wires to get me to come alive!

He did not, of course, for we had entered a new stage in my life as Memmisaab's prostituted slave. Even she, as the days passed, was softer with me. As for Ishbal, it was his smiling, scarred face I first saw when I swam wearily awake next morning. I ached all over, and felt as though I had been mauled by a Brahma-bull, but Ishbal's smile, and the way he lifted me off the bed as though I were a small child, and carried me away, and bathed me and douched me out so gently, set off a warmth in my heart that made me want to kiss him and cry with contentment and happiness.

Memmisaab was a business-woman, and although I was not made to dance the next evening, there was still quite a queue for my services. I had been allowed to rest most of the day, and Ishbal had massaged me, and I had had two lovely hot baths, and Bennasira had lain gently with me, so when I was led to my cubicle I did not feel too bad. Indeed, the sight of the herd of men waiting eagerly outside my door almost made me giggle. The way their eyes widened and leered as I was led naked past them; the way they shuffled their feet, and preened; the way some even licked their lips as I drifted into the room, was just ridiculous.

If Memmisaab saw this as merely 'business', Ishbal at least felt something for me, and even though we did not have the words I saw in his eyes concern and questioning. Was I all right? Was I up to this? I stroked the hand that touched my shoulder. Yes, my eyes told him, yes, if only for you my gentle, caring trainer. I was up to it, and would survive, and be there tomorrow.

Ishbal restricted my customers to no more than a dozen or perhaps fifteen. It was not easy by any means as eager man after eager man hurried through my door, and leapt on me, and fucked me wildly. There was no subtlety about it at all, no moments of mock-flirtation and fondling and such. Why, I hardly had time to roll off my bed after one customer, and get on my knees on the floor to show obeisance in the pakka pose, as Memmisaab required, before I was being hauled up and tossed down onto my back by the next.

I know Ishbal restricted the men who wanted my services because between bouts, and even during them, I heard shouting from outside the door, and saw Ishbal pushing men away towards the cubicles of other girls.

It took perhaps a week for the excitement to die down, for the thrill of shagging a white woman to become commonplace. It was a hard week, but Ishbal nursed me, and Bennasira eased me, and I survived it. Thereafter, Memmisaab made me dance again, every other evening, and kept me a little exclusive. Perhaps she realized that letting her ordinary customers loose on me was likely to wear me out and make a raddled hag of me in no time at all. Perhaps she just found it more profitable to keep me for no more than half a dozen or so men a day, and for her black-clad bath-house women to keep me tight and flexible with their lotions. I do not know, and had no choice in it anyway.

What I do know is that it was far less wearing to devote half an hour to pleasuring each of six men than to spend ten minutes being bounced on by twenty of them one after the other.

I know also that whenever I went out and did my dance, the coffee house was always packed, and scores and scores of men watched and cheered and called out as I weaved my body about and pumped my hips and waved my feathers and rang my bells for their entertainment.

Afterwards there was always a few customers to entertain, and on the days I did not dance I had engagements like those I had experienced when I was first bought by Memmisaab - engagements with men who could pay well, and who required more than just my legs up and a quick shag.

As the weeks went by, I got used to going out on that stage before an audience of leering, calling men, and doing my dance, and ringing my bells. In fact, if I am honest I have to confess that I actually began to look forward to it. It was something I had no choice but to do, of course, but I was rewarded in it by the love of Bennasira and Ishbal as well as by my own bodily excitement.

Even though there was no longer any reason for Ishbal to let me be with Bennasira, for she no longer needed to coach me in my dancing, he found ways of getting us together. He would arrange for us to exercise beside each other; she would hold my hand in the exhausting daily high-stepping march around the walls of the training room; she would touch my arm, and smile when the exercises got strenuous, or when one or other of the trainers got too demanding. He, Ishbal, would allow us time alone together; time to melt into one another, and to sigh in our passion, and to be loving and gentle.

And when Ishbal himself took me aside, it was no longer the assertion of a trainer's rights over his animal. No longer did he just push me onto my back and thrust himself up me, or grab my hair and shove his cock into my mouth. Instead, it became love-making almost as beautiful as that between Bennasira and me. Not quite, because nothing in the history of the universe has ever been so beautiful as making love with Bennasira. But good. Oh, so good!

He still beat me, of course.

Mostly, he beat me if I did not perform well in the training room, for I still had to go there every morning even if the evening before had been busy. If I had received a lot of customers and my hips were stiff, I would inevitably do poorly in the pacing around the sides of the room, and he would strap me down over the stool. He showed little mercy. He could not really, for others were always watching, and often

Memmisaab herself - and she brooked no leniency with her girls.

I got other beatings when occasionally a customer complained that I had given less than complete satisfaction. I knew that to be out of vindictiveness rather than lack of effort on my part, for even be he the tenth or twelfth customer I always wriggled like mad beneath him, and pumped my belly against him, and pretended the most violent of climaxes, or sucked him off as though his member was the most wonderful thing on earth and gave me raptures.

Perhaps there is a quirk in some men's minds that makes them go one step further in the humiliation of the girl who has just given them the most exquisite pleasure her mouth or body is capable of, and makes them want to have her strapped as well.

These beatings were always conducted in the presence of the customer, and thus Ishbal could not be as light with me as I knew in my heart he wished. What was worse was that the offended customer had the right to decide the method of my punishment. Usually, it was no more than bending over the end of the bed and having my bottom beaten with the strap. There were two, though, who wanted more.

Both were 'regulars', if you see what I mean. I came to know them well, and when either walked through my doorway I shivered with dread, and did everything I could possibly do to please them in the hope that they would not complain. They always did.

I saw in his eyes that Ishbal knew this to be mere perversity, but if they demanded it he had to punish me, and in the manner they prescribed.

The one demanded that I be whipped on my breasts. Had I been chained and hung up to a pillar it would have been easier, but he demanded that I kneel on the bed, and put my hands behind my head, and offer my breasts up for the whip - thus adding a devilish twist to the punishment, for if I cringed away from the strokes or rounded my shoulders, he would demand further lashings. Even though Ishbal always used a whip with dozens of thin strings, the softest and least painful he had, it was still awful, and my poor breasts would be terribly sensitive when the next customer grabbed them.

The second complainer was worse. He demanded that my wrists be fixed to the chain around my waist, and that I lie on my back with my bottom out over the foot of the bed. Ishbal had then to lock my anklets to the bedposts on either side, so that my tummy and thighs and all between were spread almost painfully wide. Ishbal would then have to flog me with the worst whip of them all, the one he had used that first time he strapped me over the stool in the training room, and he would have to whip me along the insides of my thighs, from knee to knee, leaving out nothing between.

I know Ishbal hated it almost as much as me, but he had no choice for he was a slave too. Once he was too gentle, and the customer ranted, and hit him and snatched the whip from his hand, and flogged me himself, all the blows falling on my belly and quim, as though the monster was trying to cut me in half. After that horrible occasion, Ishbal beat me with a will whenever that particular customer complained. He knew as well as I that his beating of my thighs, however fierce, was infinitely more merciful than the customer's.

Only once did Ishbal beat me on his own behalf during those last months, and then I deserved it, and it was very fierce. My offence happened in the training room, and Memmisaab was present, which made it all the worse when I pulled a face and poked my tongue out at him. I still do not know what came over me. He had been really nice to me all morning, smiling and patting me, and nodding in the friendliest fashion when I performed my exercises well.

Then, I do not know why, when it came to the time for

me to ring the bell, I grabbed up the rod for myself, and inserted it into my sheath with my own hands, and rang the bell wildly. I suppose I was showing off for some reason. Whatever it was, I poked my tongue out at Ishbal when I had finished ringing the bell, and laughed aloud.

It was an appalling insult. I did not mean it to be, for I had meant it to be a loving joke, but I knew instantly from the expression on his face and the hush that fell over the other people in the training room, girls and guards and Memmisaab herself, that something unbelievable had happened.

Ishbal looked stunned, and then the veins in his neck and forehead began to swell, and his eyes blazed fury. I froze with terror at what I had done, and fell to my knees, praying for the forgiveness I knew could not come. I, a mere slave girl, an animal to be hired out for money, the lowest creature in Memmisaab's establishment, had insulted my trainer, and in front of others!

Retribution had to be public, too, and fierce enough to restore Ishbal's standing among his fellow guards.

He grabbed me by my hair and dragged me across the floor, and dumped me down at Memmisaab's feet. He spoke to her with barely suppressed fury, and kicked me in my ribs with his hard toes. Memmisaab replied slowly, and glanced down at me, and nodded. Her eyes were so cold they scared me almost as much as Ishbal's anger.

It was to be a public punishment, and all Memmisaab's slaves were assembled to witness it. It was not just to teach me my lesson, but to serve as a warning to them all not to transgress. It was almost ritualistic in its preparations.

I was first taken off to a side cubicle to wait, and the waiting made my fear grow like a weed in my heart. After an eternity, two guards came for me, and marched me into the training room. I did not resist: there would have been no point, and in any case during my wait I had realized how wrong I was to insult my sweet Ishbal.

The training room was crowded. The older black-clad women, who did the housework and the laundry and such, formed one half of a great circle. The girls, perhaps eighteen or twenty of them, naked and huge-eyed with trepidation, formed the other. Around them stood the guards and trainers. Memmisaab sat in her chair to witness what was to be done with me, and in the centre of the circle stood Ishbal, looking more terrifying than I had ever seen him.

He had removed the loose pantaloons he usually wore, and had oiled his body, and now stood massive and glistening in the middle of the room, his very nakedness making him more fearsome. In his hand he held the twelve-thonged whip I already knew too well, its ends trailing on the flagstones. My stomach tightened, for I knew Ishbal could be very fierce with that whip.

By Ishbal's feet on the floor lay a big wooden beam attached to chains. It was to this that the two guards led me. They raised my arms behind my head, but instead of fixing my wrist-manacles to my collar as was usual, they tugged my arms tight back, and fixed each wrist to the opposite elbow so that I was held painfully tight.

Then they lay me on the ground on my back, with my feet towards the beam. They each took an ankle, and stretched my legs wide apart, and fixed me to the beam. Ishbal stared down at me, his face set, cold to the tears that were already welling in my eyes.

I heard creaking and rattling, as of a wheel and pulleys. The beam began to rise from the floor, dragging me with it. I screamed when the terror of it hit me. I was to be flogged hanging by my ankles from a wooden beam, like some animal in a butcher's shop! It was inconceivable!

It was all too horribly real. When I was entirely off the floor, hanging like some strange letter 'Y' in the middle of the training room, there had come a communal gasp from the other slave girls, and even the older women, as Ishbal flexed his shoulders and cracked the whip in the air. Then he began.

First, he reached up and pushed one end of the beam. It began to spin, slowly and inexorably rotating my helpless body. Ishbal raised his whip. He brought it whistling down. Fire exploded in my head and along the inside of my left thigh, where the blow had fallen. Again and again he brought it down as I slowly span around before him. Not a single part of my tormented body from knees to breasts, front and back and sides, was neglected. I did not faint, though oh! how I wished I had. It was like being slowly seared by some huge flame. At first I screamed and struggled in my bonds, but by the end, after a thousand years of burning torment, I could do no more than hang there, limp and silent save for my exhausted sobbing.

It became unreal. My body no longer felt the strokes of the whip, because it was already one great conflagration. My mind no longer registered the sounds of the whip, nor the ring of spectators, nor Memmisaab, nor anything in the world save Ishbal standing naked and terrible before me, his great arm rising and falling.

At last it was over, and I was taken down, and carried away to be washed and oiled and comforted by Bennasira, and to fall into what was half sleep, half fainting. When I came to myself, Ishbal was gazing down at me, and in his eyes was such a tenderness, such a regret and fondness, I burst into great sobs of sorrow for what I had done, and relief that he was here with me and had not abandoned me.

With his own dear hands he smoothed unguents onto me. With his own dear ugly, loving face he watched over me and kissed me. His thick, strong finger pressed against my lips, hushing me as I whispered my love and apologies.

And when, towards the evening, he allowed me to suck

his cock to show how sorry I was for the terrible insult I had given him, and a day later, when the blaze on my skin had begun to subside, had lifted me on top of his powerful body and let me shag him, he was so gentle and forgiving, and so caring my heart swelled and I could have died for him.

There is, I am sure, a guardian angel who watches especially over me. She visited me now, for two mornings after that beating I began my time of the month. These were always welcome times for, although dragging and uncomfortable in themselves, my monthlies brought me two blessings.

First, they showed that Ishbal's daily, and sometimes more frequent, use of his douche on me had ensured that I had not been got with child by one of the customers. Second, since a woman in her cycle was forbidden to a man, I had no customers to serve for a whole four days and nights.

It was, if you wish, a little monthly holiday during which I could rest, for not even the guards would require to use me during that blessed time.

This time, it came on me two mornings after the day of my beating, and gave me time to recover from it. Time, also, to delight in the tender care of my Bennasira, and to think about Ishbal.

Nowadays, as I have said, Ishbal was as light with me as he was allowed to be, despite that terrible upside-down beating I had so thoroughly deserved. Also, he now looked softly into my eyes whenever he was obliged to thrash me, and afterwards made love to me.

It was not the taking and shagging it had begun as; not the establishing of his power over me. It had become instead a sort of mutual consoling - he consoling me for the pain he had inflicted on my backside, me consoling him for having failed him yet again.

He did console me, for despite his size and his scars

and that I was his animal, he was a gentle and sensitive lover. I realized, as I lay on my bunk recovering from that awful whipping, that lately he had always made love to me after he had beaten me. And I realized, too, that it had become a part of the ritual I responded to.

Even after I had been let down from that terrible beam, and had been carried to my cubicle, my skin on fire from my knees to my neck, some place at the back of my mind had known that Ishbal would soon appear, and would be tender with me, and at last would shag me slowly and gently, and drive me to heaven. And whenever he did, my body was always already moist and ready, and welcomed him.

It was almost as though the act of beating itself became linked with the acts of love that now always followed. If I was spanked, Bennasira would soon be there to caress and ease me. If it was not Bennasira it would be Ishbal, and he would fondle me, and open me, and fill me with his glorious heat.

Could it be that so close-linked in my head did these things become that the suffering of a beating also served to get me stirred up? Could such a thing be possible?

Honesty forces me to admit that it is. I learned it for a surety soon after my little monthly holiday was over and I was returned to business and training. I did badly in the march around the training room, and Ishbal had perforce to beat me. Even as he strapped me down on the stool, and parted my legs, and flicked out his long leather whip, I felt myself getting hot.

I know it is shameful. I know that no proper lady could ever imagine, let alone admit to such feelings. But I was not a proper lady. I was a naked slave, existing from day to day, and drawing whatever comfort I could from what came my way. People who have not had trials in their lives - ladies who managed to marry their shopkeeper or their civil servant, and who parade ostentatiously to church on Sunday mornings, and whose most trying challenge is the week's menus or a clumsy scullery-maid - people, in short, who regard themselves as proper judges, will condemn me. I reserve the right to say they are wrong!

In extreme circumstances, extreme things happen. That Ishbal was obliged to beat me was a fact. That I was obliged to go naked, and open myself for sex to any paying customer, and to dance for them on Memmisaab's stage was a fact.

But Ishbal's love for me was also a fact, and Bennasira's too. Their gentleness with me, the love in their eyes, were balm to my spirit, and I loved them for it in return.

I knew that Ishbal had no choice but to beat me sometimes. I knew also that afterwards he would make gentle love to me. Am I wrong to have associated the two, and to get aroused while he beat me, and ready for making love when he had finished? Society will condemn me; I would myself have thought it odious a year or more earlier. Now I know better, having lived through it.

It might sound like madness to say that a girl could be grateful for a spanking, but it became true of me with Ishbal, because he and Bennasira were always so loving afterwards.

Perhaps our closeness grew because it became the rainy season, and trade slacked off. With fewer customers to attend to, we had more time to be together. Ishbal still put me through my exercises each day, and still called me coquine (slut) and putain (whore) and chienne (bitch) but these words no longer sounded like the awful insults they had once been. And 'ma petite chienne', my little bitch, can sound ever so sweet if said gently, breathed through a kiss, while making love!

Our affection could only be shown in private, of course. In the training room Ishbal had no choice but to treat me the same as any of the other girls, for if Memmisaab had suspected us she would surely have given me to another guard. Thus, I performed the exercises, and sucked his fingers, and flexed my bottom and sheath on them, and pumped my belly to his cries of "Pousse! Pousse ta connasse, putain!", and rang the bell for the entertainment of the other guards and Memmisaab herself.

Ishbal introduced a delicious variation on 'ringing the bell' when we were in private. From somewhere he acquired a heavy wooden plank, which he concealed beneath the bunk in my cubicle. It was about a foot wide and six long, and planed smooth.

This plank he would prop so that it sloped down from the wall to the floor, and he would lie back on it in such a way that his loins were on a level with my own. I would kiss and fondle him until his lovely manhood was fully hard. I would then step astride him facing towards his feet, and get him inside me. With my hands behind my head, and Ishbal's warm hands stroking my body and fondling my hips and bottom, I would 'ring the bell' - except it was not a bell, but Ishbal's wonderful cock I was pumping on.

He would set the time for me, though by patting my buttocks rather than by clapping his hands, and towards the end, when he was nearing his climax, he would let me tease my clitty with my fingers to increase my own sensations, and we would come off at exactly the same moment. It was heavenly!

Although the rains meant that trade was slack, it was by no means dead. My sweet fat old man still called nearly every week, and I would spend a delicious couple of hours with him. I still had never less than three or four customers an evening, most of them 'regulars', as it were, for there were few travellers at this time of year.

I still had to dance in the coffee house several times a week, though to smaller audiences, and I found that I came to quite enjoy it. Bennasira had taught me a number of new steps and, the place being much less crowded these days, Memmisaab had me dance actually among the audience, rather than on the stage. She even gave me changes of tail-feathers - black ostrich feathers instead of white, a mixture of black, white and brown, even a plume of peacock's feathers sometimes. The customers I danced among liked to grab at them, but I became adept at dodging away from their groping hands and spinning around to waggle my breasts to distract them.

In view of my initial terror at having to dance at all, it came as something of a surprise to me that being as close to them as I now was actually increased my excitement. To see the looks in their eyes as I weaved among them swaying my hips and wriggling my feathers, to be able to tease by dancing close and dodging away when they tried to touch me, to be able to smile and tempt and get them excited got me excited too.

The dance always culminated with a long period of 'ringing the bell', for that was the most popular feature of my performance. After dancing without the rod in me for a while, I would insert it, and begin those lascivious movements Ishbal called pumping my cunt. (I came to learn, much later, that the French word 'connasse' means 'cunt' in English, and cunt is another word for quim. There are lots of others!) 'Pumping my cunt' was a simple and accurate description, for what else was I doing!

As I became more confident I got bolder, and turned the inserting of the rod itself into a lewd performance. I would wave it about, and rub it between my breasts and down over my belly to my crease. I would slide it slowly back and forth between my folds, and hold it out towards a customer as though inviting him to put it up me, then laugh and dance away when he tried to grab it.

After I had teased half a dozen men in this way, the rod

would be nice and slick with my juices, and I would pose, and part my knees wide, and open my quim with my fingertips, and slowly slide the thick rod into my sheath, moving it in and out teasingly (and, I have to confess, for my own pleasure) before inserting it fully and setting it ringing.

By now, the audience would be whooping and stamping, and you could not have heard the bell if you had tried. But it was not the sound they wanted, but the sight of this red-haired European girl, naked, her arms up, and her breasts jiggling, and her legs open, and her belly pumping faster and faster and wilder and wilder.

So immersed in this last crescendo would I become, so intent on the beat of the tambour as it speeded towards its climax, that my eyes would be closed and my mind empty of everything except the pumping of my cunt towards its own climax (for these days I nearly always had a come when ringing the bell!)

It was during just such a time that disaster struck.

I was near the climax, facing the audience and pumping wildly, when a voice rang out over the hubbub of the audience. An English voice!

"By God, that's little Amy Mansfield!"

I froze with shock. It could not be! A deathly silence fell over the audience. I opened my eyes. Frozen in mid-pump, as it were, my horrified gaze fell upon two white men. They must have entered while I was in that final, wild part of my dance, and were pushing towards me.

It was too awful! Suddenly, everything was appalling and shameful. To be discovered dancing in a brothel, naked and blatant, by Englishmen was too terrible to be born!

I screamed and ran wildly out of the room.

FOURTEEN

It was Captain Robertson. He had been one of the military men I had met when I was with my husband, Mr. Mansfield, at Benin. I had recognized him instantly, and the world crashed around me.

I had long ago given up any thoughts of rescue, of ever hearing English spoken again, of my former life. I had closed my mind to the possibility of any existence save that of a dancing-girl whose body was prostituted for the profit of her owner. Now, it all smashed in on me in one shattering flash of realization; realization of what I was, and what I had been. If ever I came close to a collapse of my sanity, it was then.

Ishbal grabbed me as I rushed out of the coffee house, tears already stinging my eyes. He did not understand, and we had no words for me to tell him - not that I would have been capable of it at that moment - but he caught me up and hugged me to him as I sobbed. He carried me through to Bennasira, and she too hushed and comforted me as best she could.

Thinking back on it I know my reactions seem weird, and it is difficult to explain them, even to myself.

I had been captured by rebels. I had been raped and then sold in exchange for guns, and finally auctioned off to Memmisaab, and brought here to her brothel, to be hired out willy-nilly to anybody who had the cash to hire my body. I had been exercised in the lewdest of ways, and trained like an animal. Had been beaten like one too. I had been compelled to give my body to any man who could afford it, and in any manner they chose. I had been made to dance naked and in the most outrageous manner imaginable for the pleasure of hundreds of strangers. The same strangers who had then rented my quim and my hands and my mouth, and had their pleasure of me in the full knowledge that I was a slave, and would be whipped if I did not work hard to pleasure them.

Stated thus, it sounds entirely horrible; so shaming that a woman should have died rather than submit to it. Yet I had found deep comfort there, and strength. Comfort in the love of Ishbal and Bennasira and even, in her cold way, Memmisaab. Strength in that I had survived it, and even got used to it, and in the knowledge that if I tried hard to please I would be looked after.

My world had become, in fact, the walls of my cubicle, and Ishbal, and the coffee house, and my queue of customers, and my little bunk, and the love of Bennasira. Now, Captain Robertson had invaded it, and I was thrown into a maelstrom of emotions.

The other side of my emotional storm became clear to me when Ishbal came to take me to Memmisaab.

There had been confusion throughout the brothel at my hysterical reactions. Guards rushed about. The other girls whispered tensely together, peering round my door and turning wide-eyed to question one another.

Things calmed somewhat after a couple of hours, and I even began to calm down myself. Then Ishbal came for me, his face very serious, and led me towards Memmisaab's quarters, and I began to panic again.

And the reason I panicked was that somehow I knew that Captain Robertson would be there, and that I was naked, with chain and manacles and collar. I was even still wearing my tail-feathers!

It was stupid! I should have been delighted, Captain Robertson would use his power as a British officer to get me away from this world of whips and submission and sexual slavery. Instead, all that was in my head was that Captain Robertson, whom I had known only as a client of my husband, and who had only ever seen me as the chaste and busy young wife of an English merchant, would now be seeing me naked and revealed: would know, for had he not visited the place as a customer, that I was no more than a girl of the house, a body to be shown off and hired; a prostitute, in fact.

That is all that filled my head as I was hurried into Memmisaab's presence. Captain Robertson was indeed there, with his fellow officer, and all I could think of was to try to hide my nudity behind my hands.

Impressions come too fast to register in times of stress. It became as though I were seeing through thick glass, and hearing under water. Captain Robertson's face was flushed, and I remember thinking - though I have no idea why - that his moustaches were thicker than they had been. The braids and buttons on his uniform seemed to glow. He seemed to find it difficult to look in my direction, yet difficult, too, to look away.

Memmisaab was not looking at me at all, but at some papers on the table by her chair. The Captain's companion, though, did look at me, and as he eyes swept over me from toes to crown and back, I was horribly conscious of the picture I presented - a picture of absolute debasement.

From a distance, I heard the Captain's voice telling me that they had long thought me dead, had given up hope of me after I had disappeared almost a year ago. I remember being surprised at how long it had been, and thinking that I must have missed my nineteenth birthday.

(How strange that irrelevant thoughts crowd one's head in such times of stress.)

He told me that they had come across me by accident, and that all would be well now, for they would be taking me away from this den of iniquity. I had not thought of it as a den of iniquity for a long, long time, and was puzzled by the term. But then, everything in those moments was puzzling, for my head seemed to have spun off somewhere, and to be unwilling to encompass all this.

With Captain Robertson's voice still echoing round in my head, and the eyes of his companion burning into the skin of my back, I was led off, moving like some automaton, but suddenly desperately conscious of my lewd and ridiculous tail-feathers waving at them as I walked away.

As he led me off to the blacksmith's workshop, pausing only to remove my feathers and toss them aside, Ishbal's face was a mask. He would not look at me, and I began to cry. The blacksmith broke the rivet that held my iron collar. He filed off the bands around my wrists and ankles. It was an utterly strange feeling, for although my collar and manacles had been outward and visible signs of my state of slavery, as he cut them off me I began to feel, more and more strongly, a sense of terrible loss - loss of a world I had come to know and feel secure in, and worse, loss of Ishbal and Bennasira.

My tears welled up anew, and did not stop even when the blacksmith asked Ishbal something and, at Ishbal's shrug of indifference, laid me down across his work-bench among his rasps and hammers and spread my legs. He was a big man, and energetic, and he fucked me really hard, but it was as though I was a million miles away and the sheath he pumped in belonged to somebody else.

It did not matter. I was still a slave; I still had my chain around my waist. What mattered was that Ishbal had not cared, had not even looked at me when he had given his consent for the blacksmith to shag me. I felt devastated!

The blacksmith did not take long, though he was a bit rough on me, and my spine was scratched by the roughness of the bench I was crushed against. Afterwards, when he lifted me to my feet and made to cut off the chain around my waist, I had a sudden panic, and would not let him.

I do not know why. Perhaps it was fright at the unknown, or at the loss of the world I knew, or what I would face when I was returned to 'civilization' as a fallen woman. Whatever it was, the thought of being without the chain that seemed to have become part of me filled me with panic, and I cried, and pushed the blacksmith's hands away, and made him leave it on me.

I am still wearing it as I write these words years later, and will take it with me to my tomb. That sounds perverse I know, but to me it symbolizes a part of my life which, despite the training and the beatings, and the queues of men lining up to use me, gave me to know what inner strength a woman can have, and brought me, also, the love of Ishbal and my wonderful Bennasira.

I never even glimpsed that beloved woman again, and a part of my heart died. Ishbal led me back to Memmisaab's quarters stony faced. I wanted to touch him, to show him that I loved him and did not want this. Somehow I was incapable of it, and he led me into Memmisaab's room, and handed me over to Captain Robertson without a word, or even a glance. Oh, how I wanted to feel my beloved Ishbal's hand on me, and to see his eyes light with pleasure, and even to hear him call me his petite chienne , his little bitch, one last time!

There was none of it. Captain Robertson and Memmisaab were all business and briskness. Whether he had bought me or got me by some other means, it seemed I now belonged to Captain Robertson. The Captain's companion threw his tunic about my shoulders, for I was still naked save for my chain, and they took me off.

I learned, days later, that the Captain had actually used threats at first, and when they did not work, had supplemented them with a promissory note drawn on a fictitious bank in Lagos. My price had been one hundred guineas sterling, to be paid in gold, which seemed outrageously high to me. It meant, of course, that he would have to get me away from there before Memmisaab found out she had been duped.

The shock and emotional tumult had exhausted me, and I can remember little of that night save being got into some kind of carriage, and driven through dark streets for a time, and going into a building, and into a room with a bed, and collapsing onto it and crying myself to sleep.

My dazed, trance-like emotional state continued next morning, for I did not yet fully register that I was no longer at Memmisaab's, and her property. When I awoke to full daylight, I simply rubbed my eyes, and got out of the bed, and went downstairs, wondering vaguely where I was.

I heard noises from a room and went in, to find Captain Robertson busy with some papers. Only when he said "Oh my God!" and grabbed up a tablecloth, spilling the crockery that was on the table, and held it out to me, turning his head away, did I realize that I had nothing on. I was so used to going about naked that it had not occurred to me to cover myself. I had not worn any clothes to speak of for nearly a year. Indeed, during that period, the only times clothing had been put on me was when I was being presented for the pleasure of some eager customer.

Oh, how much I had to learn!

Captain Robertson and the companion with whom he had 'bought' me, a younger officer called Lieutenant Grant, behaved in the manner summed up by the phrase 'perfect gentlemen'. They did not question me about my being at Memmisaab's brothel. They gave me as much time as I wanted alone in my room "to recover myself", as the Captain put it. When I did get up and about, they ensured that I had trays of tea brought to me, and talked only of the rains, and native unrest, and the failings of the cook. But never,

never about what was so obviously at the fronts of their minds.

And never, never were they able to look me in the eyes. It became an object of great impatience to me.

I have said somewhere that the human spirit is a strange and wonderful thing. Instead of being engulfed in shame, as 'society' would insist I should be, I actually began to become irritated. I was not to blame for what I had become! I had been given no choice in it, yet the two 'gentlemen' could not look me in the eye, treated me silently as though I were some kind of pariah, as if I was in some way responsible. Yet at the same time, from the very first, I caught them looking at me as a man does a woman.

When he gave me that tablecloth to wrap myself in, Captain Robertson had coughed and hurrumphed and run a finger round his neck as though his collar had become too tight, and had been unable to prevent his eyes flicking every few seconds to where the material clung to my figure.

Later, when I had been given one of his shirts to wear, for there were no women's garments about of course, both the Captain and Lieutenant Grant became more obvious in their appraisal of me, though they still tried to be surreptitious about it. Already irritated by their embarrassed manner with me, I found this crafty peeping, and pretending they were not doing so, quite infuriating. Then, by the evening of my third day with them, I began to see it as ridiculous.

We had spoken very little that day, for the two men avoided me as much as they could in their cramped quarters. I spent most of the time in the bedroom I had slept in, and it gave me much time to think. By the time evening came my mind was clear, and I was resolved. I went in to where they were having their supper determined to beard them.

"And what is to be done with me?" I said, cutting through yet another embarrassed silence. The two officers reddened and coughed and shuffled, and avoided looking at me. "This

140

is too much! You may well have bought me, sir, which makes me your property, but I am still a human being and an Englishwoman. Look at me when I am talking to you!"

The two men started as though I had slapped their faces. I was actually surprised myself at my vehemence; clearly I had changed in more ways than I thought. I would never have dreamed of speaking thus firmly to any man before, much less my owner - which is how I regarded the Captain then. My new-found boldness stayed with me during the conversation which then ensued.

They did not know what to say to me, nor how they were going to deal with the problem of my being among them, and what I had been before my rescue, nor the idea that I was now their property. It was I who cut through the cant.

"I am here, and you have rescued me, and I am grateful, but I am not a leper!" I said. "True, I have been a naked dancing girl, and yes a brothel girl too, but it was as a slave and not by choice. I suppose, since you have bought me, that I am still a slave, but -"

Even as I poured out my tirade, their faces and their attitudes changed, and the Captain suddenly interrupted me.

"No, no! Nothing of the kind!" he said, all fluster. "You are an Englishwoman, and such a thing cannot be!"

It was the first time it had occurred to me that I was free, so used to being a slave had I become. The thought staggered me and at first I could not encompass it. I stared from face to face, and suddenly burst into helpless sobs.

Men always become awkward and uncomfortable when a woman cries, and these were no different. They cleared their throats, and shuffled in their seats, and the Captain reached out to pat my shoulder, but otherwise just sat uselessly by while I cried myself out.

By the time I had finished crying, the knowledge that I was no longer a slave, was no longer the property of others to do with as they wished, that I was free, had so swelled in me that I felt like to die of joy. I threw myself on the Captain and hugged him in my gratitude. At that moment I would have done anything for him!

All I did do was to embarrass him terribly. He went red, and choked, and almost shoved me in his efforts to get me off his lap. I recovered myself at last, and became serious, and we talked.

After an hour or more of earnest conversation about what was to become of me now, they were treating me in a much more friendly way, and as near to an equal as English-men ever seem to treat a woman. They were even accepting the points I made with good grace.

They agreed that I should not be sent back south to Mr. Mansfield, or to my father in Lagos, for I would be scorned and shunned for what my slavery had made of me - it is always the woman who is condemned. Better, they agreed, to find some other way, though what way we could not yet discover. They proposed that I should stay there in their quarters for the time being, for I could hardly go about the town until they had got me some proper clothes - and even then only with an escort, lest I be carried off again.

So much did our long conversation change the officers' manner towards me that Captain Robertson actually offered me a glass of port-wine. He was blushing as he did so, and called me "m'dear", and looked so sweet and awkward I nearly kissed him.

I had not drunk port-wine more than twice in my life, once secretly when I was quite young, and again at my wedding breakfast. It was far more delicious than I remembered, and far more warming.

Such had been the shocks and stresses of the last couple of days that none of the three of us felt like retiring. Our long conversation, too, had made us less reserved with one another. Now, we sat together in their little sitting room, and sipped port-wine, and talked in the friendliest of fashions.

Captain Robertson told me about his regiment, and the mission he and the Lieutenant were on, and how he had come to be in Timboktou - which was apparently the name of this town. He told me how he had tricked Memmisaab, which made me giggle and the gentlemen guffaw.

He told me something of his background. He was, it seemed, forty-seven years of age, an officer of Her Majesty's Own Third of Foot, and hailed originally from Buckinghamshire. He was a married man, with a wife and five children 'back home', as he put it.

It occurred to me, as he talked, that he had hardly ever addressed me when I had been Mr. Mansfield's little wife, yet here he was chatting away like anything. It could have been the effects the port-wine, of course. I thought it more likely, though, that it was because all I had on was one of his shirts, and though it was voluminous it only reached my knees, and clung rather to my bosom.

I know that this was surely the case with Lieutenant Grant, for he hardly said a word, and rarely took his eyes off my legs or the front of the shirt.

Something else that had changed in me during the past year, or perhaps had just been set free by my circumstances, was that I had a new found boldness, a sense of naughtiness if you will.

I became very aware of the way Lieutenant Grant was looking at me, and I knew what was going through his mind. Captain Robertson's, too, though he controlled himself better. I began to enjoy the attention. Call me perverse and wanton if you wish, but there was something deliciously naughty in being sitting of an evening with two presentable men, wearing nothing but a man's shirt to cover my body, and

143

feeling them reining back their growing excitement.

After the last year, when I had been at the beck and call of any man who got a fancy for me or could afford what Memmisaab charged for my body, and had been obliged to get my legs open at the merest click of his fingers, it was utterly thrilling to feel these two holding themselves back, and to be able to tease them.

And tease them I did, I am afraid. Not blatantly, of course. That would have been too cruel. All I did, really, was to move about a little as I talked, and to make the hem of the shirt ride up my legs a bit, and get it a bit tighter at the chest so that it let them see the shape of my titties, and gaze at them admiringly.

Even that was cruel, of course, for they had rescued me from my slavery, and were behaving like gentlemen should, even though when they had first seen me it had been as a naked dancing girl, ringing a bell wildly by pumping her belly for the entertainment of an audience of lecherous men. Honesty forces me, though, to confess that I was enjoying myself immensely, and getting a little heady on the port-wine - and getting a bit stirred up too, I have to admit.

Inevitably, my flirtatiousness led to repercussions after I retired to bed for the night. I had gone up alone, a little tipsy both from the port-wine and the officers' excitement. I had taken off the shirt, for I had not yet learned to find clothes comfortable, and snuggled down beneath the sheets, and fallen instantly to sleep.

I was awakened in dead of night by a hand touching my shoulder, and a voice whispering in my ear.

It was Lieutenant Grant.

For a moment I did not know who it was, or where I was, and simply reacted as naturally as I had done back in the brothel, by rolling onto my back and getting my knees up. Then, all in the same instant it seemed, I was swept over by such a tornado of feelings that I began to giggle.

I was shocked that he should have invaded my bedroom. I was flattered that he had done so. I remembered his tight 'gentlemanliness' of earlier. I was amused that he was no different from other men.

All in the same moment.

When I began to giggle he snatched his hand off me, and I felt him begin to stand up and move away. Instantly, I felt sorry for him. He had not meant any harm. Indeed, for the first time in a year, a man was asking me if he could join me, rather than ordering it as I was accustomed to. To be asked rather than ordered was a novelty, and a moving one.

And I had got the giggles!

I threw out my arm and managed to grab what felt like his night-shirt. I held on to him.

"Sorry," I whispered, trying desperately to stifle my giggles. "I didn't mean to laugh. Please don't go! I was not laughing at you!"

How fragile is a man's self esteem! Lieutenant Grant had sneaked into my room in the dead of night, clearly intent on a single objective. In the confusion of my awakening sensations I had got the giggles and now, even in the dark, I could sense that he had gone all hang-dog.

I actually had to persuade him to stay. To coax him into the bed he had been all set to invade anyway. And to kiss him, and snuggle myself against him, and put my hand down between his legs to let him know all was well for him. Mind you, it did not take many moments, and then I was having to hold him off.

He was clumsy and very quick, but also quite young and in his full vigour. After that first tussle, from which I had got little save the pleasure of his excitement (and the very copious jettings of his jism - which reminded me that I really must do something about getting myself a douche) he made as if to depart, but I persuaded him to stay by getting my leg across his, and kissing him ardently.

I got him to pull off his night-shirt. He had an excellent, firm body, with a fuzz of hair on his chest, and hard thighs, and at the join of them a most impressive set of male equipment. Oh, how horrified Mr. Mansfield would have been at my thoughts as I ran my hands deliciously over the Lieutenant, and he began to rise and thicken under my touches.

During my six-month marriage, I had never actually touched my husband in a lascivious manner. He never wanted it, never suggested it as a possibility. All he had ever done was climb on me, get his little bit of warmth and pleasure, and climb off me again. Now how much better I knew!

Life as a slave might have 'ruined' me in the eyes of society, but it had certainly given me a great deal of experience in the pleasures of the body.

I kept my Lieutenant with me most of the night. It must had been quite a time since he had enjoyed a woman, for I was able to shag him three more times - the third and fourth long and slow and lovely.

I truly believe that when he had sneaked into my bedroom, his heart was in his mouth. I know for a fact that he had never met a woman like me, or at least an Englishwoman, who joined in shagging rather than just allowing it to be done to her. He had come to me with the intention of testing whether he could fuck me; he was astonished when it became me fucking him.

That second time, when he had got roused up under my hands and kisses, I indulged myself and got astride him - always the best way for a girl, I have found. There was the tiniest glimmer of moonlight coming through the window, and I could just see the expression of surprise, and then delight, which suffused his features. He had clearly not known that anything other than having the girl on her back was possible.

I rode him deliciously, and to the rhythms dictated by my own sensations. His body was hard, and delighted my quim and my clitty, while his cock was substantial enough to please any girl. It felt good when he reached up with both hands and began roll and squeeze my breasts just exactly hard enough to delight them and stir my nipples up like excited little pegs.

Once again, he came off just a little too soon, for I had only just begun spiralling up towards my own delight. Ishbal's exercises now proved to be heaven sent, for I was able to flex and squeeze with my sheath, and keep him in me, and milk him, and work for my own pleasure until he groaned and begged me to stop.

He did not attempt to get out of my bed this time. Rather, he put his arm around me, and kissed me, and told me I was marvellous and the most amazing woman that ever lived. I knew better, knew that he was only talking in the euphoria that follows a good shag, but it was nice to hear anyway - and certainly much more pleasant than I was used to.

Our third and fourth couplings were with me on my back, but with the last one I whispered guidance to him, and he let me get my legs together once he was in me, and got his own outside mine, so that everything was nicely squeezed together, which is almost as good as being on top.

He sneaked off then, for neither of us wished our little encounter to be discovered. I slept deliciously, and woke feeling happy and relaxed. Around mid-morning, though, the poor Lieutenant managed to whisper to me that I had exhausted him and that his balls ached, and I nearly had a fit of the giggles. Mind you, he might well have been complaining that I had drained him and his balls hurt but I did feel a distinct twitch of interest when I playfully rubbed my hand over the front of his breeches!

147

FIFTEEN

You may think me an empty creature, entirely lacking in moral fibre, but I now entered on a period of great contentment. I was free from my slavery, and a way was to be found to get me back to England without being encumbered with Mr. Mansfield and a reputation as a whore. In addition, I had delightful companionship, for both the Captain and the Lieutenant turned out to be most congenial, if you see what I mean. The only pangs I sometimes knew were those from missing Ishbal and my beloved Bennasira.

Lieutenant Grant, Peter, as he asked me to call him, came to my bed again on my fourth night with them, and for several nights thereafter, and it was most pleasant. It took the Captain several more days to succumb to his natural instincts - and even then I had to lead him on more than a little.

Again you will think poorly of me, for it was I who pressed matters, and women are not supposed to be capable of such things. But he was a sweet man. He was clearly in a heat of indecisiveness in the face of temptation, and I have to confess that I was behaving as temptingly as I could. Besides, I did owe him a great debt, and what else did I have to pay it with than sex?

My strategy was to behave so as to increase his heat until that indecisiveness broke. On the surface, I behaved entirely respectfully towards him, and even according to what rules I remembered of 'polite company'. I called him 'Captain Robertson' or 'sir' with apparent humility, though always with a little sideways look beneath my eyelashes. I moved about with the appearance of as much discretion and modesty as was possible wearing only one of his shirts, and

148

apologized profusely on those occasions I 'accidentally' bumped into him (the quarters were, happily, quite cramped). I made myself useful by cleaning and dusting and serving him pots of coffee, knowing all the while that when I bent to dust a table-top the front of the shirt would hang down, and give him the chance to catch a glimpse of my bare breasts or, if he were behind me, the tail would ride up so he could see high up the backs of my legs.

The man was made of stone! I well know that I am not unattractive to men. Witness how popular I was with Memmisaab's customers. Witness dear Peter; witness the Captain's own reactions. Yet his gentlemanly upbringing was so deeply embedded in him that he forbade himself any advance upon my person - a person that smiled and fluttered her eyelashes at him, and gazed at him admiringly, and ensured that the shirts she wore always had a button or two undone!

In the end I had to very nearly ask him outright. It was in the evening. Peter was out on some errand or other and the Captain and I were taking coffee together. I decided to become sad and withdrawn.

I spoke only little, and then quietly and with a sigh. I sat across from him in the second armchair, and kept half-turned away. I kept my eyes looking down rather than at him, and repeatedly tugged at the tails of my shirt to make sure they covered what they could of me but in the process, of course, drawing his attention to those very parts.

My little bit of play-acting to appeal to his softer nature worked far better than my efforts to stir his lusts. After only about ten minutes he coughed, and shuffled in his armchair.

"Is something the matter, my dear?" he said, his voice solicitous and a little gruff. "You seem very low this evening."

I put down my cup, and bowed my head, and turned even further away from him, and began to whimper. In an instant he was on one knee beside me, his hand on my shoul-

149

der, begging me to confide what was wrong.

I dredged up that talent for acting which every woman keeps within her. I began to weep, quietly and as though trying desperately not to. I made no reply. His arm went about my shoulders, and he pulled my head to his chest.

"There, there, my dear," he murmured, and stroked my hair with his other hand. "You can tell me. I am your friend."

It was the opening I had been praying for. "Yes," I spluttered, managing even to hiccough as I spoke. "You are my true friend, but you do not like me. You think me ruined, a fallen woman, and are ashamed of me."

"No, no, my dear, it is not so!"

"It is! It is! You are ashamed of me! You are kind to me, and you rescued me, and I love you for it, but you keep so cold towards me!

I will not burden you with all the petty details, for I am sure you know well how a woman can trick and tempt a man when she has a mind to. Suffice it to say that it was not long before he was soothing away my tears, and I was in his lap, curled up and resting my cheek to his chest, and telling him he was wonderful and that I would do anything to show my gratitude and love.

Even then, it was a long time before he kissed me. It was the tiniest of kisses; nervous; like a boy with his first sweetheart. A second kiss soon followed, one that lasted long enough for me to respond with my own lips, but just as soft. They began to come quicker then, and increasingly passionate. Soon he was crushing my lips and exploring me with a hot tongue. Then, with a suddenness that startled me, he pulled back and took his arms from around me. It was amazing because even though our kisses had clearly set him on fire for me, and the lump in his breeches was practically lifting me into the air, he still tried to hold himself back.

For a moment I was nonplussed. I was determined to

have him though, so I persisted. I made myself soft and small. I snuggled against him and stroked the buttons of his tunic with my finger. I sighed and whispered that he was wonderful. I reached up with my face and kissed him under his chin. I kept my face there, letting my warm breath play over his skin.

At last, his arm slipped around my shoulders again. He kissed me gently on my forehead, and soon our mouths were once again expressing our passion, though I could still feel him fighting against it. I did not let him go. I put my hand on the back of his head and held him to my kisses. I sighed and wriggled my bottom against the hardness of his cock.

By the time I managed to get his hand on my breast he was actually trembling. I had to soothe and coax him, and let him know without words that he was welcome. Like Peter, the Captain was a product of tight-laced English morality, and could not believe that his advances would not be rebuffed. And certainly not that they would be welcomed.

I knew he had to think that it was I surrendering to him, rather than the reverse, and I behaved accordingly. I went a little shy and awed when he began to touch my breasts, but at the same time wriggled so that the organ my bottom was pressing on got even more excited than it already was. With each little advance of his hand, I kissed him, and peeped up at him beneath my eyelashes in worship and doubt. By the time he got his hand on my thigh I was being all breathless and soft.

It was silly really, for he knew what I had been; knew I had been bedded by hundreds of men; knew, for had he not seen it that night he blundered into the coffee house, that I was a wanton with my body. Yet his background and upbringing made it necessary for him to believe he was 'taking advantage', and being persuasive, and that I was surrendering to him.

Such are the charades our society obliges us to play!

He wanted my body I knew. Every fibre of his being was telling me so. And I wanted his, but he could not admit it to himself - could not admit that this English girl who was sitting in his lap, and whose breasts he had caressed, and whose thigh he was even now stroking, could possibly be willing for what he was doing. It was as if he felt he had to sneak from me that which, in truth, I would have offered him right out had not 'civilized manners' made it impossible. He needed his illusions though - show me a man who does not! - and we played the charade of him melting me, and me being persuaded, and being at last carried - he did indeed pick me up and carry me, kissing me all the while - to his bed.

Oh, had I been married off to Captain Robertson instead of Mr. Mansfield I would never have wanted to go on that fateful journey that led to my capture. He was so gentle. So careful of my feelings.

He was nigh on panting with lust for me, yet he laid me gently on his bed. He pulled the coverlet up over me, and looked into my eyes with something that was half softness, half requesting. He blew the lamp out, and undressed quietly, and slipped into the bed as though any sudden movement might scare me.

I, too, felt strangely tentative now that we had reached the crux. When he slipped in beside me, I half expected, from past experience, that he would throw my legs up and get to it. He did not. He put his arm around me, and cuddled me and kissed my brow and my lips. His hand found my breast again. He was so warm, so gentle. I wanted to reach my hand down to the organ that was pressing against my side so tantalizingly, but I held back. I knew that any forward action on my part would break his mood. It was he, for his own self esteem, who needed to take me, and I could only help him do it without him knowing.

I did not even help him when he fumbled clumsily at the buttons of my shirt. Personally, I wanted to rip the thing off my body and writhe against him, but that would not have done at all.

Even when he got his hand on my thigh, he only stroked it, up and down, from my knee towards the centre that was increasingly eager for him, each time a little closer to the top, but always stopping and moving down again, only to move up just a little closer. It was as though he was trying to camouflage his intentions, or as though he really was nervous of touching that part of me which was his focus. And mine, for I was very aroused and had to fight off the desire to take his hand and guide it home to my already throbbing clitty.

So pent up was I that when he did at last slip his hand onto me, and reward my body for all its waiting, I was already in the build-up towards a delicious come. I could not help but gasp and sigh and buck my hips a little in gratitude, and it was as though a gun had gone off. He was on me and in me on the instant.

He was wild! When such reserve as his is breached, unleash the hounds!

I was coming even as he thrust into me. His wildness drove me higher. He went at me as though he had not had a shag in years, and it was wonderful. I had at last broken down his barriers, and he fucked me as though he was mad, and I bucked and writhed along with him, and loved him for his sweet wildness.

The aftermath, that lovely gentling down from passion, was beautiful. The Captain relaxed beside me. He had an arm about me, and I rested my head on his deep chest. He stroked my hair with a gentle hand. He talked quietly about this and that, his deep voice rumbling into my ear through his chest. I felt a depth of comfort and of happiness I had not known except with Bennasira and Ishbal, and drifted off into a delicious slumber.

I awoke in full dark. The Captain's hands were moving on me, moving so lightly they were hardly touching me at all. We had removed my shirt earlier, and I now lay naked as he softly explored me. The cup of his warm hand eased over the swell of my breast, setting me tingling. A fingertip traced the curve of my shoulder and my neck, and moved down over my collar-bone and on through the valley between my breasts.

With the flat of his hand, he followed the swell of my belly, dipping a fingertip into my navel before moving down to cup the vee of my mound. As though in my sleep, for I knew he thought I was not aware of what he was doing, I sighed and moved a little. Just enough to make myself more open to him. For a moment he snatched his hand away, scared he had awakened me, but soon, deliciously, it returned.

I had bent one knee so that my thighs were now a little apart. The Captain's gentle hand traced the curve of my hip, and the crease where my thigh joined it. He smoothed his fingertips along the inside of my bent thigh, and up to the swell of my mound again. He followed the shape of my vee, moving down until at last he was touching the crease of my body-lips - lips which were already eager for him.

He slipped his fingertip between my moist folds and gently moved it along the length of my crease, softly, back and forth, dipping a little into my opening, even teasing my clitty. In the soft languor of my half-dreaming state it came to me that the Captain's wife, back in England, was a very lucky woman indeed, for this man really knew how to touch a girl to work her up.

He was getting me worked up now, very thoroughly, and it was difficult to pretend to be still asleep. Very carefully, he shifted his position on the bed, and eased my legs further apart. I was on my back now, my arms up and my legs parted so that I was fully open to him. He kissed my breasts while his fingers worked between the folds of my quim. Gently, he moved until he was between my legs. I felt the warm plum of his engorged member touch against me, slip between my swollen lips, find my entrance, press in.

As he slid slowly into my grateful sheath I 'came awake', and sighed a "thank you", and wrapped myself around him. That second shag was slow and deep and loving. Neither of us was in any hurry, but moved gently on and in each other, revelling in our bodies' union as we slowly rose towards the sky and the stars.

We three, my two officers and me, were close after that, with the quiet closeness of real friends and lovers. Even when the Captain - strange how I still think of him as 'the Captain' even though I know his name was Albert, and he wanted me to call him that - found out that his Lieutenant had been with me before him, and indeed was still active in my bed, he did not react with the hurt jealousy that would be expected.

Rather, he smiled at me and shrugged his shoulders, and made love to me. And I have to say now that my lovely Captain made love to me, Amy Mansfield, rather than just a female body that was available for his pleasure. I knew from his eyes that it was me as a person he made love to, and not just what I have between my legs. With him, it was not just shagging, for we swam in each other's eyes, and revelled in one another's bodies, and it was a compact between people who knew and liked one another.

I have had and been had by a great many people, both before and since my Captain, but honesty compels me to say he was one of the nicest. Not the most vigorous, nor the most substantial, but definitely among the nicest, for with him it was a gentleness and a building and a sensitivity to each other's reactions such as is all too sadly rare.

After our first bout - which was as quick and anxious

as the first time with a new man always seems to be - we lay together not as people wound up for sex. Relaxed by it, rather, for after that second, gentle, movingly tender fuck, I slept as deep and easy as I had since I was a little girl. And in the morning, when we rolled into each other's arms, and folded each other's body into our own, and he slipped inside me, and we gently and lovingly rocked each other towards Nirvana, I felt as warm and as loved and as cherished as I ever had, even with Bennasira.

I stayed with the Captain and Lieutenant for several weeks while they tried to arrange some means for me to get away from Timboktou. I am not entirely convinced that, at first anyway, they tried particularly hard to get me away. It would have been surprising if they had really, for what men who have an available girl at their disposal, and one who was at least as eager to shag as they were, will strive hard to get rid of her?

That I should share my favours with two British army officers, and be openly shared by them will seem shocking to 'proper society'. Even Peter and the Captain were shocked in the beginning. At first neither knew that the other was shagging me, though I myself did nothing to hide it. Then, two days after that first lovely night with the Captain, Peter returned early from whatever duties he had been engaged upon. Naturally, since he was a lusty fellow, he reached for me and we were soon hard at it up against the wall, with my arms about his neck, and my legs locked around his hips, and him bucking deep inside me. Then the door opened and in walked the Captain.

I saw him at once, but Peter was thrusting away like a mule and knew nothing until the Captain bellowed. Then he froze, on his face an expression of sheer horror. The Captain, too, seemed paralysed, and for long moments we were like some mad tableau. What would have happened if I had not suddenly got the giggles I know not, but giggle I did. It was too ridiculous!

Here I was, with my shirt all undone, wrapped around my young Lieutenant and with his cock rapidly shrinking inside me, and my other lover standing across the room looking as though he had been shot. Neither man unfroze for an age as, with tears streaming down my face and almost hiccoughing with laughter, my arms got too weak to hold me, and I slipped down between Peter and the wall, to huddle shaking with giggles at his feet.

I tried to control myself, for when I looked up the Captain was still standing like a red-faced model of shock. Then I glanced up towards Peter and was instantly set off again, for he still had his cock hanging out, and looked really silly.

It says much for their characters that soon both my lovers joined me in laughter, and it was not long before all three of us were happily entwined upon the Captain's bed as they took turns shagging me. Or perhaps it was me shagging them!

By the by, lest you think I am maligning my two lovely men by suggesting that they delayed getting me passage out, there were signs other than my own suspicions to judge by. For example, once I had explained its design and function, they managed quite quickly to get me some bits and pieces from which we could rig up a pretty effective douche, but they seemed to find it rather more difficult to find me suitable clothes to wear. Also, the shirts I was given to wear in lieu of clothes seemed suddenly to be of the style that buttons all down the front instead of just to the chest, and to have more than the occasional button missing.

I deduced that they were as against my being got with child as I was, but at the same time they liked having me about the place scantily clad. So you see, there was evidence that they were being just a little naughty. I did not mind though; it was quite exciting to have two men feeling thus about me, and I too enjoy a little naughtiness, as you well know by now.

The things they got to make my douche with were very simple, and showed great ingenuity. For the tube which has to be inserted into my sheath, Peter got a small native fife or flute. It was made of wood, and he cut it down to an appropriate length, and filled the finger-holes with little wooden pegs, and rubbed it with a piece of sandstone to make it nice and smooth. And you may be sure that some naughty games ensued when he tried it in me for size and comfort.

For the bag to hold the water, the Captain came up with a sort of little sack of soft leather. He pierced little holes around the top, and put a bootlace through them to serve as a drawstring. When it was fitted over the bell-end of the transformed flute and the string wrapped around tight, it was perfectly effective. It still is, in fact, for I still have it by me - and these days it is as much a necessity as ever, thank heavens.

My two lovers could not delay too long in finding a way out for me, for when Memmisaab discovered how she had been tricked about the money for me there would be terrible trouble. She was a powerful woman in the town, and even two British officers would not have been able to prevent her getting me back. The plan the Captain at last arranged was that I should be taken north to somewhere called Algiers, from whence passage could be arranged to get me back to England. To effect it, he had contacted an officer he knew in the French garrison. This gentleman had just completed a 'tour of duty', whatever that was, and would be leading his platoon north across the desert to Algiers, starting in a couple of day's time.

This officer had agreed to take me with him, thinking me to be an Arab woman. To this end, Peter had acquired for me a couple of those voluminous black garments called locally chadours, which cover the wearer from the top of her head to the ground, with only a narrow slit at the eyes to see out of. Those, apart from a pair of sandals, was all they were able to get me, and the Captain gave me a couple of his shirts so I would not be naked underneath my chadour - though what difference that could possibly make escaped me; no-one could have seen a thing through the heavy black cotton.

They also filled my heart and made me weepy with gratitude by giving me two more things.

From the Captain I got a letter of introduction to his family in Buckinghamshire, with a plea for them to put me up should I need accommodations. In it, he gave me the name I have gone by ever since - Amy Hurst - and concocted the story of how I was the widow of one of his junior officers who had died of a fever, and had no family of my own.

From dear Peter I got a similar letter, and also a thick envelope addressed to his elder brother, Sir Arthur Grant, in Hampstead near London. He also gave me a banker's draft for fifty guineas - enough to keep me going for quite a long time once I reached civilization.

My last two days and nights with my lovely officers were sad and sweet, and loving and melancholy. Although we were, if anything, less active in bed than hitherto, we seemed hardly able to stop touching one another. In moving past, a hand would stroke a shoulder or touch an arm. In taking coffee, hands that reached for the pot would clasp and hold for a moment. In the evenings, I would sit in one or other of their laps, and rest my head on their chest, and we would cuddle and exchange gentle kisses.

Very few words were spoken. In my case it was because my throat felt more and more constricted, and I was sure I would choke and burst into sobs if I tried to speak.

I did not want to leave these lovely men. My whole life seemed to have become a series of departings. First from my father to Mr. Mansfield; then from Ishbal and Bennasira; now from dear Peter and the Captain.

I had no way of thanking them for what they had done for me. I had come to them naked, and had no gifts I could give except myself. I determined to make our last evening together one of love; to give them as much pleasure as it was possible for me to give, as proof of my love and gratitude.

Though I had no paint for my body, nor bells or feathers to adorn myself with, I danced for them. Not as wildly as I had been obliged to dance in the coffee house, but slower, and just as naked, and more personally if you see my meaning. This was for them alone, and I danced as well as I had ever done, weaving about, and flexing my body, and swaying my thighs and my breasts, and rolling my belly in a manner that even Ishbal would have approved. And while I danced I was able to look into their eyes, and smile, and show them that this was my thanks to them.

After my dance, when we began to make love, all three of us together, I discovered that neither of them had ever known the pleasure a woman's mouth can give. I was astonished, and delighted too, for this could be my gift of love to them.

I took the Captain first, partly because he happened to be the nearest, but mostly because I loved him the more. When I caressed him and moved my mouth down to his pale, beautiful cock, he tensed and made as though to stop me. I shook my head, and insisted, and kissed his plum and took him between my lips.

When a girl is sucking a man she is in control, unless he is foolish enough to buck and hold her head. My sweet Captain did not make that mistake. He kept still. He let me love him with my mouth, with my tongue and my lips, and with my hands enjoying his root and his balls and all about his tight thighs and belly.

I kept him going for as long as I could, easing up when I felt his sweet member twitch as though rising to a climax, moving more avidly when he relaxed a little; manipulating him, if you wish, so that my gift to him could take as long as possible.

When at last I felt he could take no more, I took him as deep as I could, and writhed my tongue about his shaft, and sucked hard, and pressed the heel of my hand in below his balls. His climax was beautifully wild, and his whole frame seemed to jerk as though electrified, and he groaned as I milked him with my tongue. Oh, it was beautiful! And the expression on his face when I released him, and sat back on my heels and wiped my mouth with the back of my hand, was as much reward as a girl could ever dream of.

When I turned towards Peter, his manhood was in such a state I knew that, if I was not careful, he would explode before I even got him between my lips. But then, the wicked part of my mind told me, if I got my mouth on him quickly, he could come, and I could swallow it and work on him longer to give him his second one. Oh, how much more knowledge I had after my life as a slave-whore, and how much pleasure it could now give me!

I locked my mouth on him, and he instantly burst into his transports, and I swallowed it all, and kept moving on him. Like the darling I knew him to be, he groaned, and wriggled a little as though in discomfort, but let me have my way with him.

To run one's hands over a firm body; to caress that lovely warm valley just below a man's balls, and feel them tighten at one's touch; to breathe in the scent of his excitement; to feel his member moving on one's tongue; to sense him rising in passion, and feel him thicken and grow stiff because what one is doing for him, is irresistible: oh, all these are glorious pleasures for a skilful girl!

I felt all these joys now with Peter. Felt him rise, and grow, and become tense. Felt him begin to move helplessly, and controlled it with my hands and with my mouth. I sucked him, and drank him, and worked him, until with a groan he shuddered and spurted his second blessing onto my tongue.

By then I, too, had been in a slow, breathtaking orgasm for about a thousand years, and was too weak to do ought else save rest my head upon the swell of his hard thigh, and delight in the way his fingers riffled through my hair and his sated member lolled softly against my cheek.

SIXTEEN

I was given over to Lieutenant Jean-Louis Debrot's care next morning. He arrived with his Sergeant and several troops quite early, and almost took us by surprise. The Captain had gone to meet the French party, but had apparently missed them, and dear Peter and I were just enjoying a last, delicious fuck in the parlour. He was sitting on one of the straight-backed chair and I was astride him, bouncing gently and lasciviously as we kissed and he fondled my bottom.

The bang on the door came as a shock, especially as it came just as I was about to come. Luckily, a voluminous garment such as a chadour can hide many things - including the fact that I must have been quite red-faced when I stood up (regretfully!) and went to open the door. Peter had managed to do up his breeches by the time I returned with the French soldiers.

Lieutenant Debrot was all business, hardly glancing in my direction while he talked briskly with Lieutenant Grant. Unfortunately, it was all in French, and too rapid for my limited grasp, so I knew not what they were saying. Captain Robertson returned at that point, and joined in the discussion. Soon, their business was done, and they shook hands, and with a sort of half-bow, half-nod the Lieutenant swept out his arm to gesture me towards the door.

The Captain requested a delay (I understood that bit) and told me he had something to give me in the back room. What he had to give me was a lot of passionate farewell kisses, having whipped off my chadour without ceremony, and a very thorough fingering of my parts which finished off the climax Peter had nearly got me to.

He told me I was wonderful and that under different circumstances he would have loved me, then helped me back on with my chadour. I was still throbbing between my legs as I went back into the parlour to my French escort. I picked up the little bundle which contained my spare shirts, my second chadour, my douche, my 'lucky coin' from the brothel and - most precious of all - my letters, and walked out to where the little body of soldiers waited.

My heart was low, but I knew that if I did not go I would be carried off to Memmisaab's brothel again, never to be free. I walked in the midst of the soldiers with my head down and tears in my eyes. I dared not look back lest my resolution desert me, for I loved my Captain and dear Peter very dearly by now.

Seeing a group such as ours, soldiers clad in blue tunics, with white, straight-sided caps with square tails at the back - to protect their necks against the sun, I supposed - with, in their midst, a black-shrouded woman with her head bowed, must have been a common sight hereabouts, for nobody seemed to take much notice of us as we navigated through the narrow streets.

After a while, we came to a walled enclosure, and entered it. Inside were more soldiers, more than a dozen of them, and camels. A veritable herd of camels. I had only ever glimpsed a camel through the high, narrow slits that served as windows in the walls of the brothel. Close up, they were huge and frightening. And smelly!

I had to ride one. I was terrified, but the French officer was urgent and impatient, and generally treated me as though I were a rather stupid burden to him - which, in all fairness, I suppose I was. What more of a burden can you have than a silly little woman hanging back when you are urgent to start a journey?

I defy anybody who has not ridden a camel to imagine it. I had ridden horseback many times, but this was different. With a horse you bounce, as it were, and so long as you keep your back straight and flexible you will be all right. With a camel, you sway; forward and back to one rhythm, side to side to another. It is as though the beast were trying to swing you round and round until your spine came unconnected, and you were seasick. I know the notion of being seasick sounds mad when I am talking of the edge of a dry desert, but seasick is how it felt.

It was awful. The beast I was on was being led on a halter by Lieutenant Debrot's camel. That too was swaying, and I soon felt dizzy and ill, and my back hurt with the effort of keeping upright. Only the way the Lieutenant had been so impatient and dismissive at the start of our journey kept me going. My pride told me that if I weakened he would feel triumph. I refused to let him.

Even so, by the time the Lieutenant called a halt late in the morning, I was so weak that when he called to the camel to kneel - to get off a camel, you make it kneel down with its front legs and step off the saddle - I was unready, and simply tumbled down across its neck in a sorry heap.

I did not realise it at the time, being somewhat groggy, but that tumble sent the skirts of my chadour flying and gave the lieutenant a good look at my calves and ankles. Luckily, nobody other than the Lieutenant saw, else my situation would have become much more difficult much more quickly. What I did realise was that as he helped me to my feet, Lieutenant Debrot's hands found and squeezed my breasts. At the time I thought it was accidental. I was to learn better!

Nearly as bad as the swaying of my camel had been my growing dryness. It is not so much the heat, though that was draining enough, as the aridity of the air that drains you. I had not even known there was a water-bag on my saddle, and had thought the Lieutenant a monster to thus drag out the torment of my growing thirst until my lips had begun to crack.

The Lieutenant's manner towards me was oddly different, less impatient as it were, as he handed me the water-bag. In order to get my mouth to the spout, I had to pull down the slit in the chadour that allowed me to see out. In doing so, I knew the Lieutenant would get his first sight of my face, and that my dear Captain's little deception that I was an old Arab woman would be exposed.

That he already knew became obvious when, despite my efforts at concealment, he saw my face, for instead of being astonished or annoyed he stared at me with hard eyes and gave a slow grin. I learned the significance of that grin within an hour.

He got his men to rig up a tent, and put me into its shade, with a water-bag by my hand. I thought this a blessed kindness and relished the coolness and the frequent little sips of water I took. I had enough sense not to remove my chadour, but could not resist wetting the hem of its voluminous skirt and using it to wipe the dust from my face. As I was doing so the tent-flap parted and the Lieutenant came in.

His manner was tense. For a moment I was puzzled then, with a rush of blood to my cheeks, I recognised the all too familiar signs. He was in the heat of excitement. I was a young woman, as he now knew. The bulge in his breeches told all!

He was rough, almost frantic. Before I could even protest, I was on my back and my chadour was up around my
chest. He fucked me quick and hard, intent on nothing save
his own satisfaction. In no more than a few minutes he bucked
into his come. He pulled out of me, put himself away and
left the tent without a word.

There is no pleasure for a woman in such an encounter.
He had not even looked me in the eyes, being intent only on
satisfying his lust. Even my hundreds of customers in
Memmisaab's brothel had treated me better! There was no
pleasure for me either in the realisation of my new situation.

Inevitably, he came into my tent again that first night.
We kept up the pretence that I was a little old Arab woman
for the afternoon camel-journey, and I overheard him telling
his men that I wished for seclusion, so that my tent was
erected a little way off from the men's, and that I ate alone. I
knew he would come and tried to ready myself for him, at
least mentally.

I already had my chadour off when he crept into the
little tent, though I was still wearing my shirt. He cast me a
salacious glance before blowing out my candle. In the pitch
black of the night his hands were on me in an instant. I knew
that my flight from Timboktou depended on this man, and I
did not resist as he hauled up the tails of my shirt and groped
for my breasts. Indeed, it was in my interest to please him.

I had learned lots of tricks in the brothel, and I used
them. He began as frantically as he had when he fucked me
during the day, but I managed to slow him down. As he was
feeling my breasts I wriggled against him and reached down
to his groin. I whispered to him and kissed him, making
little noises of pleasure - they had to be little noises in case
any of his men heard.

I stroked his cock through his breeches with one hand

166

while the other fumbled with his buttons and belt-buckle. By the time I had him undone and his cock sprang out from its confines he was more than ready. My legs were already high and wide. He grunted as I guided him home and he came into me with a rush.

That first fuck was quick, hardly more than a dozen frantic thrusts before his body stiffened and he shot his heat into me. I had thought that if I gave him a good, quick shag he would be satisfied and sneak back to his own tent, leaving me to get the sleep my camel-weary body so badly needed. Instead, he rolled over and lay beside me, clearly intent on more than just a single fuck.

Whispering, he told me what I already knew - that this had to be kept secret from his men. He went on to add that which gave me great relief, saying he would conduct me across the desert to Algiers even though he was annoyed at the way Captain Robertson had deceived him. In return, I was to keep up my disguise and, inevitably, pleasure him whenever he desired it.

At the same time as he whispered these words to me his hands were moving. I squirmed out of my shirt and gave him access to my naked body. Having fucked me once, he took his time now. He had not seen anything of me except my legs and part of my face, but now he made himself familiar with every part of me he could touch. I have to confess that although his touches were not gentle, my unruly body soon began to respond to them.

He spent a long time toying with my breasts, kneading them, rolling them, pulling at my nipples. I have always been very sensitive in my bosoms and nipples and he soon had me panting a little. When his hands slid down over my tummy and he began to work on my thighs and between them, I was quickly panting more than a little. He eased several fingers into me and I heard him chuckle at how wet I already was. As he fingered me rhythmically, bringing little gasps from my slackening mouth, my hand found its way down to where his cock lolled from his open breeches.

He was only half hard, but soon began to stir under my fingers. He was not the biggest I had ever encountered, but when fully erect was quite acceptable. My eager cunny accepted him gratefully when at last he climbed between my already splayed thighs and commenced upon our second fuck of the night. It was longer and slower than the first and his fingers had got me thoroughly worked up, and the rocking of my hips and the writhing of my sheath on his weapon soon became entirely genuine as I fucked him in rhythm to his delicious shafting.

I tried to hold back but the stirrings in my body were too much for me, and I shuddered into a glorious come well before he bucked and shot his essence deep inside me, giving me a second, gentler orgasm which continued rippling through my senses even after he pulled out and crept away from my tent.

The next morning Lieutenant Debrot treated me exactly as though I was indeed the little Arab lady I was supposed to be. He was polite but impersonal; his camel led mine as it had done before; when our party stopped for the break in the middle of the day he handed me down from my camel as though he thought me a lady. Nobody looking on would have suspected that 24 hours ago he had virtually raped me, and that he had spent last night bucking and bouncing between my legs!

He had his men erect the little tent for me and I was sure he would find a chance to sneak in for a quick shag, but he did not. Naturally, he did come for me that night and fucked me very thoroughly in the pitch darkness. Again, the next day he was polite and impersonal towards me and, as I rode my swaying camel, I wondered how long he would be able to keep up this pretence.

It was not long, and it was my own fault. The

Lieutenant's manner towards me changed, as did the attitude of his soldiery, on the fourth morning, when I made my mistake.

We had camped that third night near a watering place called an 'oasis', and the men had put up tents for us, and cooked an evening meal which I ate ravenously even though it was a mysterious and rather greasy stew. The Lieutenant came for me early and only required a single, rather quick, fuck, so that I was able to sleep through the whole night and awoke feeling much better than I had for the last few days and nights. All that disturbed my good feeling was that I was undeniably grimy.

The desert dust had got everywhere, and I do mean everywhere. Inside the stifling chadour I had perspired, and the dust had stuck to me, and was itchy and uncomfortable. The residues of the Lieutenant's emissions - and, I confess, my own - between my legs did not help matters either. I needed above all things to wash myself; to get rid of the grit in my hair and about my person; to feel fresh and clean. Then, I could outface the world. Without a bath, I felt itchy and scruffy.

It was very early, not long after dawn, and when I peeped out of my little tent it seemed that everyone was still sleeping. The pool that made the oasis was large, wide at one end then narrowing and bending round before widening again, to form what was almost a second pool. This second pool was well hidden from the tents by thick shrubs. I thought my venture would be safe. Clasping the skirts of my chadour about me, I crept off to that part.

The water looked so beautiful. Still, and clear, and mirroring the thorny shrubs that grew close to its banks as though it were really a looking-glass, rather than limpid waters. I looked about me. Nobody was to be seen. I pulled off the heavy chadour and dropped it to the ground, keeping on my shirt for I thought to wash it at the same time as I bathed myself, and waded into the pool. It felt so good!

The sun was up, but it was not yet hot. The water was icy, and sent my blood racing. I ducked myself under, and wallowed on my back, and scrubbed at myself with the little piece of soap my dear Captain had given me.

So wrapped up in my luxury did I become that it was the most terrible of shocks when, just as I had dipped my head under after I had finished washing my hair, and shaken my head to throw the water off it, and got ready to climb out of the pool, I saw faces peering over the tops of the bushes. The faces of soldiers. Grinning faces. Faces with that leer I had come to know only too well over the last year.

I squealed in shock, and ducked back beneath the water up to my neck. I looked up in panic. The men had come through the bushes and were lining the bank, half a dozen of them, and they were being joined by more.

They began to call and wave to me, just like the men in the coffee house used to when I danced for them. I was scared, for I knew full well what the result would be if I dared to climb out of the water.

I shrank back, and covered what I could of myself with my hands. The grinning soldiers got right to the edge of the bank, and waved and called and leered. A couple of them even made as though to wade in to get me, and I backed away scared.

It was their noise that alerted the Lieutenant. Even as I shrank back, the water now chilling rather than welcoming me, I heard a voice shouting, and he ran up. He had his sword out, and was shouting orders as though he thought we were under attack. When he saw the cause of the riot, he stopped in his tracks and stared aghast. After a long minute, he bowed his head, and touched his fingers to the side of his nose as though gathering himself.

He straightened up and gave more orders, not shouting

now, but coldly stern. His soldiers did not like the orders, that much was plain by their mumbling and surly looks, but they obeyed them. They backed away, still keeping their eyes on where I crouched in the pool. The Lieutenant spat his orders again, and they drifted reluctantly away - but not so far away that they could not see me.

Lieutenant Debrot waved his hand imperiously. "Come out of there, you stupid, stupid woman!" he said.

I had to climb out of the pool, and if the truth be told I have never felt so small and stupid in my life. The men had got what vantage-points they could. The Lieutenant was standing above me on the bank of the pool. My shirt was drenched, and the white cotton of it clung to me as I climbed out of the water, becoming transparent where it stuck to my skin - which was more or less everywhere. I felt more naked at those moments than I had ever felt in my life. Ashamed; pierced by the hungry eyes of the soldiers; humbled by the angry looks of the Lieutenant, I searched around for my black chadour.

It was nowhere to be found. One of the soldiers must have taken it away. Blushing to my hair, and horribly aware of how the soaking cotton of my white shirt clung to my body, I bowed my head and tried to hide myself behind my hands. Lieutenant Debrot shouted at me, but in such rapid French I did not understand. Then he waved his sword and pointed. I understood. Horribly aware of the eyes of the watching soldiers I clasped a hand to my loins and, with my other arm across my chest, scurried back to my tent.

As I scrabbled about in my bundle for my second chadour, I could hear a lot of shouting outside. I knew I had made a terrible mistake, and that there would be repercussions. When the Lieutenant threw aside the flap of my tent he was in a towering fury.

He stood in the middle of the tent, his face livid with

rage, and stormed at me as I cowered on the floor. I could not understand what he said, for it was in rapid French incomprehensible to me, though I did recognize the words coquine and putain, for he said them repeatedly. The last time I had heard those words they were said with affection, when Ishbal had called me his 'little slut' and his 'sweet whore' towards the end of my time in the brothel. Now, they were said with deep contempt, almost with loathing. I began to weep.

The cause of his fury was not that I was a whore and a slut, but that his men had found out I was not the Arab woman he had told them I was. It was his authority that was at stake. There was an appalling logic to what he went on to explain. If his men thought that he knew about me and had kept the knowledge secret, they would surely mutiny. If they even suspected that we had lain together, blood would be shed - his blood and possibly mine too.

Therefore I was to be publicly disciplined.

He ordered me to remove my chadour. I made to remove my shirt as well, but he stopped me. Then he led me out of the tent. All his men were assembled. I was put on trial, but a very quick one and conducted in such a rapid French that I could not keep up. I was not invited to speak in my own defence, not that I would have been capable of it. It was all so unfair!

Although their speech was too quick for me to follow properly, I managed to get the gist of it - and it frightened me greatly. The Lieutenant told his men I was guilty of deception, and must therefore be punished according to military discipline. After the punishment he would decide what to do about me.

I stood facing the 'court' clad in just my shirt, and my heart began to pump wildly. I knew without being told what kind of punishment military discipline meant. The men had formed a wide circle around me and I could veritably feel their tense excitement as their eyes raked over me. The Lieutenant looked me in the eyes, his expression hard, and held out a hand. What choice did I have? It would happen anyway, and if I seemed to co-operate it might make things a little easier on me.

I lifted my shirt off over my head, acutely conscious of the low growls from the circle of soldiers as they saw my naked body. I handed it to Lieutenant Debrot and stood with my head bowed and my hands at my sides; there was no point in trying to hide myself with my hands. The sun beating down on my skin was no hotter than the looks of the men surrounding me, and the thought sent a flush of equal heat through my insides.

At an order from the Lieutenant two grinning men ran forward, their eyes greedy. One of them had a rope and my arms were grabbed and pulled forward. They tied my wrists together and dragged me over to the front of the largest of the several tents. At its front was a thick pole eight feet or more high. They looped the rope around the top and hauled on it, pulling my arms high above my head until I was on my very tip-toes.

The soldiers crowded around, muttering and whispering. I knew what kind of sight I presented to them, dangling there naked and helpless, and also knew exactly what was going through their minds. I steeled myself. Even this, I told myself, was better than being sent back to Timboktou.

It was the sergeant, Sergeant Duclos, who inflicted the punishment. He was a big man, and laid it on heavy with the whippy stick used to control the camels. I had determined to be strong. I had been beaten many times before since my capture and was sure I could bear up, but with the very first stroke I screamed like a banshee and I know that my body and legs flailed around madly.

It felt as though I had been cut in half! There were more

strokes, each landing on my writhing backside like an explosion of white-hot fire, setting me dancing and wailing. Much later I counted my stripes. There were only ten of them, but it felt like a thousand! I was vaguely aware of being cut down from the tent pole and carted back to my tent, to be dumped face down on the canvas sheet which covered the ground. I felt rough hands rub over my burning buttocks and flinched afresh, for I was very, very sore. I heard the Lieutenant's voice saying something, but I was too far gone with the pain in my bottom to take in whatever it was he said before he left me to my agony.

The Lieutenant did not return to my little tent for what must have been well over an hour, during which space of time the conflagration in my backside dulled to a steady throb and my fears as to what would be done with me screwed horribly tight in my chest.

When he entered my tent his face was cold, and my heart sank. All was surely lost for me.

"I have spoken with my Sergeant," he said. "And he with the men. This is most unusual, but we are in unusual circumstances. I do not wish to have a mutiny on my hands. Therefore, a decision has been made."

He paused. He stood above me, filling the middle of the tent. His presence was chilling. I knew, even as he searched for words, that my future, my very life perhaps, was held in the balance of his next words.

"It has been decided - I have decided, that I will fulfil my agreement with Captain Robertson." His voice was cold, but his eyes were not as they roved over my exposed body. "I will conduct you to Algiers, and fulfil my word as a gentleman of France."

I could have kissed his boots!

"There is a condition. You have a choice in the matter," he continued, his voice getting even colder. "Two of my men have recognised you from a certain establishment in

Timboktou. Now all the men know what you are, and are muttering amongst themselves. The journey is more than two thousand miles. I have twenty soldiers. You have been what you have been, and will understand me when I say that certain requirements will be made of you, should you wish to continue this journey."

I did indeed understand, instantly and only too well. Lieutenant Debrot made it plain. There were twenty men, twenty-two if you counted the Lieutenant and the Sergeant. The journey would take weeks. If I went on, the soldiers would require me to 'work my passage', as the naval phrase has it. If I declined, I would be returned to Memmisaab and a certain, awful future. Although the prospect of the journey was daunting, the alternative was too awful to be contemplated.

I was cut by the scorn in the Lieutenant's eyes when I made my reply. There was only one possible reply, and I gave it, and confirmed the Lieutenant's opinion that I was indeed a whore. I asked please to be allowed to continue on to Algiers, even if it meant I had to entertain his troops.

The expression of contempt on the man's face horrified me. What a hypocrite he was! He had sneaked into my tent several times and told me to keep it secret. No doubt he would have kept on secretly shagging me all through the journey had I not made my silly mistake in the pool. Now he'd had me flogged in front of their goggling eyes, and was expressing disgust that I was prepared to let his troops fuck me rather than go back to Timboktou!

He did not understand my decision. He obviously did not know what fate awaited me if I went back, only that I had been seen by some of his men dancing in a whore-house. He was raised in a society where whores were whores, and good women good. Yet he had not known I had been a prostitute when he raped me that first day nor when he had crept into my tent each night! Blind, hypocritical fool!

When the Lieutenant stalked out of the tent, all straight back and stiff knees, to announce my choice, I expected to be engulfed by lustful soldiers. Instead, controlled I think by Sergeant Duclos' strength and the discipline that had been instilled into them by their military training, they were very civilized about it. Or at least, as civilized as a situation in which they held, and were set on using, power over a helpless woman allowed.

They had drawn lots for me, to decide the order of access, as it were. The Sergeant explained it to me in very broken English, aided by my poor schoolgirl French. They had divided themselves into shifts, or rosters, or teams if you will. Each roster numbered seven in all. Each night, I was to hold myself available for that day's roster, thus ensuring that every man got his relief at least every third day. He, the Sergeant, would by right of rank have me outside the roster he was numbered among as well, should he feel the need.

It would not only be at night, either, for there was always a long break, three hours or more, during the hottest part of the day. I was to be available to them during that period also.

It was a daunting requirement. I tried to bargain him down, to perhaps only three, maybe five men a day, or perhaps only being used at night rather than in the middle of the day as well. Trying to bargain with a man who knows he has you in his power, and is at that moment intent on shagging you very soon, is not easy and he was not to be moved. I bowed to the inevitable. I had survived worse in Memmisaab's brothel. I would survive this. Seven a day was not too bad, even though I knew most of them would want it more than once. I accepted his terms.

Then I learned how our bargain was to be sealed. The lieutenant had agreed with his Sergeant that the troop would

176

remain at the oasis until the morrow. In the meantime, he had given his men the freedom of me so they could work off their state of excitement.

Even as he had been explaining all this to me the Sergeant got me down onto the ground, and began vigorously working off his own state of excitement. He was quite a big man, if you see what I mean, and far from gentle. Why should he be? As far as he was concerned he was only shagging a whore. Although the fire had died somewhat my bottom was still very sore. At his very first thrust he crushed me against the hard ground and a jolt of pain in my abused buttocks caused me to squeal and jerk my hips upwards. He must have thought my reaction came from some kind of pleasure, for he proceeded to fuck me very hard indeed, grunting as he shafted me and oblivious to my little whimpers as my backside slapped on to the ground with each thrust.

He bellowed when he came, shoving even harder as he pumped his stuff into me. Then, without a word, he stood up, put himself away and opened the tent-flap. His soldiers were waiting outside to take their turns on me. They had even formed a line, and while one was shagging me, the leering face of his successor would be peering over his shoulder.

It was a nightmare. I lay naked on the sandy floor of the tent while soldier after soldier ducked through the entrance, and waited his turn, then fell on me and got his pleasures.

They were all rough and over-eager. Even when most in demand in Memmisaab's, even when I had first danced in the coffee house and Memmisaab had let all-comers at me, I had not experienced this. Garlic-laden breath swamped my senses. Hard hands pulled at my breasts and my bruised buttocks. The metal buttons of their tunics grazed my ribs. The cloth of their breeches chaffed my thighs.

I went away from myself. I became no more than a receptacle for them to rut in. Only when one of them was especially big, or very vigorous, or - worse - very smelly, did I

177

come back to myself and register what was happening. The mind does that in extremis, runs off, avoids the immediate, finds ways to survive.

The immediate, that which was happening to me now, was too awful to think about. Twenty soldiers were queuing for me, all of them very worked up, some of them I am sure coming back for a second turn at me. I lapsed into a trance long before they finished on me.

After that first, frenzied orgy they allowed me to go back to the pool to bathe and ease the aches their wild shagging had given me. They managed to turn it into an entertainment, though, for they had me walk naked to the pool and all stood on the bank to watch me bathe, laughing and making lewd gestures, and all followed me as I limped wet and naked back to my tent.

I cannot describe the detail of that exhausting journey for, as you can imagine, I had other things on my mind. It lasted more than a month, I think, through rocky deserts and sandy wastes, from water-hole to water-hole, sometimes with several days travel between. There were mountainous stretches, especially near the end. We hardly ever saw other travellers, and only in the last week did we even see any villages or towns.

The soldiers kept strictly to their bargain, and I 'worked my passage' in the manner they had prescribed. There was no point in protesting, and having matters regulated was infinitely better than the free-for-all there might have been.

At the midday break, I would go into my tent and spread out a blanket on the ground, and get my chadour off. I did not bother wearing a shirt underneath it now. The men always wanted me naked, and for the rest of the journey the only time I wore anything was when I was actually riding my camel. After that first strenuous day when the Lieutenant had let the whole lot of them at me, there was little rushing, for they all knew I was theirs for the taking.

Sometimes, only three or four might come for me during the day, though I never got less than all seven during the nights. I made matters as easy for myself as I could by using all the little tricks and ploys I had learned as Memmisaab's brothel girl. I would wriggle voluptuously underneath them, and pump my hips and flex the muscles of my sheath to bring them off as quickly as I could. If they wanted my mouth - which became increasingly in demand - I would suck and lick them as though drinking at a fountain of ambrosia, and hold their shafts, and press that place beneath their balls that is so useful in bringing a man off quickly. Some of them, though only a handful thank heavens, seemed to prefer using me as though I was a boy, which I had never really enjoyed but had learned to accommodate while with Memmisaab.

All in all, I confirmed their opinion of me by playing the whore as though what they were doing to me was the most wonderful thing on earth. They thought I was wild for them, and would sigh and wriggle at their very touch. In reality, I played the part of a 'good fuck' to get it over as fast as possible, and make things easier for myself.

I even danced for them each night, on the desert floor in the flickering light of the campfire. Those two soldiers who had seen me in Memmisaab's coffee house told the others about seeing me 'ring the bell', and they all agreed it would be entertaining if I performed for them, too. Thus, every evening after about a week an observer, had there been one, would have seen a squad of soldiers sitting in a wide circle eating their evening meal, while inside the circle a woman danced around, naked, weaving her arms and gyrating her belly and waggling her breasts and bottom for their entertainment.

Lieutenant Debrot never stopped regarding me as a

whore, and always treated me with cold contempt when he could not avoid addressing me. He never came near me now; that would have been beneath his dignity as an officer. I did sometimes see him, though, glancing through the open flap of my tent while one or another of his men was bucking and grunting between my thighs.

Sergeant Duclos, on the other hand, turned out to be quite friendly in his rough soldier's way. Naturally, he took advantage of his rank to fuck me pretty well every day, and such was the regard in which he was held by his men that only one or two seemed to resent him his extra shags.

He became much less rough with me than those first couple of times, and would stroke my breasts, rather than grab them as if they were bread rolls like too many of the others did. When I was sucking him off, he never grabbed my head. And, sometimes, with him my climaxes were not pretended.

It was Sergeant Duclos who had the day-by-day management of me, who organized my food and water-ration, who got me onto my camel each time we set off, and behind whom I rode for weary hours each day. It shows how quick a person can learn and change, for I soon became no longer afraid of my camel, nor made sick by its swaying. Indeed, I soon learned to actually sleep while in its saddle - a blessing indeed, for as you can imagine I got little rest at night or during the midday breaks.

To sleep and, often, to let my mind wander. It is strange, considering all that had happened to me, that when it wandered off in a sort of half-dream it reflected on only the good things, the lovely moments, the sweet people. As I sat there rocking and swaying on my camel, I dreamed of all those lovely moments when Ishbal kissed me, and caught me up and hugged me if I had danced well, and of my times with beloved Bennasira, loving and making love.

180

Such reveries would send me into a strange sort of melancholy happiness. Others would make me giggle. Especially the one concerning a wonderful evening towards the end of my time with Captain Robertson and Peter. We had got really close and relaxed with each other and were chatting away after supper. Peter made me laugh while I was eating a biscuit, and I spurted some crumbs from my mouth, and he made a remark about not getting crumbs in my pussy, which in turn set Captain Robertson off into a fit of guffaws which had him coughing and red-faced.

The look of blank puzzlement on my face set Peter off, too. We did not have a cat in the house, so how could I get crumbs in my pussy? After their hilarity subsided there ensued a conversation which had me wide eyed with amazement, and frequently giggling helplessly. The conversation was about words and terms and names for things, and became a hilarious vocabulary lesson.

It transpired that 'pussy' was one of the seemingly endless names for what a girl has between her legs. There were lots of others, many of which I have forgotten because at the time my two lovely men were demonstrating by playing with the part of me in question - which was very nice, but also very distracting. They soon had me naked and were putting their hands on me, each seemingly in competition to think up a name that would allow him to feel me - not that they needed any excuse as far as I was concerned!

These, Peter told me, handling me softly, were called my titties. Also, my Captain said, his hands replacing Peter's, my boobies. Also my dugs, my jugs, my tits and my mams. This, fondling another place, was my pussy, and my quim, and my fuck-tunnel, and my cunt, and my minge. What they had - and yes, I was allowed, indeed encouraged to touch! - was called a cock or a prick or a todger. What happened when the two got together was called shagging or fucking. Not exactly beautiful names for such beautiful things, but that did not matter at all by the end of the evening because my Captain was fucking me beautifully while I rubbed Peter's cock in my hand in preparation to 'gobble' him - which is apparently a name for the delightful activity in which a girl uses her mouth on her lover's cock.

But to return to my story -

Our journey across the Sahara continued drearily, with the Lieutenant still disdaining me, the teams of seven lusty soldiers exercising their daily rights, and Sergeant Duclos becoming almost fatherly towards me.

Only once did the Sergeant bellow at me and become frightening, and that was when he came upon me as I was using my douche behind my tent.

"Stupide! Chienne stupide! Pas de l'eau! Pas de l'eau!" he bellowed, frightening the wits out of me.

Water was precious. I was stupid to use it to rinse myself out. He grabbed me up in one arm as though I were no more than a doll. In an instant, I was spun round and thrown down across his knee. He spanked me very fiercely, setting my poor squirming bottom aflame, and making me wail aloud.

Lieutenant Debrot heard my cries and hurried up, demanding to know what was amiss. A gleam came into his eyes as the sergeant explained, and I felt a chill run through me at its malice. He had clearly become frustrated that his 'officer's dignity' could not allow him to shag the woman all his men were fucking, and was intent on taking out that frustration by wreaking revenge on me. It was another public beating hanging naked from the tent-pole.

He did it himself this time, and he laid it on very hard. My shrieks hurt my throat despite my determination to keep quiet, and when he finished I could only hang from my bonds gasping for breath. When I gathered myself, fiercely determined that this malicious, hypocritical man should not think he had broken my spirit, I became aware of two things.

The first was that there was no audience of soldiers. They had all moved away and were going about other business. There was a strange silence about the camp. The second was a stain of wetness at the top of the left leg of Lieutenant Debrot's breeches. For an instant it meant nothing to me, then its meaning hit me and despite my circumstances I burst into a fit of helpless giggles. He had come! He had messed his breeches in his excitement at beating my bottom! What price his officer's dignity now!

Algiers seemed vast and cacophonous after the emptiness of the desert, but I was hugely relieved when we reached it. The Lieutenant led us straight to the barracks, and took me into the quarters of the commanding officer. I was told to wait in an ante-room while he spoke to his superior.

I could not tell what they were saying, for it was in rapid French, but I could tell from the clipped coldness of the Lieutenant's voice and the words prostitue and putain, which I did manage to make out they were repeated so often, that he was not holding back on any of his contempt for me.

I dreaded the worst when the Lieutenant marched out of the office, gestured coldly for me to enter, and left the room.

The man who faced me when I entered the office could not have been more different from the Lieutenant, or from what I expected. As I entered he stood up behind his desk, smiled broadly, and spoke to me in perfect English, only slightly accented.

"Well, my dear," he said, waving me towards a chair. "My young Lieutenant tells me a very strange tale. Very strange indeed. If what he tells me is true, I must offer you the humble apologies of the French military, and the French nation. An officer of France must also be a gentleman. Now,

I will send for some coffee, and perhaps a little cognac, and you will tell me what his strange tale was all about."

I gazed at the man amazed. This was the reverse of what I had expected. He was tall even when sitting down. His face was dark from the sun, his eyes were brown, and his hair and side-whiskers were showing a dusting of white among the dark brown. His smile showed a fine set of very white teeth, and there were crow's-feet by his eyes that suggested an enjoyment of laughter.

Over coffee and brandy, brought in by a soldier, I began to tell him my story.

SEVENTEEN

I told him the whole of my story, or rather the full outline of it. I could not go into the details I have revealed to you here. To write it is one thing; to tell it face to face would be too embarrassing! So, I told him of my kidnap. I told how I had been sold off, then auctioned, and made to work for Memmisaab in her brothel. I told how my Captain had rescued me, though not that we had become lovers, and how he had arranged the contract with Lieutenant Debrot to bring me across the desert. I stopped there, for he clearly already knew how I had worked my passage.

He was the nicest of men, and easy to talk to, and seemed not to judge me harshly. Indeed, he nodded sympathetically several times and, at the end of my tale, rose from his chair and patted me on the shoulder comfortingly. He was clearly a man of the world and knew without making me go into detail what my role had been with Memmisaab, but he did not condemn me for it.

He then mentioned something my ninny head had not even considered. What was I going to do now I had reached

Algiers, and how was I going to get passage back to England? I suddenly felt very small and silly. And lost. What was I to do! I was in a foreign town where English was not the language. I had no idea how to find the port, let alone book passage on a ship. The awfulness hit me like a thunderbolt and I began to sob uncontrollably.

The Colonel came at once to my rescue. He had a house outside the barracks, where he lived with his wife and two daughters, and he would take me there. It was not far, perhaps half a mile, and his wife would welcome me he was sure. My heart swelled when he added that he would see what he could do about finding me a vessel.

My sobs burst out afresh, but this time for joy and gratitude. I could have hugged him to death! He waited patiently while I controlled my emotions then, with a gentle voice, said that which showed me that, nice as he may be, the Colonel was as much a man as he was a gentleman.

"My young Lieutenant told me that he was obliged to punish you during your journey. Is that so?" At my silent nod, he gestured towards he desk and continued, just as gently. "Show me the marks my dear, if you would be so good."

There were no marks any more, or if there were they were very faint. I knew instinctively that seeing the marks was only an excuse and that he had other things in his mind. But what could I do? Just as my future had depended on the Lieutenant, it now depended on the Colonel. I stood, bent over the desk and raised the back of my voluminous chadour up to my waist.

The knowledge of the view I was giving him set off that old familiar lurch in my belly. Without even knowing it I had posed with my feet apart and my back arched downwards, so that he had an excellent view of my cleft and sex. He took full advantage of my compliant position.

I shivered as he began to stroke his hands over me. They were soft hands, yet strong, and he smoothed them over every curve of my offered hind-quarters from my waist to the tops of my thighs. He took his time, enjoying me as though I were some choice morsel. He parted the cheeks of my bottom and explored the length of my cleft with tender fingers. For a moment his fingers paused at the pucker of my rosehole, pressing a little as though seeking admission, but then they moved on.

I was already moist by the time his fingers traced the length of my crease, and I heard him give a little grunt of satisfaction as he discovered my condition. He knew exactly what he was doing and soon had me panting as he teased the inner folds of my sex-lips, and slipped the tip of a finger into the entrance to my sheath, and touched and tormented the little clitty that was already standing out eager for him.

When his hands left me he did not stand back, and I knew there was more to come. To be honest, I confess I wanted it. His touches had got me very worked-up. I gave an instinctive wriggle as I felt him touch against me, his satiny hardness sliding down my crease to find the hot wetness of my cunt. He came into me slowly, a little at a time as though he was checking to see whether my body welcomed him. That it assuredly did was signalled by the way my vagina sucked at him and my pelvis instinctively rocked back against his hardness, to get more of it.

He was big. When he got fully into me he gripped my hips and began a slow, delicious rocking motion, moving deep until his loins pressed against the cheeks of my bottom, easing back until he was almost out of me, then pushing deep again until my breath was squashed out of my lungs.

I was coming long before he started moving quicker, signalling his own impending eruption. Then he did get somewhat rough, gripping my hip-bones hard and banging the fronts of my legs against the edge of the desk in his excitement. When he did finally come, cramming into me so deep I felt my eyes must surely pop out, it was volcanic and set off yet another orgasm in my own unruly body.

I was blushing when at last he pulled out and I stood up, shaking down the skirts of my chadour. He, though, was as calm and urbane as though nothing untoward had happened. Once again he patted my shoulder in an avuncular fashion and suggested that I go with him to his home. He walked with the gait of a long-serving soldier and I had to scurry to keep up with him.

The first part of the walk, around a large parade area and out through the barrack gates, was the most difficult, for there were a great many soldiers about. It became pretty clear that the news about the woman who had worked her passage across the Sahara had spread. All eyes were on me, and I could see troops nudging one another and smirking and whispering. It was strange how, after all I had experienced, I found this scrutiny so embarrassing, and beneath my all-enveloping chadour I blushed to my roots. It was almost as though all these men could sense their Colonel's emissions as they seeped down my thighs.

The last part of the rapid walk, outside the barracks was easier, for there were lots of people about, including many women clad like myself in voluminous black chadours, and nobody took any notice of us. Colonel de Villars, for that was the officer's name, ushered me through the door of the large, two storey building that was his house, and at once called out in a cheerful tone. Straight away, a handsome, dark haired woman in her forties, carrying a brimming glass in readiness, came out of one of the rooms.

She seemed momentarily disconcerted to see what she must have thought to be an Arab woman standing there, but recovered her composure in an instant. She handed the Colonel the glass, and they conversed rapidly in French.

After only the briefest of conversations, they reverted to excellent English and I was introduced. For the time being, the Colonel told her little save that I was in need, though

I knew that my story would soon have to be told. Madame de Villars, for the lady was the Colonel's wife, gathered me in like a mother hen, calling to one of her daughters to get water heated for a bath, and to the other to hurry upstairs with me to find me some 'civilized garments', as she put it.

I felt a pang of guilt at her kindness, for hardly half an hour earlier her husband had bent me over his desk and shafted me very thoroughly and here she was being nice to me. I glanced towards the Colonel, but his expression was bland and unconcerned. I knew then that I was in for a somewhat interesting time!

I could have died for a bath, for although I had bathed at every oasis we stopped at, for the entertainment of the soldiers as well as to get rid of the dust, I had not had a proper bath, with hot water and soap, since leaving Timboktou.

Marianna, the Colonel's eldest daughter, who's clothes I was being lent, knew nothing of my story yet. Even though she must have been sorely puzzled at the sudden advent of this European woman clad in Arab garb, she asked me no questions. Such was this family's ready generosity that instead, she straight away began to rummage among her things to find something for me to wear.

She was at least six inches taller than me (most people are!) but managed to solve that problem by sorting out a separate blouse and skirt. She expressed astonishment when I pulled off the chadour which was by now odious to me, as much that I should do so with her still present, I think, as at the fact that I was stark naked underneath. When she saw the chain I still wore around my waist, her mouth became an 'O' of amazement and she stared at me, then her face went pale when she caught sight of my brand, but she still did not ask the questions that were clearly boiling in her mind.

She gave me a robe to wrap myself in and, carrying the

skirt and blouse, led me down to the scullery, where a wonderful, steaming tub awaited me. Oh, such luxury! She left me alone to bathe, and while I wallowed and soaped I am sure that she, and her mother and sister poured question after question over the Colonel.

I know that when I had dried myself, and put on the blouse and skirt, and went out to seek them, they gave me the longest, softest looks, while Madame de Villars hugged me and murmured "Pouvre petite! Pouvre petite!" over and over.

The de Villars family, the Colonel, his wife and the two girls, were the sweetest and most generous family in the world. They treated me, a stranger, with such gentle kindness that I soon wished I could be part of such a family. Except that the Colonel missed few opportunities to get at me.

He was discreet, picking his times when nobody else was around, or none of them were likely to see. He knew from my compliance when he had shagged me in his office at the barracks that I was unlikely to make any fuss, and so took every chance he got to squeeze my breasts or get a hand up my skirt.

Within the house there were few opportunities for him to actually fuck me, for although he had a small room which served as an office and he frequently took me there, ostensibly to discuss my situation and his progress in arranging papers for me, his wife and daughters were in the habit of walking in at any time, usually without even knocking on the door, to offer coffee or to convey a message.

The Colonel solved his problem in the simplest of manners. He put me to sit beside him behind his big desk, which faced the door. Papers would be strewn on the desk-top. He would be holding a quill as though about to sign something. Meanwhile, concealed by the body of the desk, his free hand would be working between my legs while my own hand would be rubbing frantically up and down the thick shaft that protruded from his breeches.

If anybody walked in all we had to do was to pretend to be examining complicated document. When they left again we would take up where we had left off. I think it was the element of danger about it that excited me. There is not much actual physical pleasure for a girl in rubbing a man's cock with her hand until he comes. Much nicer to have it in her mouth or pulsing in her cunt! But I have to confess there was a certain strange excitement in sitting behind that desk wanking the Colonel - I have heard that bringing off a man by hand is called wanking him - knowing that at any moment somebody might walk in.

Once, a junior officer entered with a message from the barracks just as I got the Colonel to his climax and feeling him spurting all over my hand and his breeches as he talked military business with his subordinate nearly sent me into hysterics! To watch him being dignified and business-like above the desk, while below it my hand was milking his throbbing cock was wonderful, and makes me giggle at the recollection even today.

Although the Colonel's wife and daughters skirted very delicately around the subject, it was clear to me that they were on hooks to know all about me. I told them my story over the next few days, in dribs and drabs at first, while Colonel de Villars sorted out papers and a passage aboard ship for me, and had his daily wank. They were so kind and warm and sympathetic that I found my resolution to tell only the barest outline dissolving, in part, I confess, because both Madame de Villars and Marianna asked quite shrewd questions.

They expressed horror about my kidnap, and how I had been sold off to Arabs in exchange for guns. When I told them about the slave-auction in Timboktou Silvie, the younger daughter, put her arms around me, and kissed me in sympathy at my suffering.

I expected 'civilized' people to sneer at me and treat me with the same contempt as had Lieutenant Debrot. Madame de Villars and her two daughters did not, and went to my heart. Even when, without going into much detail at first, I let them understand that I had been the common property of my kidnappers, and what kind of place Memmisaab's had been, they showed only kindness. It surprised and warmed me, for Madame de Villars showed by her glance that she fully understood the implications of my tale, and I think Marianna did too, a little.

I have said that the de Villars family were kind to me, and they assuredly were. That does not mean, though, that they were disinterested. I suppose it was inevitable that as they learned more and more of the details of my story, attitudes towards me should change somewhat. Those of Marianna and her sister certainly did.

It was Marianna who instigated matters. Since the de Villars household was geared for two parents and their daughters, it had only two bedrooms; one for each pair. Thus, I had perforce to share with the girls. Marianna had a double bed and Silvie a single, and it was regarded as simple and natural that I should share with the older daughter.

That first night, although things were naturally a little stiff and awkward, for I was a strange creature come among them, with a story as yet only sketchily known, Marianna was all solicitude and care, and gave me one of her own nightgowns to wear, and kissed me on my forehead by way of a goodnight.

By the second night, when she had begun to know a lot more about my experiences, though not in any great detail of course, she was even more solicitous, but not in quite the same way. This time she kissed me goodnight on my lips, a quick, soft kiss that betokened little. When she had extinguished the candle, however, Marianna snuggled in close beside me rather than taking the far side of the mattress as she had last night and began, in whispers so as not to disturb her sister Silvie, to question me about some aspects of my story she had learned.

How had I felt when I was carried off by those great African tribesman? Had they been very hard with me? Very demanding? Was it terrible to be kept as a helpless plaything; to have no choice in what became of one?

I gave her the blandest answers I could without actually lying, but it was clear that Marianna had visions in her mind of what I had experienced, and was both frightened and fascinated by them. Excited too, as became clear after I pretended to be asleep in order stop her flow of urgent questions.

I had not been pretending for many minutes when I felt her move a little away from me, for she had been lying rather close. Further movements told me that she was now lying on her back. Then the blankets shifted a little and the bed-springs began to give out a tiny, rhythmical squeaking. I continued my pretence of sleep, but all my senses were alert with astonishment.

The squeaking of the bed-springs gradually became faster and more pronounced. Marianna's breathing became quicker and grew ragged and the movements of her hands beneath the blankets more obvious. She was pleasuring herself! There, in bed beside me and thinking me asleep, the minx was bringing herself off with her fingers! Clearly she was not the little innocent she gave the appearance of being!

I learned on the third night that I was not wrong in my assessment of Marianna. It had come out during the day that I had been a brothel girl, and that I had lain with women as well as with men. Because of their obvious care for me, I had become honest with Colonel and Madame de Villars and I had let slip about my sweet Bennasira. That night, Marianna's questions were more pointed, and very persistent. And she accompanied them with little revelations of her own.

She wanted to know if it always felt strange and tense and nice when a man held you in his arms and kissed you. There was a handsome young officer who had got her in private several times, and kissed her, and she was confused about how she felt. Was it usual, she wanted to know, to feel so excited by it? To look forward to it happening again, and yet to feel so guilty? He had fondled her breasts, too, though outside her blouse, and it had felt very strange and exciting, but naughty as well, and she had been tense and jumpy for ages afterwards.

As much as anything, she wanted to know how it felt when a man touched you between your legs. She had felt a longing there, a hotness, and wondered what it signified. I knew she was dissembling with me, for had she not pleasured herself right beside me last night, but I went along with her little deception. The point of it became clear when she asked me point blank about what sex was like.

I told her what I felt I could. Told her that being a woman was a mysterious and powerful thing. That men would want her because she was beautiful (which was true) and that she would feel deep and moving emotions. To my slight surprise, she turned the questioning away from emotions to physical sensations. She wanted to know how the body felt, and not so much the mind or the heart.

Did that thing she had felt pressing against her belly when her officer kissed and caressed her really get ever so big? Did they really want to put it up inside a girl? Was it really big? Did it hurt when they put it up a girl? Had a lot of them done it to me? An awful lot?

Patiently, feeling a strange surge of motherliness even

though Marianna was actually older than me, and choosing my terms carefully, I tried to enlighten her. It was not easy, for on the one hand I did not wish to put her off by stressing the uncomfortable aspects of the kinds of sexual experiences I had lived through, neither did I want to excite her into possible indiscretions by talking too much about how glorious shagging can be.

I stuck strictly to the facts. She was enthralled, and snuggled against me. I could sense that she was becoming tense, and tried to keep things matter of fact. Then she became very curious about Bennasira. I could not help becoming lyrical about my beloved Bennasira, but stopped myself telling her any details about our actual love making.

Then Marianna touched me for the first time.

She made a snaking movement in the bed, and was close upon me, her breath on my neck, and her hand slipping onto my tummy, her leg sliding over mine. I was startled, and must have shown it, for Marianna clung to me and began to kiss me and whisper urgently.

"Please ... I don't know ... I ... you ... please help ... oh, Amy!"

All the while she was pouring out these and other incoherences, she was kissing me and pressing her body against mine, her hand urgent on my breast. Something in my heart swelled to bursting point. She was the sweetest of girls, and in desperate confusion about the needs of her body and her burgeoning womanly sensations. It would not have done to speak, and so, gentling her off me for a moment, I sat up and pulled off my nightgown and lay back again, naked and open for her.

It was not making love as one would normally regard it. It was more that she explored me, and at the same time explored her own senses and desires. The huge, silver African moon bathed us in gleam and shadow. Marianna pulled the sheets down from my body and kneeled up on the bed. She gazed down at me with enormous eyes. Her hand was actually trembling as her fingertips traced the swell of my breasts, and the curve of my shoulder, then down over the dip of my navel towards the join of my thighs. They lingered for several moments when they found the shape of my brand. She was obviously fascinated by it, but was reticent about asking anything.

She leaned down to kiss me on my mouth, her lips warm and soft, her long, dark hair setting off tinglings in my skin as it traced across my breasts. Her hand found my centre and slipped down to cup me. She was tentative, nervous even, but it was clear that in touching me thus she was repeating how she had touched herself in the past, for her fingers were skilful.

She parted my outer lips with gentle fingers. She explored the length of my inner folds so softly it took my breath away, then found the swelling cowl of my clitty and began to circle and dominate me. Her lips were on my cheek and my neck and my mouth. Her body was curled against mine. Her breath was hot against my skin. Her hand was wreaking tender havoc between my thighs. Suddenly, even before I reached my own rapture, her thighs were clamped about my hip and she was gasping and grinding her loins against me, pulsing and gyrating as she shuddered into her climax, thrusting fingers deep into me and setting off my own unexpectedly violent come.

The rest of that night was exhausting, for Marianna wanted me to show her what I had done with Bennasira; more than wanted, demanded. She had a lovely body and smelled and tasted delicious, but she was awfully greedy. After I had kissed and caressed her from head to toe she got me to play with her cunny while I sucked and nibbled at her tiny nipples. Then she got my face between her thighs and kept me working there for ages, while she spasmed into come after come.

I fell into an exhausted sleep in the early hours, but luckily, I woke up at the first light of dawn with my head still between Marianna's legs. I hurried to shake her into consciousness so we could both get our nightgowns back on before Silvie awoke. What a disaster it would have been if she had caught us!

How wrong we were.

The next day was spent busy with needles and thread, altering skirts and blouses and such to fit me. There were moments when Marianna looked at me in a new way, less gentle than before, and her tone when telling me to move this way or that for the fittings had a commanding edge to it.

She got me down to my chemise and drawers, and kept me that way for most of the day. While Silvie was with us Marianna was all decorum, although she did rather linger over measuring my bosom and my hips. Whenever Silvie went off on some errand or other - and Marianna thought of plenty! - the older sister made no bones about kissing me and feeling me up in the most lascivious fashion, all the while making it plain that she believed she had the right to do so.

Perhaps I had spent too long being the sexual plaything of anybody who fancied me; perhaps it is a sign that my nature is basically wanton. Whatever it was, the caresses and kisses did not really shock me, and before long I was certain that bedtime tonight would bring with it some strenuous activity!

We waited until Silvie seemed asleep, pretending to be asleep ourselves. Marianna was actually trembling with tension as we waited, her hand surreptitiously stroking my tummy all the while. Once Silvie's breathing became regular and she seemed asleep, Marianna curled around and kissed me, and in a trice our nightgowns were off, and our hands and mouths were busy.

Even as we were in the midst of our transports both Marianna and I froze.

"What are you doing?"

The voice was Silvie's, and it cut through like a sword even though she had only spoken in a whisper. Unnoticed, the younger girl had got out of her bed and was standing beside ours, staring down at us as we lay with our limbs entwined. I was naked. Marianna had her nightgown around her armpits. We could not pretend that we had been doing anything other than we had - making passionate love.

It might have been a disaster. Silvie might have gone rushing off to her mother, or called out, or made a loud fuss. Instead, she sat down on the bed beside us, her eyes wide with curiosity as she took in every detail of the display her sister and I made. My legs were wide. Marianna's hand was still between them, her fingers in me. My face was still between Marianna's breasts, where I had been kissing her. There was a silence that seemed eternal. I could think of nothing to say, and Marianna too remained mute with shock as she tried to pull her nightgown down to cover herself.

Then, Silvie reached out a hand and placed it full on my quim. Not salaciously, but with a sort of nervous curiosity.

"Is that what you did when you were a slave?" she said, her voice oddly throaty. "Is it good? Is it exciting? It looked it."

I was in an awkward situation, even if - looked at from another angle - it could be thought delicious. I was being sheltered under the roof of a kind family, the head of which was trying to arrange passage home to England for me - and, of course, taking every chance he could for a wank or a feel. I had submitted to the desire of one of his daughters to learn the delights of bodily sensation the night before. Now, I was doing it again, naked and spread in the bed of that same daughter, with the other one cupping my quim in her hand and showing plainly, though she did not say it, that she wanted to do what her sister had just been doing.

Perhaps I have some kind of perversity in me. Perhaps I had simply learned over the last year and more to accept the inevitable, and reshape it in my mind into something permissible. However it may be, I accepted now that for the time being I had two new young lovers. Once again, it felt as though I had no choice in the matter of the disposal of my body, for these girls wanted me, and I owed them a great debt.

In a way, I became a sort of training ground for them, for they were both in the throes of early womanhood, and experiencing the confusing awakenings of their bodies' desires, and wanted to learn. Now, with an eagerness that ignored my own desires in the matter, they wanted to touch me, to explore the body of a woman they knew to be experienced in matters of the flesh - matters that were still a great mystery to them, and about which they were enthralled. Explore me they did, lying on each side of me, kissing me and touching me with greedy hands.

While they did so, they wanted me to tell them things. They were confused as to what those things were, for like so many girls of my generation they had been told very little about what I have heard called 'the facts of life'. They knew, of course, that men had 'things', but not really what they were nor what was done with them, save that it had something to do with what they called, charmingly, their 'dinkles'. Marianna guessed something of it, for when that young officer had kissed her she had felt something hard pressing against her and she had felt that liquid hotness between her legs while he kissed her and felt her breasts. That, though, was the pretty well extent of their knowledge.

They knew I had been married, and asked me what it

was like. I described to them my wedding night, making it seem rather nicer than it actually was. Silvie had a finger inside me as I described my husband's cock, and what he had done with it.

"What?" she gasped. "In here! And so big! It must have been agony! Nobody is ever going to do that to me!"

"Oh, yes they will," I chuckled, kissing her. "They will, and though it might hurt the first time it will soon feel wonderful!"

And judging from what she was doing now, and the fascination she showed with the subject, and the way her nipples perked hard against me through the cotton of her nightgown, it would happen sooner rather than later. Though younger than Marianna, Silvie was taller and had a riper, fuller figure. It would not be long, I thought with a little smile, before some young officer would take her aside just as Marianna's had. Perhaps, though, Silvie would not be so confused after what we were doing.

What we, or rather they, were doing was becoming somewhat frustrating. It was clear from the knowing way their hands moved between my legs, that both girls had caressed themselves more than once, and knew how nice it feels to excite one's clitty, and thrust a finger or two in one's sheath. That seemed to be all, however, and - nice as it is - it can become frustrating if that is all that is happening.

I decided I should become more active. I chose Silvie, for Marianna had already enjoyed a climax. I whispered to her, and after only a moment of nervous shyness she sat up and pulled off her nightgown. Her body was indeed superb, shining almost silver in the moonlight. Her breasts were full and up-tilted, and her nipples stood out like little nuts. Her back was long and her waist slender, and below her softly rounded belly was a neat triangle of dark curls that entirely concealed her crease.

She lay back, gazing up at me nervously as I moved to her. I kissed her softly on her ripe lips, and she responded almost at once, her mouth eager. She gave a little shiver as my hand moved over her breast and I rolled her hard nipple with the ball of my thumb. I moved my head down, trailing my hair over her skin, enjoying her little gasps of excitation, and began to kiss and lick her other breast, circling her with my tongue, slowly, deliberately slowly, approaching closer to her nub.

When I closed my mouth over her nipple, and sucked gently and rasped my tongue over its tip, she gave a soft moan and her body moved with a sort of slow shudder. I stayed on her breasts for some time, moving my mouth from one to the other, timing my movements by her quiet gasps and the way her body began to move.

My free hand had slipped down over Silvie's soft belly. Her hips had given a wriggle as my hand moved further down, but I was not ready to touch between her legs yet. I smoothed my palm down over her hip and the outside of her long thigh, almost down to her knee, before trailing my fingers back up along the inner side. As I did so, she parted her thighs and I felt her pelvis rise towards me.

I was still not ready yet. I wanted this sweet girl to learn that there is as much pleasure in the building up as in the culmination; more, if anything. She gave a little mewl of disappointment when my fingers avoided the place she had opened to me, and her own hand sneaked down. I moved it away. This was for me to do.

Releasing her breast, I traced my lips down the midline of her ribs and to her navel. I teased the tip of my tongue around and into it while my hand returned to her thighs, which by now had fallen wide. I scratched my fingernails softly over their sensitive inner curves, and was rewarded with a gasp and a little shudder.

Silvie's pelvis had taken up a motion of its own, flexing

softly as though she were pressing herself against something. I moved my mouth down over her belly. I planted a kiss on the soft curls of her triangle. My hand slid up her inner thigh and my fingers parted the love-lips that were already swollen and slick for me.

Her inner folds were glistening like swollen petals, and her little clitty was straining out at me. She shuddered as I slipped my fingertips onto her pouting, virgin cunny, then jerked and groaned aloud as my lips found her clit and my tongue rasped across its perking tip.

Her orgasm was slow and powerful. Her pelvis rolled rather than bucked against my mouth. Her juices covered my fingers and my mouth and chin, and oozed down over the cleft of her pale buttocks. All the while I could hear her ragged voice groaning "Ah, je t'aime! Je t'aime, Amie, je t'aime. Mon Dieu, je t'aime!"

Her hand riffled in my hair as I gentled her down, not grabbing but touching, as though the feel of my hair in her fingers was yet another heady sensation to add to all the others she was experiencing. When at last I let her go, and kissed her on each thigh-top and breast, and knelt up so that I could look at her face, her hooded eyes were shining with the light of new understanding.

She sat up, and her arms went about me. She crushed herself against me, a sob in her throat as she hugged me and kissed my shoulder.

Beyond her, Marianna lay unaware of us. Her nightgown was once again above her waist. Her eyes were shut. On her face there was that expression of half agony, half ecstasy as her hand delved and delved and delved between her thighs, and she groaned towards her climax. I eased Silvie away from me and turned to Marianna. I took her hands and pulled them away. Her cunny was plump and lovely, gaping from her attentions to it. I leaned my face down towards the splay of her thighs, my tongue ready. It was only fair.

It took only a second for Marianna to go over the top, to swirl and churn into the delicious cramps of her passion. Hardly had I rasped my tongue along the length of her folds towards her straining clitty, and grasped that glorious nub with my lips and began to suck, than her hands were in my hair and her belly was bucking, and she too was gasping "Mon Dieu! Ah, mon Dieu!"

I had not known the need for secrecy before. With my husband, in Timboktou and during the journey across the Sahara, I had had nothing to hide, and indeed no way of hiding anything. Now, I was in a difficulty, and felt very uncomfortable in the presence of Mme de Villars. I managed to get through the morning after my night with her two daughters without discomfort because I only saw her for a few moments. At luncheon, however, I noticed her once or twice looking at me rather sharply, and became a little uncomfortable. She said nothing, and so I could only wonder, with some trepidation, whether she had found out about her husband and I. It turned out to be nothing of the kind.

Because I did not wish to disrupt the family routine too much, it had become my practice to take my bath in the afternoons. I heated the water myself in the boiler in the corner of the scullery, poured it into the hip bath with the bucket, and generally sorted matters out myself. It was, of course, a solitary activity, taking up most of the afternoon.

On this afternoon, my fifth with the family, it became not solitary. As I was sitting in the bath having soaped and washed myself, and was just considering getting out and towelling myself dry, Mme de Villars walked in.

As I have said, I was already feeling rather uncomfortable about that lady and, as she greeted me and leaned against the side of the boiler, regarding me shrewdly, I began to feel more so. Being wet and naked in a hip-bath, in the presence of an older woman about whom one feels guilty, is distinctly disturbing. The expression in her eyes told me that something was afoot, and I quite dreaded what it might be. There was a long pause before Mme de Villars spoke.

"I hope my daughters are not being too demanding of you."

I stared, not comprehending at first what she meant. Then I blushed to my ankles. She had found out in some way! Seeing my discomfiture, Mme de Villars smiled - a smile with an edge to it. I became even more nervous. "You all stayed late in your room. You missed breakfast. I looked in to see if matters were right with you all."

Into my head flashed the scene she must have witnessed, for Marianna, Silvie and I had collapsed into sleep naked and wrapped around each other as we had descended from our transports, and woken up in the same state. To even the simplest observer it would have been blatantly clear what we had been up to on that bed. The observer was Mme de Villars, and she was far from simple - as the way she was looking at me now confirmed.

I shrank back as far as I could in the little hip-bath, wishing that the floor would open and swallow me up. There was a long silence.

"Well get out and dry yourself, child," she said, folding her arms beneath her ample bosom. "Your water will be going cold."

Numbly, I obeyed her. I felt very small and young and embarrassed as she watched me dry myself, her eyes frankly appraising my figure. She was standing between me and where I had piled my clothes on a little stool by the wall, and somehow I felt too embarrassed to brush past her to get them. I also felt very awkward and foolish just standing there clutching a towel to hide at least some of my nudity.

"You are very pretty," she said, reaching forward to pluck the towel from my fingers and looking me over from head to heels. "I cannot blame my daughters for wanting to play with you, but it is very naughty of you to let them, isn't it."

It was a statement rather than a question but I felt myself nodding dumbly anyway. I knew what was going to happen the moment she swept my clothes off the stool and sat down on it. Her gaze swept over me once more and then, her eyes locking on to mine, she patted her lap with both hands. Feeling like a cross between a naughty little girl and a hypnotized rabbit, I moved forward and draped myself across her legs.

She spanked me very hard. She used the flat of her bare hand, and it stung dreadfully as she covered both cheeks of my squirming bottom with fierce slaps that soon had me whimpering. There was no warning when she suddenly thrust her hand up between my wriggling thighs and found my quim.

She was holding me down with a strong hand in the small of my back, and I could do nothing against her sudden invasion. My thighs instinctively clamped together, but it was too late. Her hand had already found its target. She got several fingers into me and began to work them in and out with an inexorable, knowing rhythm. For a few minutes I was stunned at this sudden change, but then the stinging in my freshly spanked bottom was joined by a growing heat in my cunny.

She worked me hard, holding me down and pumping her hand in me with increasing speed - and I knew that it had become her whole hand, for I was very crammed and she got very deep. I knew by the vehemence of her pumping that Mme de Villars was not doing this for my benefit but her own. It was almost as though what she was doing in my vagina was no more than an extension of the way she had punished my bottom. Yet it drove me wild!

It hurt, but it was oh, so glorious a pain! She did not stop when she got me coming, but if anything pushed even deeper until it felt as though she was cramming my every internal organ up into my ribs. She kept pumping at me until

I was veritably sobbing for mercy, for I had come so much and so hard I felt like to faint. She pulled her hand out of me so suddenly that there was an audible squelching sound and I screamed. I screamed again when she gave me two more hard slaps, one on each cheek of my throbbing backside.

I could hardly stand, my knees were so weak when she hoist me to my feet. Tears were streaming from my eyes and I rubbed my bottom frantically with both hands as she looked at me and smiled.

"My daughters are very lucky," she said quietly, her eyes once again wandering over me. "My husband also, I suspect."

She raised an eyebrow at my renewed blushes. Did she know? Or was she merely guessing? She smiled.

"I have noticed that he has been a little more tired than usual lately. Since your arrival, in fact. Does he fuck you every day?"

Her question, spoken as calmly as though she was asking about the weather, shook me. Before I could even think I blurted out "Only once. I mean he's only done me once, ma'am."

She leaned back against the wall, regarding me shrewdly. "Done you. Hmm, an amusing way of putting it, my dear."

It was as though I was mesmerized by this astonishing woman as she proceeded to question me. She was very calm, but I was boiling with embarrassment as I found myself describing how he had bent me over his desk and fucked me that first day in Algiers, and how he never missed an opportunity to feel my titties or grope my bottom and quim. It was worse when I told her about how we would sit at his desk pretending to work through papers while in reality I would be wanking him beneath the desk-top, for she burst into peals of laughter.

The really astonishing thing was that Mme de Villars did not demonstrate any resentment at all at my revelations of what I did with her husband, but rather seemed amused by it. Indeed, she expressed surprise that he had only fucked me on one occasion, and smilingly predicted that the score would rise pretty soon.

It was Mme de Villars herself who ensured that the 'score', as she called it, began to rise that very same evening. Dinner was over and Marianna and Silvie had gone to the scullery to do the washing up. Mme de Villars, who was sitting next to her husband on the other side of the table from me, took his hand and leaned towards him in a confidential manner.

"Don't you think our little Amy is rather beautiful?" she said, teasingly. "I'm astonished you've been able to keep your hands off her!"

The Colonel, her husband, was as put about by her astounding words as I was, but recovered more quickly. He coughed and cleared his throat and hurrumphed a bit then looked at his wife, who was smiling almost smugly. They clearly knew one another very well, as happily married couples should.

The long and short of it was that Mme de Villars practically instructed her husband to take me upstairs while the girls were busy!

I went with him, stunned that a wife should offer her husband the services of another girl, indeed almost insist that he took her. At the time it did not enter my head that I had not been asked; that it had been simply assumed that I would go along with it all. But then, had that not been my condition for a long while now?

I walked in front of him up the stairs and before we got to the top his hand was on my bottom. The Colonel's bedroom was about the same size as their daughters' but seemed more spacious because there was only one bed, a large one with a thick mattress and lots of pillows. He sat down upon the bed and watched in silence as I took off my clothes.

I was still tender between my legs from what Mme de Villars had done to me only hours earlier and now, on her orders almost, I was going to have to shag with her husband! The whole situation was so outrageous as to be unbelievable, and I gave up all thought. I became a marionette and as though witnessing this from a distance.

When I had finished taking off my clothes he reached for me. His mouth was hot on mine, and on my breasts. He hurt me a bit when he thrust into me, because I was still a little sore down there, and he fucked me hard. It was over in ten minutes at the most, and then I had to drag on my clothes and follow him down the stairs to make polite conversation with Marianna and Silvie when they returned from their washing-up and with Mme de Villars, who smiled and talked as though nothing of significance had occurred.

I was, as you may imagine, rather subdued and could not really pay much attention as Marianna and Silvie tried to teach me a card-game called 'bezique'. Ever since my father had married me off to Mr Mansfield my body had been at the disposal of others, with little or no thought for my own wishes in the matter. And now this family, generous and kind as they were, had joined the list - the seemingly endless list! - of people who required my service for their sexual desires.

Mme de Villars smiled and nodded when Marianna suggested that we retire to the bed-chamber. It was early, not much after half past nine. Mme de Villars gave me a significant look as I followed her daughters from the room, and actually winked at me. It was clear that she knew, and was happy about, what would happen to me when we got upstairs!

My head span at what an extraordinary woman she was. In the last, what, six hours she had spanked me across her knee then made my quim sore with her fingering of me; then she had virtually instructed her husband to take me upstairs and fuck me; now she was sending me to bed with her daughters knowing full well that they would want sex as well!

EIGHTEEN

It took Colonel de Villars almost a month longer to organize papers for me, and arrange a sea passage. It was a strange and exhausting month!

I slept each night with Marianna and Silvie. As I have said, they were both beautiful, with glossy, dark brown hair which they wore in ringlets. Both had dark eyes fringed with long, curling eyelashes (and knew how to use them to advantage!) and full-lipped, smiling mouths. Though Silvie was the taller and had a riper figure, they were both deliciously shapely. This, together with their light-hearted gaiety, already turned many a head, as was obvious when they took me about on their daily engagements once we had got my European-style clothes sorted out.

By day they were the sweetest and most demure of girls, but at night they became positively naughty. None of us bothered to wear nightgowns, and Silvie's single bed was hardly slept in. Sometimes my jaw ached from all the licking I did between virgin thighs, but at least they insisted on pleasuring me in return.

They made a game of it and always worked on me both at the same time. I confess it was a thrilling and voluptuous experience to have two beautiful, naked girls kissing and stroking and licking me. I also confess that the sensations they aroused in me were so glorious that I often held back as long as I could to prolong them. They were always thrilled when they made me come and kept me going as long as they could, giggling with excitement and clapping their hands and, nicest of all, lapping up my juices greedily.

Another example of their innate naughtiness, and of their sense of humour as well came on the evening I asked Marianna if she had a pair of scissors I could borrow. She stroked the hair on my head, and said it was lovely and that I must not cut it. And that my fingernails did not need doing either.

Blushing, I explained that it was not my head-hair nor my fingernails that needed trimming but my other hair. There was a moment of puzzlement, then Marianna's eyes got so wide as she suddenly understood that I got a fit of the giggles. I told her, truthfully, that I had got so used to being as bare as a young girl down there during my servitude in the brothel that now my bush had grown back, thicker and coarser, I found it ugly and uncomfortable. I did not have a razor available to me, but with sharp scissors I would be able to trim it short and neat.

The girls listened to me with eyes like saucers and mouths hanging open in amazement. The thought of such a thing was astonishing to them. Then they took up the idea with enthusiasm and it became a game. Silvie rummaged in the dressing-table drawer and came back with a comb and the scissors they used when they trimmed their hair. They insisted, vieing with one another, on performing the task for me.

Lying back on a bed with one's knees as wide as they can get, while two loving, giggling girls comb and stroke and coo is luxurious. They trimmed me with such enormous caution lest they nick me that it was almost comic. Marianna insisted on putting the curls they clipped so carefully into a handkerchief on the excuse that she wanted to keep them as a souvenir.

Then they discovered my brand.

It had been hidden by my thick fuzz, and the trimming revealed it. I had almost forgotten its existence but the sisters were horrified. They stared from my eyes to my crotch and back to my eyes, and then both began to weep, relapsing into French and sobbing "Pouvre Aimie! Pouvre Aimie!"

I had to cuddle and comfort them. They asked if it had been absolute agony, which it had been but I played down the fact. I assured them that it had not been too bad, and that once healed I did not feel it. I told them I thought it was really rather pretty. This thought startled them. They set to it to finish clipping me.

When they had done and my curls were neatly knotted into the handkerchief, they spent a long time tracing the shape of the brand with their fingertips and cooing over it and kissing it. That, naturally, turned into more pointed activity and soon the three of us were entwined.

The next afternoon Marianna came to me when I was alone in the bedroom and blushingly offered me a present. She had bought it, she said, when she had gone to the market that morning, and hoped I would not refuse it. It was a little leather case held closed with a narrow strap and a little brass buckle. Inside was a gentleman's travelling set - a badger-hair shaving brush with a horn handle, a brass cylinder containing a stick of shaving soap, and a small, ivory-handled razor. There was even a rolled-up strap of leather to use as a strop.

It was a beautiful present, and so thoughtful! I hugged the dear girl, and we both wept a little.

The girls absorbed everything I could teach them as if they were scholars mugging up for an examination. The one would watch while I played with the other, and they would both practice on me - with more enthusiasm as each night passed.

Silvie was fascinated with the idea of the cock, and

kept asking me about sizes and how it felt when a sturdy member thrust its way up. She simply could not believe something of the dimensions I described could possibly fit into the soft sheath even two fingers seemed to fill. Then one night she suddenly produced a candle from under her pillow.

It was a large candle, over a foot in length and tapering from about an inch across at the top to fully double that at the other end. She was wide-eyed and blushing as she showed it to me, and suddenly looked even younger than her seventeen years. She stumbled over her words, but my understanding of her fascination, and the way her eyes flicked nervously from mine to the object in her hand and to the place between my legs, made it perfectly clear to me what was in her mind.

It was outrageous, but at the same time it was sweet and even a little comic. I indulged her, and Marianna too, for the older girl was watching with fascination. I lay back and caressed myself to get moist. I parted my love-lips with my fingers and addressed the tip of the candle to the opening of my sheath. As I pressed the cool, rigid tallow cylinder into myself, pushing it in a little, pulling back, then pressing further, Silvie's eyes grew enormous. By the time I had got perhaps half the length into myself, her mouth was an 'O' of amazement and her eyes were like to fall out of her head.

I moved the candle in imitation of shagging for a little while, then slowly eased it out. I was not getting much from it, save the pleasure of the girls' reactions. Silvie took it from me with trembling fingers, and held it up and stared at it. The sheen of my moisture covered about eight inches of the tallow, and Silvie's eyes ran back and forth along it as if measuring it in her head.

"C'est vrai!" she said, in an awed whisper that almost made me giggle. "C'est vingt centimetres! Plus! Mon Dieu!"

With a suddenness that took me by surprise, she span round, threw herself back onto the bed and moved the candle towards her quim. I grabbed her impetuous hand to stop her.

"No, Silvie. No!" I said urgently. She was a virgin, and could not do what I had done without damaging her maidenhead. I tried to explain to her, told her what her virginity was, and about that little barrier of skin which preserves it. I told her how it would be torn by entry, and would hurt at least a bit, and cause a little bleeding. To my surprise she blushed, and then giggled.

"It is of no concern," she said through her giggles. "It happened to me a long while ago, the first time I tried to put two fingers in. I was quite young, and it frightened me a little because I had got carried away and did not mean to do it. But I've got two fingers in lots of times since. Even three once or twice!"

What a minx! Clearly, she had been delighting herself for a long time, and what I did with her was icing on the cake, as the saying goes.

Even as she was speaking she had brought the candle to her cunny and was already pressing it slowly home. She copied exactly what she had seen me do, pushing, retreating a little, pushing further. Unlike me, Silvie's fingers began to circle and excite her clitty as she moved the candle in and out. She was gripping the butt in a tense fist and was moving the candle several inches at a time, her eyes tight shut.

Slowly, Silvie's eyebrows arched and her soft mouth drooped open and her breathing became ragged. I felt Marianna move close beside me as we watched enthralled. Silvie was quite gone away from us. Nothing in the world existed for her except the fingers that were on her visibly pulsing clitty, and the thick candle with which she was shagging herself, faster and harder, until she caught her breath and spasms rippled through the muscles of her belly and thighs, and she sobbed into a violent come.

It was I who removed the candle from Silvie's oozing, swollen quim, for she was utterly spent and lay like a rag doll. She had got a considerable amount into herself, nearly as much as I had in fact, and I became somewhat worried lest she had harmed herself. In fact she had not, for the next day, although she moved a little gingerly and rolled her eyes at me in mock-agony, she professed nothing save delight at her experience - an experience she was eager to repeat most nights. I did wonder how she was going to persuade whatever husband she eventually found that she was a virgin, for soon she was getting nearly the whole candle up her sheath; but then, she was a resourceful girl and would probably think of something.

If the girls were natural and enthusiastic - if demanding - in their relation to me, matters were very different with their mother.

Apart from contriving to ensure that her husband got plenty of time alone with me in his study each day, of which I shall say more later, she re-organised my bath-time to the mornings. The girls were always out then, at the market or visiting friends, and she always had several hours alone with me.

She lightened my task in one respect, for the water in the boiler would already be hot, but made bathing something of a trial in other respects. She sat on the stool by the wall and watched me as I removed my clothes, her eyes piercing. Sometimes she chose to soap my body herself, but usually just watched as I stood up in the hip-bath and poured water over myself and worked up a lather with the soap, before sitting down to rinse off.

It was obvious to me that she regarded this as a performance for her lascivious entertainment. She enjoyed observing my nakedness, watching me move and turn and run my hands over myself. She exclaimed aloud with delight the first time I bathed before her after I had shaved myself with Marianna's gift, and spent a long while exploring my brand in close detail, with her fingers as well as her eyes. Drying myself also became a performance, she breathing more and more quickly, me becoming increasingly tense, for I knew full well what the next step was to be.

At this stage she would become very commanding. I was required, once I had towelled myself dry and deposited the used towels into the laundry basket, to stand before her with my hands behind my head and relate what her daughters and I had got up to in bed, and what her husband had done with me the last time she had arranged for us to be together. I also had to tell her whether I had come or not, and confess that I was a very naughty girl.

Then she would get me over her knee and spank my bottom. She seldom spanked me as hard as that first time, but it was always hard enough to bring tears to my eyes and make me yelp a little. What followed varied according to her mood.

Occasionally she would hold me down over her knees and finger me until I came. Sometimes she would undo her blouse to reveal beautiful, matronly breasts with aureolae the size of crown coins and nipples like nuts, and I would suck and nibble at them while she stroked my hair. More often, she would slip forward a little on the stool, and lean back against the wall and part her knees. Then, I would crawl up beneath her skirts and do for her what I had done for her daughters last night.

She was a ripe woman, full and mature. The lips of her sex were plump and soft, and so welcoming that I could get my nose as well as my mouth between them. Her clitoris was the size of a peanut, and always ready at attention for me. Her orgasms were controlled, never more than a rippling against my face, and she never held my head, but her juices were copious and I sometimes felt like to drown in them - but they were delicious and often times I had a quiet little come myself while I was delving in her.

Often, if I had given her an especially good orgasm, she

would spank me again afterwards, as though the act of spanking my bare bottom was all part of her thrill - which, when you think about it, it was!

As regards to her husband, as I have said Mme de Villars contrived daily occasions when he could be alone with me. She usually managed matters by taking her daughters out somewhere for an hour or sending them off on some errand or other.

The Colonel took very full advantage of the new arrangements you may be sure! If all three of his womenfolk were going out, the front door would hardly have shut behind them before he was hurrying me towards the stairs and fumbling with my clothes. Sometimes I was half naked even before we got to the bedroom!

He need not really have got so frantic and eager, of course, for he was obviously going to get his shag anyway. But it seemed that the secretiveness of our enterprise, and probably the easy availability of a compliant young woman, excited him greatly.

Our bouts took on a pattern. As soon as we were in the bedroom and the last of my clothes were off, he would have me on my back on the bed with my feet in the air for his first fuck. These were invariably quick and rather frantic, and he sometimes hurt me a little in his eagerness. Then, when we had time - which we usually did when Mme de Villars had taken her daughters out - we got down to the real business of the session.

He too would get himself naked and, knowing I had been a brothel-girl, required me to massage him while he toyed with my body. It was not a massage such as one would get in a Turkish bath, to relax the muscles. This massage, rather, was designed to bring a particular muscle out of relaxation, and included mouth and dangling breasts as well as kneading hands.

He liked me to rub my breasts across his body and face while I was caressing his other parts with my hands. Often he would suck and nibble my nipples quite sharply, which hurt a little but was nice just the same. He liked me to use my mouth on him, not only to get him up again, but quite frequently in lieu of the second fuck with which our sessions usually concluded.

He also introduced me to what at first I thought a strange act. A few times he got me on my back and knelt astride my ribs. He would place his cock in the valley between my breasts, and I would squash them down on it, and then he would rut. It was as though he was shagging my titties, and he seemed to go wild for it. With all my experience, nobody had ever wanted that before, and I confess that looking up at his straining body while I squeezed my breasts around his thrusting cock did not leave me un-aroused. When he came, which he did each time and explosively too, his jism spurted right up to my chin and, knowing what men like, I then scooped it up with my fingers and popped it into my mouth. His eyes shone each time he watched me swallow the essence of his come, as though he were some kind of conqueror. If only he had known that I actually found the act as erotic as he did!

Despite Mme de Villars' machinations, there were still occasions when the Colonel and I had no recourse but to retire to his office. We still usually had time for fairly protracted activity, though naturally most of my clothes stayed on. He still took great pleasure in having me rub him with my hand, and occasionally had me bend over the desk with my skirts up on my back and my drawers around my knees while he shafted me heartily from the rear.

His favourite activity, though, was to push his chair back from the desk and get me kneeling between his spread knees, cupping his balls in my hands and sucking hard on his cock.

He could never resist me long when I sucked him off, and would buck into his come after little more than five minutes. He told me once that his wife, although she would sometimes kiss and lick him as part of their build-up to sex, never actually took him into her mouth and certainly never let him come down her throat as I did. He thought me wonderful because of it. Little did he know that I enjoyed it almost as much as he did!

Came the day Mme de Villars sent me to the Colonel's barracks with a message for him. It was the first time I had been back to there, but it was not difficult to find the way. She gave me a note to present at the gate and I had no problem gaining entry, though I thought one of the guards looked at me rather peculiarly.

I gave him the envelope I had brought for him and waited while he read its contents. Then he stood up and gave me that look of his. I knew already what he wanted - what else could it have been? - and was ready to give it to him. I had not even bothered to wear any drawers, and had on a front-buttoning blouse. I was not wrong in my assumption, and in moments the Colonel had me on my back on the floor of his office, my skirts above my waist, and his cock firmly planted up me.

He did not take long and the floor-boards were hard under my back, but it was nice all the same. Afterwards he sent his steward for coffee and cognac and we sat and chatted amiably. He told me that my papers were nearly ready, and that he had arranged passage for me on a dhow from Algiers to Gibraltar and a British merchantman from thence to England.

It suddenly struck me that he must have had to lay out money for it all, and I got rather flustered about how I was going to repay him. He laughed and told me I already had, giving my knee a squeeze. I was, for a minute, overcome with the sweet generosity of this man, and indeed his whole family, and wept a little. Then, before I left him I insisted upon adding a little more to my 'repayment' by insisting on giving him as nice a gobble as I could. Since he had fucked me to a finish only ten minutes ago he took a little while to get hard and then quite a long while to reach his come, which made it rather nice for both of us.

It was only when I left the barracks that I learned why that soldier at the gate had looked at me so sharply. Stupidly, it had not occurred to me that I might be recognized if I went back there. That I had been became shockingly obvious when, walking past an alleyway outside the barracks, I was grabbed and dragged in. For a moment I was terrified I was about to be robbed, or have my throat cut. Instead, I was thrown breathless against a mud-brick wall, and found myself staring into the greedy eyes of a group of soldiers.

I recognized a couple of them from the journey across the desert. They knew who I was. Knew what I had been. What could I do? I am hardly over five feet tall, and female. These were great hulking soldiers, five of them, all towering over me. Had they wanted to, they could have raped me then and there in the alley, and I could never have fought them off. When one of them grabbed my arm and began to tug me along the alley, I went with them. Once again, I had no choice. All I could do was pray they would not be too rough with me.

I was marched along the alley, my progress made ungainly by the way I had to twist away from the hands that groped at my breasts and backside. They took me through a door and across a room that looked to be some kind of poky coffee parlour or drinking house. Another door, and I was spun into a dingy room, with the soldiers crowding in after me. The door banged shut. The only light was from a wide, unglazed window high in one wall.

I backed against the wall as hands reached for me. There was no escape. They were going to have me whether I wished it or no. All I could do was save my clothes from getting ripped, and make them as easy on me as I could. I held out my hands to hold them off.

"Arretez! Attend! Je vais faire!" I cried, hoping I had got the French right. 'Stop! Wait! I will do it!'

I stared at them as appealingly as I could, and moved my fingers to the buttons of my blouse. Mercifully, they stopped and held off, watching like a pack of dogs as I undressed myself for them. I had chosen clothes that were easy for the Colonel to get off me. Thus it was quick and simple for me now. In a moment, my blouse was off and I was stepping out of my skirts.

Hardly had I dropped the garments onto a wooden chair than they were on me. There was no bed or couch. I was borne to the floor. Rough hands were all over me. Rank breath assailed my face as greedy lips captured my mouth. My legs were dragged apart. Rough cloth grazed the insides of my thighs as the first of them thrust into me.

They took turns, the one having me being urged on by his fellows to speed up so they could have their turns. They had me on my back. They had me from behind, kneeling on all fours. They had my mouth. Several had my bottom. Although there were only five of them they spurred each other on, and they all had me two or three times. By the time they had finished and left me, laughing and clapping one another on the back as if at a job well done, I lay sprawled on the floor exhausted.

Then, as I began to drag myself to my knees, I heard a low chuckle. I looked around dizzily. Around the door peered several grinning faces, two bearded Arabs and one a tribal African. They crept through the portal, their intentions obvious. I resigned myself. I was naked, and too weak to fight them off anyway.

I made to roll over onto my back and spread my legs, but they preferred the other way, the way some men like women for what they have in common with boys. They got me onto all fours, my knees wide, and took turns on me in my bottom. I was too weary to resist, nor to co-operate neither. I could do no more than crouch there on all fours as they parted my cheeks, and bumped against me until they found my entrance, then gripped me by my hips and thrust in.

One of them, the African I suspect, was bigger than the other two and made me cry out with his size as his balls slapped against my body with the force of his rutting. I bore it. I did not come; they were too quick and too rough. I did, though - call it my survival instinct! - push back against them and wriggle my hips and clench myself to try to bring them off as quickly as I could. It seemed to work, for none of them took long before spurting into me.

And then they were gone.

Wearily, I dragged myself up and struggled to pull on my discarded clothes. On trembling legs, I crept to the door and peeped out. No-one was about, thank heavens, and I managed to escape the place and the alley without further molestation. I got back to the house safely, and hurried to wash off the sticky mess they had left on me and to use my douche.

When I came out of the scullery Marianna expressed concern that I looked pale and unwell, but I put her off by saying I had probably been in the sun too much. That night I had to be careful lest Marianna or Silvie notice the scratches my ravishers had left on my thighs and breasts, but I got away with it undetected, even though they both now paid a great deal of attention to my now-shaven cunny.

Came the day I was to leave and the whole family came to see me off. Right to the end they had remained generous to a degree that was almost embarrassing. Marianna had given me several frocks and skirts and blouses, which she, Silvie and Mme de Villars had altered to fit me properly. I had also been given lots of petticoats and underthings, really pretty ones, and Mme de Villars had taken me into the local market and bought me several pairs of shoes.

Silvie gave me two hairbrushes and a lovely set of combs made of tortoiseshell, and the Colonel gave me a sturdy leather hatbox with a lock, in which I put Silvie's gifts as well as Marianna's and the precious contents of the little bundle I had arrived here with.

With a suitcase packed with my new clothes and my hatbox of personal treasures, I was better fitted out to face the world than I had ever been before. First, though, I had to kiss these generous people good-bye, and it was a great wrench.

All three of we girls were blubbing again as we kissed and hugged, and promised to write to one another very often. Mme de Villars' eyes were moist as she crushed me in a motherly embrace. Even the Colonel looked emotional as he too kissed and hugged me.

He escorted me up. or rather along, the gangplank, for the vessel he had found for me was not large. It was of the kind I have since learned is called a 'dhow', a type of boat common in the Mediterranean and Arab seas, with a single mast and a big, triangular sail called a 'lateen'.

Colonel de Villars introduced me to the captain, an olive-skinned man, squat and stocky of build, and with enormous black moustaches. This gentleman smiled broadly, shook hands with the Colonel and bowed deeply to me, and led us to the stern end of the boat and my little cabin.

The Colonel apologized for the smallness of my accommodations, explaining that we should be in Gibraltar within twenty-four hours given a fair wind, and supervised the stowing of my case by the sailor who had carried it for me. That done and the captain and sailor having left us, he gave me that look of his.

I felt my spirit droop a little, for I was very tired. Last night, our last night ever together for sure, Silvie and Marianna had been very active and persistent with their hands and their tongues and their candles, and had kept me coming for ages. Then this morning, after breakfast, Mme de Villars had taken me up to her room to give me, as she put it, 'something to remember her by'. The 'souvenir', if one may call it that, was a very thorough spanking with her hairbrush followed by half an hour with my head bobbing beneath her skirts.

Thus, when the Colonel gave me his look I was not enthusiastic. Nevertheless, I bent over, hoist my skirts up onto my back, and pulled down my drawers for him.

He expressed astonishment at the glowing redness of my backside, and even more astonishment when I explained about his wife's habit of spanking me for being naughty. He found it amusing!

He also found it exciting, to judge from the vigour with which he then proceeded to shaft me. As I have said before, he was quite substantial as to his cock. Now, gripping me by my waist and thrusting so hard his breeches slapped against my stinging buttocks, he got very deep; deep enough to get me going in only half a dozen thrusts, and have me coming in half a dozen more. He changed his grip to my hip-bones when he neared his own climax, pulling me on really hard, and he came with a series of low grunts matched by my own as my quim milked him.

He kissed me gently before he left, on the cheek, almost like a fond uncle. It was nice, even though he could not resist giving my left breast a bit of a squeeze in parting.

The vessel cast off almost immediately. I was too weary to go out on deck to wave goodbye and, I confess, too heart-

222

swollen with happiness at the prospect which now lay before me. I had my passage booked; I had my letters of introduction from my dear Captain and Lieutenant, and even the money-order, all of which would give me respectability. I would be able to shrug off my past. I had a future!

I was soon to learn that a woman travelling alone can take nothing for granted ...

BONUS PAGES OVERLEAF

We start with the first chapter of our next book, THE GENTLEMAN'S CLUB by a new author, John Angus:

1

Sir Edward Rawlins stared eagerly out the window of the helicopter as the island came into view. There was little to see, for the aircraft approach lane was designed to minimize sightseeing from the air. All he could catch sight of was the lush tropical greenery, the long, lush white sanded beaches, and the red tiled roof of the large and beautiful main residence building.

His chest was gripped by an anxious tightness as the helicopter came into land, and he still found it hard to believe the fanciful tales which had been told him about The Viceroy Club, the gentleman's association of which he was now a probationary member.

The helicopter landed perfectly and he, its only passenger stepped out to be greeted by a thin faced older man in a three piece suit. If the warmth bothered him he gave no sign as he bowed, actually bowed to Sir Edward before directing two other men in ties and tails into the helicopter for his bags.

"Sir Edward, my name is Anthony. On behalf of the staff let me be the first to greet you and welcome you to the Viceroy."

"Um, er, well, thank you," Edward said, licking his lips a trifle nervously.

His particular, well, preferences had been a long held secret, and he was uncomfortable with anyone knowing about them. He was still far from certain how the Viceroy had come to be aware of them.

"I'm at your disposal, Sir, if you'd like a tour of the facilities. Or I'll show you to your suite if you'd like to relax."

"I'd, er, rather like a quick tour actually," Edward said hesitantly.

"Of course, sir. Your bags will be taken to your suite and your things made ready for you. In the meantime, if you would come this way please, sir?"

Edward smiled as the man bowed again and swept his arm towards a Rolls sitting a few yards away. He was happy that this place, at least, had help which knew its place. That was something of a rarity even in London's better shops and clubs. He walked to the Rolls, where a Chauffeur bowed and held the door for him. Anthony got in beside him and the chauffeur pulled away from the helicopter.

The ride was a brief one, ending at a small garage set amongst the trees. The chauffeur hopped out and opened the door on his side, bowing again as Anthony got out. Edward preened at this respect, for he seldom experienced it back home, where, despite his wealth and undeniable physical attractiveness he was something of an outcast, the butt of jokes amongst his peers and even in the mass media.

Edward was in his early thirties, yet his boyish, handsome face was far from the only thing about him which was immature. He had a tendency to sulk when he didn't get his way, was a well-known coward and bully, and had a cruel streak which made him such a tyrant to his servants that it had proved almost impossible to keep any, even at triple wages.

Anthony led him down a winding, flower-lined path and thence into another building, where they were met by a small, gruff man in working clothes.

"A carriage for two, in Sir Edward's name," Anthony said.

"Right away, Sir Edward," the man said respectfully, bowing and tipping his hat before hurrying away.

Anthony and Edward followed, and Edward suddenly halted, brought up short in astonishment as the man opened what appeared to be cages and brought out two women.

The women were both quite tall, and muscular, and entirely nude. Their bodies gleamed darkly, heavily tanned, and each had a sort of harness about her upper torso.

The leather harness was composed of straps over their shoulders and around their chests. Both women had their arms bound in leather sleeves which pulled them behind their backs and then up high, the tops of the sleeves, obviously containing their hands, bound to collars at the back of their necks.

Neither woman struggled or made any effort to protest as they were led towards a small, low-slung carriage and their harnesses attached to the front. As Edward's wide-eyed stare took in every detail he watched the man attach lead lines to small rings in their nipples. These lines led under their arms and back to the carriage.

"Step aboard, Sir Edward," Anthony said, bowing and motioning him towards the carriage.

Edward obeyed in a daze, climbing up and taking his place on a heavily padded seat while Anthony got aboard next to him.

"These are their reins, of course," Anthony said.

Edward took them, staring at them, then ahead at the tight, firm buttocks of the two women now attached to the carriage.

"And that's for encouragement, of course," Anthony said, pointing at the buggy whip protruding from a small holder next to Edward's seat.

"How, I mean to say, how um -"

"As you would horses or oxen," Anthony smiled.

Edward swallowed then snapped the reins. The two women started walking forward, then began to jog, leading them along a paved, cobblestone path through the grounds.

"My God," he said, shaking his head.

"Our membership prefers a civilized mode of transportation rather than smelly cars or unsightly golf carts," Anthony said with a smile.

The carriage took them to the edge of a rolling eighteen hole golf course, where Anthony explained a few of the finer points, then to a large, beautiful pool of water below a waterfall, then down to the beaches before turning towards what he called the barn.

"We're quite proud of the barn, really," Anthony said. "Our breeding program is well underway now. Our ambition is to be self-sustaining. That's not to say occasional new blood won't added into the mix, but we won't need the constant recruitment we now require to satisfy our members' needs."

"How do you er, uh, get your new recruits?"

"Oh we have a number of ways. We have contacts out there, people who recruit for us, who are on the watch for just the right kind of girl for the Viceroy. Usually these are young ladies with little if any family who will not really cause much of a stir when they disappear. Sometimes, of course, we recruit what we call special girls."

"Special?"

"Oh, certain young ladies whom a member or members considers especially deserving of such treatment, if you know what I mean."

"So I could have a particular girl, er, imported then if I wanted?"

"Certainly, for a price."

"I have just the one in mind," he said. He licked his lips at the thought of Amanda...

Now for the next dip into the Victorian Scrapbook, vignettes from a sterner age, by Stephen Rawlings, author of the very popular 'Jane and Her Master'. Mr Rawlings also has a library of unpublished books on our web site.

THE CORRECTION OF THE DAUGHTERS OF THE WELL-TO-DO

Though it was not unusual for mothers, even of the highest classes, to chastise their daughters themselves, it was also quite normal for the duty to be delegated to a governess or the principal of a 'finishing school' where young ladies were taught those accomplishments that would prepare them to be mistresses of their husbands households, and hostesses for the entertainments he gave. Some of these 'schools' catered specially for erring daughters who required to be 'straightened out' or punished for some misdemeanour, and which advertised openly in such respect able magazines as 'The Family Herald,' 'Queen' and 'The Englishwoman's Domestic Magazine', the latter published by Samuel Beeton, husband of the famous Mrs Beeton of cookbook fame.

The Misses Fulcher on Chiswick, and Mrs Walter Smith of Clifton, were among those who offered courses of correction for erring girls, ranging from a short visit of a few days, for a summary correction, to stays of several months so that the lessons learnt from birch and cane could be absorbed and retained.

The following is an imaginary account of what may well have taken place in just such an establishment, when a girl was caught in 'the shameful act', as masturbation was known, or nurturing romantic feelings about some man (or, indeed, woman) other than one selected for her by her parents or Guardian.

228

The regime described is based on the published advice to mothers by a leading physician of the time for girls in this position.

"Celeste, your parents, quite rightly, will not tolerate this mooning calf love in one who, at nineteen years of age, should be acquiring the ways of womanhood. Your stupid antics might just be forgivable, though deplorable, in a thirteen year old, enamoured of her gym mistress, or an unseasoned girl of six teen, swept away by her first awareness of male beauty, but you are past that age, and it is now my duty to see that you approach these matters in the way of the grown woman you are."

She bent her gaze even more sternly on the pink cheeked delinquent, standing nervously on the small Persian carpet that adorned the polished parquet in front of her desk.

"While you are in my care, I shall furnish you with a comprehensive programme of study, exercise, and firm discipline," she promised, "you will benefit from a simple diet, regular purging of your bowels, and a cold shower on rising every morning. It is also well known that too close confinement of the female parts can lead to inflammation and overstimulation so, from now on, you will go without drawers at all times, allowing the air to circulate and cool your blood. There will be other practical measures as well, novels will be forbidden you, they only inflame a young girl's passions, and lead to unhealthy exuberance of your female parts but, above all, I think your moral fibre will best be stiffened by systematic applications of the rod."

Celeste's eyes widened at the word, but her mentor chose to ignore the unspoken appeal.

"It is an exercise in mental control," she continued, "that I have always found effective in firming up minds softened by exposure to too much romantic nonsense, and you will start with six cuts of the rod, each night before retiring, to dispel any weak thoughts that you may be prey to. We will commence your rehabilitation at once," she announced firmly, "kindly remove your drawers."

"But Madame..."

"Do you question my judgement, girl?"

"No, no. Of course not, Madame."

"Then bare yourself at once, and prepare to suffer. Believe me, I only do this in your best interests."

Seemingly resolved to maintain something of her dignity in the light of the uselessness of further protest, Celeste gracefully opened her wrapper, revealing a delicious figure encased in a tightly laced satin corset, that lent elegance and a certain voluptuousness to her natural feminine charms.

Her smooth and ample breasts seemed set to spill over the top of the lacy cups, that formed the top of the figure moulding garment while, below the narrow whalebone constricted waist, the jut of her buttocks was discernible through the soft batiste of the thigh long drawers, with their pretty blue ribbons at knee and waist.

With fingers that trembled a little, despite her resolve, she loosened the blue satin bow at her hip and, hesitating but slightly, slipped the soft undergarment over her swelling haunches. Somehow, in her agitation, the garment had worked it self into her crotch, the thin material penetrating the plump moist gash of her Venus lips in front, the deep rose divide of her buttock cheeks behind.   Her cheeks above flamed even more hotly, a she tugged the damp gusset from its musky seat, and down her straight slim thighs, until she could step out of it and make to add the soft damp scrap to the folds of the wrapper she had placed on a chair nearby.

"You will not be needing those in future," Madame reminded her, holding out the wicker basket from beneath her desk, and the girl, covered in confusion, hastily dropped the delicate garment in amongst the waste paper.

Now she stood, her blushes scarlet, naked below the

waist, save for her little buttoned boots, with their rows of glistening fastenings, and the embroidered black silk stockings, tight gartered below the knee, her buttocks quite nude, the air cool upon them.

And what a pretty little bottom she boasted - or, perhaps one should say, how delightfully compact, for Celeste was a woman, not a half formed child and there was, in their neat tight masses, a certain feminine fullness. The rounds were perfectly formed tight ivory flesh, deeply divided, and the thighs so slim and straight that there was a little arch between them through which the careful observer, and who would not give careful regard to such a subject, might just detect a soft stray curl of dark fur, the deepest reach of that luxuriant tangle that formed the enticing delta between her thighs in front.

Above this amorous thicket the deep cut busk blade of the rigid corset held her belly flat and encouraged her to maintain that upright posture that is the true grace of a lovely woman. Now that posture was still held, as she pointed her chin bravely up, but her underlip was caught between her sharp white teeth, that it might not tremble and betray her state of inner turmoil.

Celeste had never been corrected in the manner proposed before. As a child, of course, she had felt hand or slipper on her girlish bottom, and hairbrush, or even the strap, as befitted one of her station, but she had grown beyond all that, or so she had thought. Now the prospect of a return to physical chastisement set her belly fluttering. In any case, she had never suffered the rod before and her fellow pretty 'penionieres' at the Academy had made it clear to her that it was something to be feared and avoided at all costs, even though they might attempt a sort of bravado to cover their terror of its application.

Even if she had had any doubts about the veracity of their accounts, they could have been no more than a tease for a newcomer joining the house at rather more than the usual age of entrance, she had had ample opportunity to observe the stiff legged gait, the red-rimmed eyes, the bitten lips and pained wincing, as a recently corrected girl placed her ridged and glowing bottom on a hard seated chair. At this austere academy all chairs had hard seats, and straight backs, to encourage good posture, and such revealing squirms and squeals were almost inevitable with a well-whipped posterior, though woe betide a girl who could not adequately control her reactions in Madame's presence, as her bruises were crushed against the unforgiving wood. It was not unknown for an unfortunate girl to be ordered a further dose of the same medicine, who had done no more than moan, or make an unladylike grunt of pain, as she had contacted the comfortless perch with the newly raised welts on her bottom.

Now, as Celeste awaited her first experience of this painful condition, that same careful observer, who had spotted the frail pubic fronds from behind the shapely thighs, would not fail to detect the slight, but unmistakable, clenching of the trim buttocks, mute testimony to the tension within, despite the cool exterior, though the iron grip of the busk bone on her belly obscured its incipient fluttering.

Madame viewed the pale faced maiden, standing half naked before her.

"If I did no know it already, the fact that you have not received corporal correction here before would have been apparent from your deportment to date alone," she observed, drily.

"Let me explain. These corrections are intended not so much to punish, although there is of course a penal element involved in your very presence here, but equally to temper a girl's steel, and enable her to display the fortitude and resolution appropriate to a young woman of her station. You are expected to strip quickly, modestly, and without delay or fuss.

"The position to be taken at all times, requires a degree of will to maintain. You will find it helps you to develop and bring out your hidden reserves.

"No deviation of any kind is allowed, no flinching, no clenching of the buttocks, no turning away of the flank, no outcry or pleading. It goes without saying that it is a very serious offence to try and protect your buttocks with your hands, or to rise without permission. The former will lead inevitably to, at least, the caning of the offending hand or hands, the latter to extra strokes or even to the strokes already taken being disregarded, and the whole count to be taken again."

Throughout this dire recital Celeste had tried to maintain her composure and her pride, but her first flush had changed to a paling of her cheek, and the sharp white teeth had bitten even deeper into her lip. She pressed her dimpled knees tightly together to try and overcome the trembling in her legs.

"Normally a girl of your age would be expected to take up her position without further instruction," Madame observed, "but you are new here and I will explain matters just this once. You advance to the chair there," pointing to a heavy straight backed and armless structure of age blackened oak, "and bend from the waist to grip the seat on either side. Keep your heels together, your legs braced back, quite straight, your waist dipped a little to cant up your buttocks to accept the rod, and tilt back your head, so that you may see yourself in the mirror. Eyes open at all times, please, and maintain your position at throughout, exactly. As I have said, this is as much an exercise in fortitude and strength of will, as a correction."

She gestured to the chair in question, an unspoken invitation to the trembling novice to submit herself to the test, and Celeste advanced as instructed on shaky legs, bending to grip the seat with a hand on either side. She shuffled her feet, until the leather of her boots touched, then braced back her knees until her legs were quite straight, from naked thighs to booted ankles. She threw back her head, pulling back her shoulders and letting her waist dip. As she did so she could feel the skin on her buttocks stretching, her pelvis tilting to throw her ivory nates into even greater prominence. She gave an involuntary shiver as the cold air reminded her that they were bare and vulnerable, and that they were completely open to the cut of the Madame's rod. The cool caress had brought home to her why she was bent here like this, and what was to be done to her and, if she had had a lingering doubts on the subject, they fled away as she stared, open eyed as ordered, into the mirror in front of her and saw Madame standing behind her, flexing a dismal length of black misery in her hands.

"Now," Madam announced, as if declaring a sudden new truth, rather than the doleful fate that Celeste was already only too aware of, and awaiting in dread, "I am going to give you six cuts across your naked bottom. I shall use my best whalebone rod since, despite your inexperience, you are already a well-formed young woman, and will take no harm from it. Anything less would not be as effective in hastening your progress, and I shall make sure you obtain the utmost benefit of its corrective powers which, I can assure you, are well attested to by your predecessors in this exercise. Call up your courage, ma petite, brace back those legs, and prepare to demonstrate that courage and self-discipline that are the true hallmark of all those who have passed through my house."

And here is the next episode of ERICA by Rex Saviour. This can be enjoyed wherever you start! Rex is trying to cure Erica of her hangups by systematic desentisation - exposing the subject in increasingly strong doses to what she fears most - it isn't working too well:-

"Well how do you like that?" exclaimed Hank. "Uses the belt on you most days, eh?! Bare assed?"

She nodded, blushing.

"Wowee!" He licked his lips, but evidently thought it best to change the subject. "I like the jewellery, all those snakes, but aren't they a bit - well, nasty?"

As well as the medallion he could see the snake bangles at wrists and ankles. The bands round her arms above the elbow were hidden by the jersey. They all have inconspicuous rings and hooks that snap together as required, but the miniature padlocks are symbolic only.

We were both silent, and he glanced at me enquiringly. "Is there something I missed here? Does she go for snakes, then?" He turned to Erica. "Fond of snakes, are you, girlie?"

"NO!"

"No?"

"No, I -"

"Yes, girlie? Go on?"

"Oh God, I'm so scared of them, they're horrible, horrible, I hate wearing them, it makes me think real ones are creeping all over me, slimy -"

"Snakes aren't slimy," I said. I was always pointing that out to her, but she never seemed to take it in.

"Slimy and slithery. Slither slither slither!"

The very thought of it was making a squirm more than the dildo was. "It's a hang-over from an unfortunate childhood," I explained. "A very unfortunate childhood ... hush dear, you're getting too excited."

"Sorry, Uncle Rex," she said meekly, but I saw tears in those bright blue eyes of hers.

"You'd better tell Hank about systematic desensitising."

"Uncle believes in this systematic desensitisation therapy - it's very scientific, he's shown me books about it, it means if I wear more and more snakes it will cure me of my fear of snakes. In the end. So being with snakes is good for

235

me, just like being dressed like this will make me less shy. He believes."

I do believe that. "We!" I said. "We believe!"

She hesitated. "We believe."

"And about beating? I wouldn't want him to think I am unkind to you."

"And - and - and so, you see, if I don't accept the desensitisation gracefully - well then Uncle Rex has to beat me till I do."

"Great stuff," he said. "And is all this, er, this therapy stuff, is it working?"

"Well no, no not very well, not yet. I think I'm worse." She glanced at me. "But Uncle says we have to keep trying."

"Another thing is, she doesn't like being touched by a man," I said.

"So being touched is good for her? It will cure her if it is done enough?"

"That's right," I said encouragingly. "She wriggles a bit, which proves it must be doing good."

The man winked at me, and Erica shrank back as he reached out to lay a hand on her knee. I didn't object. It must be good for her. She didn't seem to be any better, but the method surely can't be wrong. Indeed, I know it isn't. An Aunt of mine was cured of a fear of spiders by looking at a little one from a long way off, then coming closer and closer, and then doing the same with a bigger one, until at last she could even touch it.

Hank finished his beer then raised a hand to her chest. "Is it my imagination, or does the little lady have rings in her nipples?"

"Ask her," I said.

"Well, angel?"

"Yes," she said. "But there aren't any bells of them to-day."

"And no bra?"

236

She wriggled. "No!"

He glanced round to be sure nobody was watching, then reached out and pinched the left nipple through her jersey. We both noticed how she flinched away.

"God, it's true! I like that, very sexy. Er -" For the first time he seemed a little embarrassed. "Do you mind if I ask - is she wearing knickers?"

"No," she said, "no, because Uncle considers them unnecessary."

He whistled. "And does she have labial rings too as well as nipple rings? Do you, girlie?"

Erica glanced at me, but I didn't help her out.

"Uncle did put some on me, but I don't have them on now, because -"

"Because what?"

She hesitated. "Because - they got in the way of the chain -"

"Chain? What chain?" His eyes were glistening.

"To keep the snake in -"

"Snake? What snake, for God's sake?"

"It's her name for a special dildo," I explained. "I made it look as much like a snake as possible."

"Jesus! A snake dildo - she wears it all the time?"

I nudged her into speech. "Well, you see, that's what the chain is for, it comes between my legs from one round my waist. It's locked by a padlock at the back."

"My God! And no, eh? Considers them unnecessary, does he?"

She was blushing furiously as she nodded. "Unnecessary, yes, well, actually, it's more than that I suppose, he burned the ones I had and - well, actually, I don't think I'm allowed -"

"Come now," I said. "Not allowed? That's not true, Erica dear. I got some special ones for you when you first came to me, don't you remember?"

"Oh!"

"Of course you remember!"

"Yes, Uncle, you did get some for me -"

"Yes, go on, tell him."

"They had snakes embroidered on them. I just couldn't wear them, he tried to make me, he beat me every day for ages because I wouldn't but it was no good, ugh, snakes crawling over me down there - oh God, I couldn't, I couldn't, not down there -"

"You still have them, my dear," I said mildly. "They were quite expensive. You could wear them if you wanted."

"I can't, I can't, not more snakes down there!"

"But the dildo?"

"He put it in. I can't get it out because of the chain. It's horrible, it's getting warm and that will wake it up!" She was nearly in tears.

"No knickers under that apology for a mini-skirt! Wowee! This I must see!"

"Well," I said, "her chain is certainly something we're proud of, aren't we dear?"

"Yes Uncle Rex." She sounded very reluctant, but I decided to speak to her about that later.

"So you'll be glad to show our friend Hank?"

"Yes, Uncle, I suppose so." Even more reluctant, almost mutinous. I would not forget that, and she saw the prospect of the belt in my face. She would not aggravate me any further, I knew. I looked round the lounge. It would be somewhat embarrassing to do it here in the cafeteria, and we mustn't miss the flight by causing a disturbance.

"Come on," I said. "Over by the wall." I could see that a few men were curious as we walked over, but not enough to matter. "That's right, you two face each other. Now, Erica dear, lift your skirt, come on, right up, don't worry about that lot over there, I'll stand behind you to block them out."

Ever so reluctantly the little skirt inched up, and Hank

whistled.

"God sakes, look at that!"

"Turn round for him, dear," I said, "and you'd better damn well stop blushing or I'll change that chain for the snake one." She knows I have a chain made of little gold snakes: I have never made her wear it, but the threat certainly bothers her.

In the meanwhile, Hank's eyes were almost popping out. "God, what a neat little bottom. But isn't that chain too tight?"

She turned back to face him, and glanced at me. "Uncle doesn't think so!" That was as near to a complaint as she dare go.

"And he keeps you shaved?"

Just a little whisper. "Yes!"

She was still blushing, but she was also still holding her skirt up. She was doing quite well. He tore his gaze away and looked at me.

"I have to touch, OK?"

At that moment the flight was called.

"Maybe on the plane," I said.

Titles (listed overleaf) can be ordered from any bookshop in the UK and an increasing number in the USA and Australia by quoting the title and ISBN, or directly from us by post. Credit cards show as EBS (Electronic Book Services - £ converted to $ and back!): Price of book (see over) plus postage and packing UK £2 first book then £1.30 each; Europe £3.50 then £2; USA $6 then $4. Please make US cheques payable to DS Sales Ltd. All titles (including out-of-print) are also available on floppy disc (PC unless Mac requested) £5 or $8.50 inc. postage.

TITLES IN PRINT

Silver Moon

Silver Mink

*UK £4.99 except *£5.99 --USA $8.95 except *$9.95*